# THE OVERLOOKER

# THE OVERLOOKER

Fay Sampson

This first world edition published 2012
in Great Britain and 2013 in the USA by
SEVERN HOUSE PUBLISHERS LTD of
19 Cedar Road, Sutton, Surrey, England, SM2 5DA.

British Library Cataloguing in Publication Data

Sampson, Fay.
   The overlooker.
   1. Fewings, Suzie (Fictitious character)–Fiction.
   2. Women genealogists–England–Fiction. 3. Detective and
   mystery stories.
   I. Title
   823.9'14-dc23


ISBN-13: 978-0-7278-8241-7 (cased)

*All Severn House titles are printed on acid-free paper.*

Severn House Publishers support the Forest Stewardship Council [FSC], the
leading international forest certification organisation. All our titles that are printed
on Greenpeace-approved FSC-certified paper carry the FSC logo.

Typeset by Palimpsest Book Production Ltd.,
Falkirk, Stirlingshire, Scotland.
Printed and bound in Great Britain by
MPG Books Ltd., Bodmin, Cornwall.

# ONE

Nick drove them up the winding road between stone walls. The fields on either side were dappled with sheep. At the top of the hill, the view he had been anticipating sprang up to meet him in all its grandeur. The massive block of Skygill Hill, which he remembered climbing with his parents as a boy. The hollow plain at its foot, with the former cotton-weaving town clustered around the river and climbing the lower slopes.

He stopped the car and lowered the windows. He took a deep breath of the chill autumn air.

'Ah! You never get it this fresh down south.'

'Dad!' Millie protested from the back seat. 'You don't have to put on that northern accent every time you cross the Mersey. You've never actually lived here, have you?'

'*Touché.*' Nick grinned at his daughter's elfin face in the rear-view mirror. 'It's in the blood, though. I may not have been born in the north, but my grandparents were. I was brought up to think of myself as a northerner.'

'What a view!' said Suzie beside him. 'Only, sixty years ago, you wouldn't have been able to see it for smoke. And there would have been over a hundred mill chimneys, instead of . . . what? Half a dozen?'

Nick sighed. 'No. It's dying on its feet. The only working mill left is a museum.'

He closed the windows and started the engine. 'Come on. Let's see if we can find High Bank. If I know Cousin Thelma, she'll have a proper Lancashire tea waiting. There was always at least one fresh-baked cake.'

Suzie looked at him oddly. 'Nick. You don't eat cake.'

'I do here.'

He took the steep downward gradient slowly. There was little traffic on this back road. His eyes were going from side to side. Could he really find High Bank again? He had tried to program the satnav, but it hadn't recognized the name. Just a row of three terraced houses perched above the valley, where a branch of his family had lived for more than a century. Great-uncle Martin and his daughter, Thelma, were the last of their line to cling on.

His breath caught at the sudden glimpse of the little terrace of smoke-blackened stone.

'Is that it?' Suzie asked at the same moment.

The same precipitous slope of the garden he remembered. Gooseberry and currant bushes. The broad leaves of rhubarb. A late row of beans. And a bright crop of dahlias outside the front door.

He swung off the road on to the gravelled approach and stopped the car.

Millie was swiftly out of the door. Her hands were thrust into the pockets of her green wool jacket. Her slight shoulders hunched against the wind.

'You did say tea, didn't you?'

Nick strode to the front door of the third house and rang the bell. For good measure, he thumped the brass knocker as well.

He had expected the door to spring open immediately and his father's cousin to greet him with open arms.

It was a little while before anyone answered. Had he told her the right day?

The door opened more slowly than he had anticipated. Thelma Fewings stood there, like and yet unlike the woman he remembered. She was only ten years older than him, but she looked more. Her grey hair was curled against her head in an old-fashioned perm. Suzie's brown hair had a soft natural curl, but most of her friends wore their hair straight these days. Behind the pink-framed glasses, Thelma's face looked flushed. She might have been crying.

'Hi, Thelma! How are you doing?' He leaned forward to clasp her shoulders and kiss her powdery face. 'How's Uncle Martin?'

'Oh, Nick,' she said, her voice shaking. 'I've only just got back from the hospital. Dad's had a stroke. He's in a coma.'

Nick felt the bottom fall out of the cheery family reunion

he had been looking forward to. Great-uncle Martin was the last of his grandparents' generation still alive.

Nick had only recently come to share Suzie's interest in family history. He had been amazed to realize that, now in his nineties, Martin Fewings' lifespan reached back so far that he must have known people who had been born in the nineteenth century. The same people Suzie turned up in the old censuses. The Fewings, the Bootles, and their related families. Nick's mind reeled at the thought. Uncle Martin might even have talked to the children of the ancestor who interested Nick most. James Bootle, the handloom weaver turned herbalist in the Industrial Revolution.

And now that last frail link with the past was teetering on the edge of extinction. With the sorrow of one who has come late to family history, Nick felt bitter regret at all the questions he could have asked Uncle Martin while he was still alive and well, and now might never get the chance to.

This purely selfish reaction passed through his mind in a second, before conscience smote him. He felt Thelma trembling under his hands.

'Here, come and sit down. Suzie, can you make us a cup of tea?' He led Thelma to an armchair in the front room. A bow window looked out across the grey-roofed town, with its few isolated chimneys, to the solid bulk of Skygill Hill. 'When did it happen?'

'This afternoon. After dinner. I was just getting ready to go back to work. He was sitting in his chair, and I thought he was having a nap. Then I noticed he was breathing sort of noisily, and one side of his face seemed to have slipped. I tried to wake him, but I couldn't. So I called the ambulance. They rushed him into hospital. I went too, of course, but then I was worried about you coming and finding nobody in. And the doctor told me I shouldn't wait, because he might not come round for a long time . . . if he ever does.' She dabbed the corner of her eye with a tissue.

Nick clasped her cold hands in his. 'You shouldn't have worried about us. I'm sure the neighbours would have seen the ambulance arriving and told us.'

'Oh, Geoffrey Banks next door was out like a flash when

the ambulance came. He's a cousin on my mother's side. We're all related up here in High Bank. Geoffrey's been a big help to me now that Dad's getting on. He's got a key. But I didn't like to think of you coming all this way to an empty house.'

'Nonsense. We'd have quite understood,' Suzie said. 'And we could have found somewhere else to stay. We still can. You'll need to spend time with your father. You won't want to be bothered with visitors at a time like this.'

'No! I never heard the like! I invited you to come and stay with us. I've got the beds all made up and I've baked a cake.'

Just for a moment, Nick caught the ghost of a smile Millie shot at him.

Thelma got to her feet with difficulty. 'I'll come and show you where things are, Suzie.'

'I can help,' Millie said, starting forward.

Nick stayed her with a hand. As Thelma went out into the kitchen, he whispered, 'Let her do it. It's better if she has something to take her mind off Uncle Martin.'

When the two women came back, Suzie was carrying a tray of teacups with an embroidered cloth. Thelma had an uncut fruit cake on a glass stand and a plate of iced buns. They set them down on a table under the window and Suzie poured the strong tea.

'I'll run you down to the hospital this evening,' Nick said. 'We can see if he's any better.'

'That's kind,' said Thelma. 'I was thinking of going on the bus. I don't really feel safe to drive. My nerves are all over the place.'

'That's only to be expected. You've had a shock.'

'And here you are, coming all the way from down south to talk to him. It's such a shame. He was really looking forward to seeing you. Well, he talks to me about the old days some-times. But I've no children to pass it on to. You're the future.' She glanced across at Millie and managed a smile. 'He had me rummage about in the loft. You should have seen me afterwards, covered with dust and cobwebs. There was a suit-case he was after. It's full of old papers, letters and certificates and such. He's been looking forward to showing you. He wanted to tell you about them. I think he was going to pass them over to you to keep.'

Nick felt a start of surprise, a sudden surge of hope. Maybe it wasn't a total loss, after all. Then he thought of Great-uncle Martin lying white and still in a hospital bed, his ancient face disfigured by a stroke. The old man was more than just a source of information, a link with history. He was a human being who had shared Thelma's life for all her fifty-eight years. Hovering now on the brink of departure.

Thelma looked around with a mild surprise. 'Tom isn't with you? No, I remember. You said it was just you and Millie till the weekend.'

'Tom's at university,' Suzie said. 'His first term. But it's only thirty miles away. He's coming over on the train on Friday. It's good of you to put us up for so long. But really, we can find a B and B. Leave you in peace.'

'I wouldn't hear of it! You're family. I can just imagine what Dad would say if he came round and found I'd turned you out of the house, just because he was taken poorly. Millie, another slice of cake? You look as if you could do with fattening up.'

Millie's pointed face under its cap of blonde hair broke into a smile. 'That's the nicest thing anyone's said to me this week. And here was me, thinking I was putting on weight. Yes, please. I can't think when was the last time Mum baked a fruit cake. It's really good.'

Suzie raised her eyebrows, but Nick saw the flush of pleasure on Thelma's face.

There was a knock at the front door, but it opened immediately. A man about Thelma's age put his head round the sitting room door. A scraggy neck protruded from a checked flannel shirt. A bony chin and prominent cheekbones seemed to thrust his face forward ahead of his shoulders. Yellowish hair, streaked with grey, fell over his forehead.

'I saw you were back. How is he?'

'He hasn't come round yet. They sent me home. They say they'll ring me if there's any news.'

'It's a bad do. But he's getting on a bit, isn't he? Ninety-three? I'll be glad if I'm as sprightly as that when I'm his age, or as he was till today, anyroad . . . And these'll be your cousins from down south.'

His quick and curious eyes raked over the Fewings.

Thelma seemed to come to herself with a start. 'I'm sorry! Look at me! I'll be forgetting my own name next. This is Geoffrey, the cousin from next door I was telling you about. Not on the Fewings side. Banks was my mother's family. And this is Nick, and Suzie. And this bonny little girl is Millie.'

'Not so little nowadays,' said Nick hastily, before fourteen-year-old Millie could protest.

'So you've come all this way up to Lancashire, have you? Thelma tells me you're into this family history business.'

'That's right. I'm a late convert, I'm afraid. So I'm trying to make up for lost time. Suzie here's the expert. She's looked up loads of stuff on the internet. I didn't know how much you could find out about people who lived more than a hundred years ago.'

'Actually, more than a century is easier,' Suzie said. 'The censuses are embargoed for a hundred years. And they're full of information about people. Where they lived, what jobs they did, where they were born.'

Geoffrey Banks shook his head slowly. 'You want to be careful. Once you start poking your nose into all that, you never know what you're going to find. Things aren't always what they seem. Do you watch *Who Do You Think You Are?*'

'Yes,' said Suzie.

'Sometimes,' Nick said.

'Well, some of them have had a shock, I can tell you. There was a fellow discovered his ancestor had three wives, all at the same time. And then he ran off with one of his slaves. And another one was responsible for massacring Indians in North America. If I was you, I'd leave well alone.'

Nick felt an inward shiver that was part apprehension, part stimulated curiosity. Did Geoffrey Banks know something about the Fewings family he wasn't telling them?

'Actually,' Suzie said bravely, 'it's the more disreputable bits of family history most people enjoy. I know I shouldn't, but when I found one of my forebears had three illegitimate children in a row, and was probably a prostitute, I felt a sort of one-upmanship. Something to liven up all those everyday births, marriages and deaths.'

Geoffrey Banks's bony face looked shocked. He glanced across at Thelma. 'Well, maybe they have different morals down south, but if that was me, I'd be ashamed to tell people. We're good Methodists in this family, aren't we, Thelma?'

'It's in the family, yes. Stoneyham Methodist Church. Our folk have been stewards and trustees for generations, so I've heard. And before that, I think it was Baptists, out at Briershaw in the Dales.'

'*Every tree that bringeth not forth good fruit is hewn down and cast into the fire.* Matthew seven, verse nineteen,' Geoffrey said.

There was an awkward silence.

'Well, I only came in to see how Martin was.'

'We'll know more in the morning.'

'I'll leave you to your visitors, then.' Geoffrey cast a lingering look over Nick, Suzie and Millie. 'I hope you find what you came for, since you're set on it. And no nasty surprises . . . I'll let myself out.'

When the door had closed behind him, Thelma said, 'Don't mind him. Geoffrey's a good sort, really. He keeps an eye out for me and Dad.'

'He's right, of course,' Suzie said. 'Once you get involved with family history, you don't know what you're going to turn up. And that's even supposing you can believe everything you're told. People didn't always tell the truth to census enumerators. Even the inscriptions on gravestones may not be true. There probably isn't a family that hasn't got something to hide.'

'Well,' said Thelma, rallying. 'I'd better show you where you're sleeping.'

There were two smallish bedrooms at the back of the house, facing up the hill. A double bed for Suzie and Nick took up most of one. Thelma had made up a folding bed in her own room for Millie. Nick saw the anxious glance Suzie cast at their daughter when she found Millie would be sharing a room. But Millie smiled gamely.

There was a narrow bathroom. The largest room, at the front of the house, must be Uncle Martin's. Nick wondered if he would ever come back to it.

# TWO

I t was dark when Nick drove Thelma down the steep hill towards the town centre. An autumn mist was thickening over the river, blurring the street lamps. At the foot of the hill, the road passed in quick succession over the canal bridge and then the river. A solitary mill chimney rose into the darkness, like a memorial to the industrial past.

At a crossroads, his eye briefly registered a brown-and-white tourist signpost that read *Thorncliffe Mill Museum.*

'You'll need to turn left in the town centre,' Thelma was saying. 'The hospital's a bit up the hill on the other side.'

The centre of the town seemed quiet in the early evening. There were pub signs here and there, but no evidence on the pavements of customers. Perhaps they were all inside, enjoying the warmth and light. In the deserted streets, Nick felt they were passing through a no man's land. He thought it must be the heaviness which was lying on his spirit. He had so much looked forward to this expedition. The meeting with Great-uncle Martin, whom he had neglected for so long. And Thelma, of course. But it was the link with the past that had drawn him. The sudden awareness of what he had nearly missed. The knowledge he had failed to ask from his own grandparents.

And now Uncle Martin lay in a limbo between life and death.

'In here,' Thelma said, startling him.

Nick had hardly noticed that they had left the streets of shops below them. He swung into the large hospital car park. Lights were on in the tall building, making it look like a liner moored alongside a dimly lit quay.

Thelma hurried over to the reception desk.

'They've put him in Crompton ward,' she said, turning to Nick. 'When I left, they were still doing all sorts of tests. I didn't know where they were taking him.'

A red line on the reception floor led them round corners and along a corridor. At the ward door, there was another desk, more questions.

The plump, dark-faced nurse shook her head. 'I'm sorry. He's still not come round. I've got a note here to ring you if there was any change. I'm afraid you've had a wasted journey, pet.'

It had been in Nick's mind all the way that this was likely. But he recognized the tense anxiety in Thelma that needed to be doing something, however futile.

She hesitated. 'Can I see him?'

The nurse looked surprised, but she got up and led the way down the ward. Blue-and-pink flowered curtains were drawn around a bed. The nurse twitched them partially aside and motioned Thelma in. The curtain fell back behind her.

Nick stood, uncertain. He had had a momentary glimpse of a lean, grey figure, connected by wires and tubes to clinical equipment. The face had been obscured by the nurse's large figure. Should he follow, or leave Thelma a few moments of privacy with her father?

He had not had time to decide before she came out. She sniffed loudly, took out a tissue and snapped her handbag shut.

'Thank you,' she said to the nurse with forced cheerfulness. 'I just wanted to say goodnight to him. Silly, really.'

'No, it's not,' said the nurse. 'Look on the bright side. He's had a setback, but he's still with us. With luck, we'll have better news for you in the morning.'

'I hope so.'

The mist was creeping up around the edge of the car park.

'I'm sorry to have dragged you all this way for nothing. And it's not a nice night for driving.'

'I'll be OK. There'll be street lamps all the way.'

'And after you've driven all that way today.'

It was beginning to hit home to Nick. That long drive up the motorway from the south-west to the other side of the Mersey. And then the blow of finding that the man he had come to see was in a coma, and might never recover. Having to care for Thelma, who was gallantly hiding her inner anguish. He suddenly wanted nothing more than to be home in bed.

Nick woke early. He slid out of bed, dressed quietly, and let himself out of the front door. On the gravelled path in front of the house he drew lungfuls of keen air.

He could not repress a wry chuckle. Last century, this air would have been full of the smoke from a hundred mill chimneys. The same smoke that had blackened the stone of the house behind him. The streets would have been noisy with the clatter of clogs along the cobbles. Klaxons would have brayed the need for workers to hurry before their pay was docked for arriving late. Go back another century, and pale-faced children would have dragged their weary bodies to another twelve-hour day.

His thoughts flew to Uncle Martin. That had been his life. A beamer in the cotton mill, whatever that was, and then an overlooker. Had he survived the night? At his age, there was the imminent risk of another stroke that would finally sever the thread of his tenacious life.

He turned indoors. Thelma met him at the foot of the stairs. Her face bore an unexpectedly beaming smile.

'He's awake! At least, they say he opened his eyes. He's not saying anything yet, but they think he'll come round.'

'That's great!' Nick kissed her spontaneously. 'I'll take you down to see him this morning, shall I?'

'There's no need. It's kind of you, but they say it might be best if I come on my own to start with. Don't overtire him.'

Nick felt a surprising disappointment. It was years since he had seen his great-uncle. They exchanged Christmas cards, but it had always been Thelma who wrote chatty letters about the family news. He was beginning to realize what Suzie had long experienced, that his new interest in family history was making him curious about his living relatives in a way he had never been before.

He felt oddly jealous of Thelma. How long would it be before he, too, could sit at Uncle Martin's bedside? Would he ever get the chance? He knew how frail the ninety-three year old's hold on life must be. Would he even be able to speak again?

He smiled politely for Thelma, covering his feelings.

'That's OK. We've got a list of things we want to do while we're here – as well as talking to you and Uncle Martin, of course. Top of the list is Thorncliffe Mill Museum. I know they've still got the old steam engine working, and at least some of the looms. It's the sort of place my grandparents worked at, and Uncle Martin, of course.'

'I wish he was here now. There was so much he could tell you about the old days. D'you know, I've never been to Thorncliffe. That's life, isn't it? You have things on your doorstep, and you never think much about them. But people like you come from the other end of the country to look at them.'

'I know what you mean. In our city, there are underground passages dating from medieval times. I'm always telling myself I must go and see them, but I never do. Just because I know they'll always be there.'

But Great-uncle Martin won't always be here, he thought.

He looked past Thelma into the front room. There was no sign of the suitcase Martin had asked her to bring down from the loft.

A figure came hurrying over from next door, hobbling slightly. Nick recognized the yellowish hair and bony chin of Geoffrey Banks.

'How is he?' he asked eagerly of Thelma. 'Have you had any news?'

'He's awake. At least, he's opened his eyes. That's about as much as they're telling me. I'm going in to see him in a bit.'

'Praise God. *The eyes of the Lord are towards the righteous. The face of the Lord is against them that do evil.* Let me know if there's anything I can do.'

'I will. Thank you, Geoff.'

The man lingered. His watery eyes were watching Thelma, as though hoping for more. Then he turned and made his way back to his own house.

'He's a good sort,' said Thelma. 'Though he does have some

weird ideas. As I remember it, the good book says God sends rain on the just and on the unjust. That's the way it looks in real life, anyway.'

'What does he do? It doesn't look as if there's much happening in the town these days. I guess the recession must be hitting pretty hard.'

'You're right there. Lucky for me, people still want fruit and vegetables. I'm pretty safe doing the accounts at Sutcliffe's, touch wood. Geoff wasn't one of the lucky ones. He was an industrial chemist at Bray and Rose. But they shut down two years ago. Not much chance of getting another job at his age. He was bitter about it at the time. Said he's served God all his life and it was the devil's work he was thrown on the scrapheap. As far as he's concerned, the whole world's going to hell in a handcart. Still, he's been kind to Dad and me.'

'I'm glad,' Nick said. 'You may need a bit more help when Uncle Martin comes home.'

If he does, he thought. Even so, the stroke may have left him partially paralysed. Thelma had said how his face seemed slack on one side. Could she manage to look after him? Would they have to move him to a nursing home? And what would that cost?

But it was too soon to ask that sort of question. For the moment, it was enough that Great-uncle Martin was alive.

The thunderous heartbeat of the steam engine thrilled Nick to the core. The Fewings watched from behind the safety line in the narrow room at the top of the mill. The huge silver piston shot forwards and back on its bed of oil. At the other end, the bright green painted mechanism it powered would be sending the leather belts whirring in the weaving shed below.

'Fantastic!' Nick raised his voice above the roar. 'She looks in as good fettle as the day she was made.'

'Aye. Not bad for a hundred and twenty years.' The volunteer engineer patted the casing with pride. 'She could have been put in yesterday.'

Suzie's long hair swung as she turned to Nick with a quizzical look. 'You do realize it was machines like this that put your great-great-great-grandfather out of work. You know, the handloom weaver. The Industrial Revolution spelt the end of his way of life.'

But Nick was in love with the pounding beast in front of him. 'That's progress. You can't expect history to stand still.'

One of the museum guides called up the stairs to them. 'You'd better hurry up if you want to see the looms under power.'

They clattered down the steps. At the bottom, fourteen-year-old Millie tugged her father's arm. Her pixie face grinned up at him. 'Seen this, Dad?'

Nick read the notice at the foot of the stairs. '. . . *Even the mill manager had to ask permission to enter the engine room.*'

'Now that's power,' Millie laughed. 'Think yourself privileged to get up there.'

The noise in the weaving shed was even more deafening. Over three hundred looms stretched away in row upon row under the tall windows. The dancing diagonals of leather belts carried the power from the engine room overhead. Just two of them were working. Their high-pitched clatter added another layer of sound to the thunder of the piston overhead. A metal grille separated the Fewings from the darting machinery.

'Just imagine,' Suzie marvelled, 'what it must have been like when all three hundred were going at once.'

Nick stared at the scene with a hungry intensity. 'My grandmother worked in a mill like this,' he told Millie. 'She had five looms to look after.'

'I'm trying to watch the shuttle,' Millie said. 'But it goes so fast I can hardly see it.'

Their guide had joined them. 'You'd have to imagine the air thick with cotton dust. And first thing on a winter morning the machines would be covered in frost. Your hands would freeze to the metal if you didn't wrap them in cloth. And the noise was so terrific, the weavers worked out a way of lip-reading.'

Suzie was silent for a while. She carried the details of Nick's family tree in her head better than he did.

'James Bootle was a handloom weaver back in the 1851 census. And then he re-invented himself. He turns up in later records as a medical herbalist. There's a trade directory that shows he had a shop on Market Street Court, in the centre of the town, where the shopping precinct is now. But he couldn't save his children from being sucked into the mills. Millicent was a cotton factory worker in the next census at the age of eight.'

Millie's eyes grew round. 'Millicent! You never told me! Did you name me after her?'

'I'm afraid not,' Suzie laughed. 'We weren't into family history then. I only discovered her a few weeks ago, when I started chasing up Dad's family history as well as my own.'

'All the same . . . But it's daft. She couldn't have managed even one of these looms at that age. She wouldn't have been big enough to reach.'

'She'd be working her socks off, supposing she had any, keeping the weavers supplied with weft for the looms, and clearing away the waste.'

'She'd learn to be a weaver when she was older,' the guide agreed. 'But if you could reach your arm over your head and touch the opposite ear, you were thought big enough to work. And they didn't stop the machinery if something needed fixing or cleaning. If she didn't look out, she could lose an arm or her scalp.'

Millie shuddered. Her hand went protectively to her own blonde head.

She gazed back at the clattering machinery with renewed intensity. 'Millie Bootle. She worked here?'

'In a mill like it, certainly.'

'It's just possible,' Nick said, 'that your Great-great-uncle Martin knew her.'

Millie swung her wondering eyes round to him. '*Really?*'

'It's possible. If she lived that long, she'd have been in her sixties when he was born.

The noise slackened overhead. Nick could hear the piston slowing to rest. The flicker of hundreds of leather belts ceased their dancing. The shuttles on the looms fell still. A strange silence held the vast weaving shed. For several moments, none of the three Fewings moved.

Then Suzie's hazel eyes smiled sympathetically at Nick. 'That was great, wasn't it? I never thought it would seem so real.'

He turned away from the looms reluctantly. 'My gran and granddad left all this to move south, soon after they got married. Apparently Granddad Fewings had been posted to Portsmouth in the First World War, and liked it. They set up a fish and chip shop. But Gran was always a Northerner at heart. She was proud that she'd worked in the mills.'

'I bet James Bootle was proud of the cloth he wove on his handloom. But his was a different world. Before all this.'

They wandered off to the café, through rooms stacked with samples of cotton cloth, the myriad sizes of shuttles for every conceivable job, arrays of weavers' tools, and the Jacquard looms that could weave more complicated patterns. Room after room opened up in the rambling mill. And there were more doors that were marked 'Private'.

Nick thought of the contrast between his own modern office in the southern cathedral city, his architect's practice designing houses and offices for the future. Until recently, he had not shared Suzie's all-consuming passion for family history. But this had gripped him. Here he was in touch with a woman who had died only a few years ago. His grandmother. A woman whose shy grey eyes had come to life as she told her children and grandchildren about her life as a cotton weaver. The knocker-up tapping the bedroom window with his pole, the clogs on the cobbled street, the close-knit community where almost everyone on the street worked at the same mill.

And now that high tide of the Industrial Revolution had receded. The mills were deserted, the chimneys cold. Here and there they were being demolished, but slowly. There was no money to replace the mills. No new industries. Half the town seemed to be on benefits. He thought of Geoffrey Banks, the embittered industrial chemist. A disappointed man whose life's work had been taken from him.

Suzie could take her mind far enough back to imagine the way of life James Bootle had lost in the 1850s. Nick could only feel sadness for the loss of his grandparents' world.

They enjoyed a homemade lunch in the museum café. Nick chased the last crumbs of a rhubarb-and-apple crumble round his bowl.

'I wonder how Thelma's getting on at the hospital. Visiting

hours don't start till the afternoon, but it sounded as if they were letting her see him this morning.'

'You could ring her.'

'I'm not even sure if she's got a mobile.'

They stepped out of the café on to the canal-side. Millie looked along the once-busy waterway. Derelict mills stretched into the distance. Only the textile museum was a hive of activity.

'What do people *do* with all these empty buildings?' Millie asked. 'There must be something going on, mustn't there?'

# THREE

Nick checked his watch. 'It's only early afternoon. If Thelma's gone to visit Uncle Martin, she won't be home yet. Do you feel like a walk along the canal? I'd like to take a look at Hugh Street, where my family used to live. We could drive round, but it'll be more interesting on foot than taking the car.'

'I'm fine with that,' Suzie said. 'Is that OK with you, Millie?'

'I suppose so.' Millie dug her hands deeper into her jacket pockets. 'It's a bit creepy, though. Those mill chimneys. If you stand too close and look up, you feel they're going to fall on top of you.'

'I'm sure they wouldn't have left them if they were unsafe,' Suzie reassured her. 'There used to be a spate of programmes on TV about blowing up chimneys like these. There's an art in getting them to collapse just where you want them to. I haven't seen one of those for a while.'

They were walking along the muddy towpath, avoiding the puddles. Nick peered through a gap in the stone wall alongside them. 'They may have left the chimney, but the rest of the mill has gone. There's just an empty space and a bit of rubble.'

Suzie looked across the canal. 'There are plenty of them still standing on the other side. But they all look empty. The lower windows are boarded up or they've got metal grilles over them.'

'Gran said they needed those big windows for the weaving sheds,' Nick said. 'It could be freezing cold in the morning, but once you got all those looms working at once, they generated a terrific heat. And they had to have good light for mending broken threads or spotting a dodgy patch in the weaving. If the overlooker said your work wasn't good enough you'd to unpick the weft and do it all again. And you were paid by the piece, so that meant you lost money.'

The stone wall of the demolished mill ended. They were walking now beneath the towering brickwork of another derelict mill, four storeys high.

'Someone's gone a bit mad with the graffiti on this one,' Millie observed. 'It's not exactly a Banksy artwork, is it?'

The dark wall of the mill overlooking the canal had been daubed with letters in black and red a metre high. Nick read one message aloud.

'*They called to the mountains and rocks, "Fall on us and hide us from the wrath of the Lord."*'

'Cheerful,' said Millie. 'How about this one? *He shall drink the wine of God's wrath, poured unmixed into the cup of his anger, and he shall be tormented with fire and brimstone in the presence of the holy angels.* It's enough to put you off religion altogether, isn't it?'

'It's from the Book of Revelation,' Suzie said. 'The last book of the bible. Written when the Church was undergoing martyrdom. John wrote it after he fled to the island of Patmos in fear of his life. He had this vision of the Roman Empire being overthrown and terrible happenings before the end of the world. Like that one up there. *Their torture was like the torture of a scorpion.*' I guess he was dreaming of seeing his persecutors persecuted.'

'Gross,' said Millie. 'I thought Christianity was all about loving people who did nasty things to you.'

'It is.'

'Anyway, whoever did this is wasting his time. He'd have done better painting it in the middle of town. Who's going to see it out here, with just a lot of empty mills?'

'Oh, I don't know. There'll be plenty of people like us who walk along this towpath.'

Even as she spoke, a man with a dog overtook them, squeezing past on the narrow path.

As the Fewings passed underneath the mill, with its louring messages, Millie ran her hand along the brickwork. Her fingers twanged the metal grilles guarding the windows.

Nick and Suzie walked on. Not far ahead, Nick could see a bridge. He was fairly sure that was where Canal Street crossed the waterway. They would need to leave the towpath there to find his grandparents' old home in Hugh Street.

A voice called from some distance behind them.

'I don't think this one is going to keep people out.'

Millie had stopped. She was pulling at the grille over the window beside her. It was red with rust. As she tugged, a corner sprang away from the wall.

'Millie!' Suzie exclaimed as she turned. 'I don't think you should be doing that. It may be empty, but this mill belongs to someone.'

Millie had prised a second corner free. A side of the grille swung away from the wall. There was no glass in the window behind it. Two boards had been nailed crookedly across the gap. But they were rotting away. There was a gap big enough for Millie to put her head through.

'It's a bit like that museum, except it's all covered in dirt.' She wriggled sideways to see better. 'Some of the machines have gone, but there's still rows of them.'

Nick strode back to join her. 'Let's have a look.'

Millie stood back to let her father peer through the hole. As he put his weight against it, a section of board broke off.

'Nick!' Suzie exploded. 'You're as bad as Millie. What if someone comes along and finds you breaking and entering?'

'I admit to the breaking. But we haven't entered yet.' He withdrew his head and grinned at Millie. 'Are you up for it? I got a bit frustrated back at the museum, with a metal screen between us and the looms. I know they have to have it for safety reasons, but I'd love to stand in front of one, just like my gran did. Even if it's not working.'

A little boy's curiosity had got the better of Nick. He

squeezed himself between the loosened grille and the window space and swung a long leg over the sill.

He dropped down on to the dusty mill floor. His heart beat faster with recognition. There were rows of disused looms, stretching away down the long dusty room. Diagonal leather belts still connected drive wheels at the side of each to a pulley overhead. It did not take much imagination to picture the threads of the warp stretched over the rollers. You would only have to set those leather belts in motion for the warp threads to lift and fall and the shuttle to fly across at twice a second.

Millie had followed him through the window. She was prowling around, her blonde head under the tall windows misted by the dust Nick had raised.

He wandered along the line of machines, picturing in his mind his grandmother in her calico-print apron, casting a sharp eye over her five looms.

He stopped short beside one, with a sudden flutter of excitement in his heart.

'Look at this! Somebody's cleaned this one up.'

Millie ran to join him. Together they studied the gleam of the newly cleaned iron frame, the signs of oil on the leather belt and the wheel it drove, the wooden shuttle lying as if ready to use.

'Mum! Come and look! Somebody's getting this one working.' Millie cried.

'All the more reason to stay outside,' Suzie's voice from the towpath scolded them, 'if somebody's trying to restore them.'

But Nick and Millie were eagerly examining the loom.

'Do you think someone's planning to start weaving here again?' Millie asked. 'Why else would they clean it up?'

'Perhaps they're going to turn it into another textile museum.' Suzie had reluctantly joined them. She was brushing at a smear of rust on her jeans.

'The whole town will be a museum soon,' Millie retorted.

'It makes money and it gives people work. Besides, we're not the only people who love to see history brought to life. School parties, dressing up and pretending to be Victorian children. Your father was in his element this morning, imagining all his forebears who worked in mills like that.'

'They'd better clear all those graffiti off the wall, then,' Millie laughed. 'Tourists aren't exactly going to want to come here, with all those threats of hellfire outside.'

'Yes, it's a bit like Geoffrey Banks last night,' Suzie mused. 'From what Thelma said, he thinks the present world is under the power of Satan.'

'Creepy.'

Nick was studying the renovated loom.

'I wonder how they'd power it? There can't be another steam engine like the one at Thorncliffe Mill Museum going spare. They said it was the last one operating looms anywhere in the world. I expect it would have to be electricity for this one.'

He wandered away to the far end of the vast room. A cry of discovery burst from him.

'Yes! Right here. There's a bank of switches. And it's not covered in dust, either. I bet if you threw one of these, those looms would jump into life. Or at least, the one that's been cleaned.'

'No, Nick!' Suzie's shout of alarm rang down the weaving shed. 'Don't touch it! You're positively not to switch any of them on. We've no idea what would happen.'

Nick looked regretfully at the bank of switches in front of him. It would be such a feeling of power to move one of them and send those leather belts spinning, just the way they had in Thorncliffe Mill. Even if only one loom here was connected up, the air would be alive with the dancing of all the other belts.

But Suzie was right. Once he threw that switch, he had no idea what would it would do. What crucial stage of renovation might the new occupant of this mill have reached? Was the cleaned-up loom even working yet?

Reluctantly, he stepped away and walked back to join the others.

He walked around the freshly oiled loom and bent down to inspect the narrow space beneath. He grimaced.

'How do you fancy it? Being a scavenger under here? Just imagine when the loom was working. You remember the speed they went, back at the museum?'

Millie's hand went instinctively to her short-cropped hair. 'And I remember what she said about getting scalped, or having your clothes caught and losing an arm. Gross!'

'The girls had to pin theirs up in a tight bun.' Suzie said. 'They only wore it loose at the weekend. That's what they meant by "letting their hair down".' She raised a thoughtful hand to her own long brown hair.

Millie shivered. 'No, Dad. I am definitely not crawling under there. Even when it's not working. It would give me nightmares.'

'Coward. Here!' He slipped off his leather jacket and handed it to her.

It was a tight squeeze. And it was indeed rather frightening to be lying underneath that silent metal beast. He could imagine all too terrifyingly what it must have been like when the wheels were turning and the iron jaws were chomping, as the threads of the warp shot up and down and the shuttle flew between them.

In a sudden panic, he slid out on his back and stood up.

'Nick! Your shirt!' Suzie's voice betrayed her tension.

'Why do you think I took my jacket off? The shirt will wash. No harm done.'

He was glad to have a diversion from the unreasonable fear he had felt in that confined space.

Millie held out his leather jacket, draped over her arm. There was a rattle as several things fell out of the upside-down pockets.

'Thanks very much!' said Nick.

They scrabbled around chasing a pen that had rolled away, scattered business cards and his mobile phone. Millie reached a reluctant arm under the loom and retrieved his diary.

'Sorry,' she said, stuffing them back into the inside pocket.

She plucked at the dustballs on her sleeve. Then she nodded further along the room. 'I noticed something when I was down on the floor. Someone's been here recently. There are footsteps in the dust.'

'Of course they have,' Suzie said. 'This loom didn't clean and oil itself, did it?'

'They lead to that door over there and back.'

Nick looked back along the way he had come from the switchboard. He had been too intent on his discovery to notice it. But it was true. There was another double line of prints beside his own. He prowled down the long room again. Millie's sharp eyes were right. The trail of footsteps led past the power switches to a door in the end wall. He tried it.

'It's locked.'

'Of course it is,' Suzie called. 'Whoever is using this will have a key. They'll have got in by the door, not the window. We shouldn't be here. It's obviously not as derelict as it looks from outside. We ought to go.'

Nick looked down at the line of footprints Millie had indicated. Large ones. Shoes? Probably trainers. The excitement of his schoolboy adventure had faded. He began to share Suzie's unease.

'Come on. Let's make ourselves scarce. I wanted to know what it felt like be a scavenger, like Millicent Bootle. Now I know. At least, I know what it's like under that loom when it's not working. It scares me to think what it must have been like for a nineteenth-century child, when this whole room was clattering with lethal machinery.' He gave a brief smile at Millie. 'Your namesake. Working here at eight years old.'

'Don't!' she said. 'I don't like thinking about it. Let's go.'

Nick put his head out of the window to check that no one was in sight on the towpath. He drew a sharp breath. A couple of teenagers had passed the window without remarking on the broken grille. He watched them walk under the railway bridge and disappear.

'All clear,' he hissed.

The three of them squeezed through and dropped back on to the path. Nick and Millie pressed the rusty grille back into position as best they could.

'Vandals,' said Suzie.

'It was worth it, wasn't it?' Millie said. 'You're the one who's always on about bringing family history to life.'

# FOUR

'Dad,' Millie said, in the patient tone of one explaining a simple fact to the obtuse, 'the further we walk away from the car, the longer we have to walk back.'

'It's not far now . . . I think. See that bridge? We can get up on to the road there. If I remember rightly, that's Canal Street. Hugh Street's just a short way up.'

'Says you.' Millie hunched her shoulders against a spatter of rain.

Suzie hesitated about opening her umbrella, then put it away again.

Steps led up from the canalside. They emerged on to the road. At once, they were in a different, noisier world. Cars flashed past. Nick led them uphill.

'I'm right! There's the Woolpack.' He pointed to a pub sign at the top of the rise. 'Hugh Street should be more or less opposite there. If it's still standing.'

Millie stopped dead on the pavement. 'Dad! You're not going to tell me you've dragged us all this way for a house that may not even *be* there?'

'Thelma said they have plans to demolish that area. But as far as she knows they haven't got to Hugh Street yet.'

'They'd better not have, is all I can say.'

'Look out, you two.'

Suzie shepherded them against the wall. A woman was hurrying down the pavement, almost dragging a small boy. She wore a brown cardigan and turquoise tunic over loose beige trousers. An indigo scarf swathed her head, but did not hide her features. In the first startled glance, Nick could see that her face was contorted, her eyes brimming with tears. The little boy, who looked no more than four, was whining and protesting as she gripped his arm and hurried him along.

'Is something wrong?' Suzie asked, as the pair drew level

and the two women were momentarily close to each other.
'Can we help?'

The woman shot them a look that Nick could only construe
as terror. 'No, no!'

She said something rapidly to the little boy in a language
Nick could not understand, as she hauled him on down the road.

Suzie stood looking uncomfortable as she watched them go.
'What was that about? She didn't just look upset; she looked
frightened. But I can't think what can have happened to her
on a busy street in the middle of the day.'

She looked up the road in the direction the woman and child
had come from.

Nick followed her gaze. 'Looks like there's a nursery school
up there. Lots of mums and toddlers just coming out. Come
to think of it, my dad said he went to one back in the forties,
when he was evacuated to his grandparents here. I can't believe
it's still functioning seventy years on!'

'Nick, we're not in your family past now. That woman's
the present. And she looked terrified of something.'

'That's rich from you, Mum!' Millie snorted. 'For years,
it's been you who's been living in the past, up to your eyebrows
in family history. Now Dad gets to make one trip to relive his
roots, and you're scolding him.'

'Well, I know. But that poor woman . . . It shook me, the
way she looked at me. I wish there had been something I
could do.'

Millie shrugged. 'You tried. It's a free country. If she didn't
want your help, that's her choice. Forget it.'

Nick turned to look back down Canal Street. The hurrying
woman dragging the child had almost reached the bridge.

'Look! She's meeting someone.'

The man was too far away for his features to be distin-
guished. From the brimless cap he wore, Nick guessed he was
a Muslim. The woman was gesticulating violently.

'Looks like some kind of argument's going on,' observed
Millie.

'Nick,' Suzie said urgently. 'Do you think we should go
back and see if she needs help? What if he's her husband and
he's abusing her?'

'He's hardly likely to attack her in the street in broad daylight.' Nick shared Suzie's unease, but it was a big step to confront a couple they did not know, in public, and attempt to defuse a situation whose origins they knew nothing about.

'I think it's all right,' Suzie said with relief. 'She's handing the boy over.'

They watched the man and the boy walk away. The pair lingered on the bridge. The man lifted the boy up. For a horrified moment, Nick wondered whether he was going to drop the child in the canal. Instead, it was the boy who was leaning over and seemed to be dropping something into the water.

'They're playing Pooh Sticks,' said Millie. 'I used to love that. Except that they can hardly dash across the traffic to see it come out on the other side. Whatever. Doesn't seem particularly violent to me.'

'It was the woman I was worried about,' Suzie said. 'Where is she?'

'She's coming back up the hill.' Nick watched her weaving her hurried way through other pedestrians back up from the bridge. 'No. She's turned off down that side street.'

'She saw us watching her,' Millie said. 'Didn't you notice? She was coming straight up the hill. Then she stopped dead. I'm sure it was because she didn't want to pass us. She thinks you're going to stop her again, Mum. Interfering do-gooder.'

Suzie's cheeks flushed. 'I'm not! I just couldn't let a woman walk past me in tears and not offer to help.'

'I mean, that's what she *thinks* you are. Whatever's up, she doesn't want to have to explain it to you.'

'She's gone now,' Nick told them. 'We might as well go on.'

They walked on up the hill. More mothers, white and Asian, were scattering from the gates of the nursery school with their children. Nick sensed, from the way Suzie turned her head to examine their faces, that she was not finding it easy to put that encounter out of her head.

Opposite the Woolpack, Nick took a deep breath and turned. Disappointment engulfed him. Instead of line after line of neat rows of millworkers' cottages, there was a vast open space. Even the rubble had been cleared away. Where the nearest terrace of houses had stood, there was a rectangle of grass.

'It's gone,' he said helplessly. 'We're too late.'

'Told you,' Millie said. 'And you've dragged us all this way for nothing.'

Suzie slipped her arm through his and squeezed it. 'I'm sorry. But we can see what it used to be like. Look, there are other streets still standing. Let's go and have a look. They were all pretty much the same, weren't they? We can get the idea.'

Disconsolately, Nick let her lead him past the patch of grass. It did not look big enough to have contained some twenty houses.

As they neared the terraces still standing, something quickened in him. He began to walk faster.

'No! I'm wrong. I had a memory that Hugh Street opened straight on to Canal Street. But it didn't. Look! That's it straight ahead. I can read the name plate.'

He couldn't explain the uprush of joy. It was silly, really. His grandmother had grown up here, but neither Nick nor his father had ever lived in the north. And yet he felt the fierce loyalty of northernness. He had never seen himself as a southerner. It was something in the blood.

'Better get your camera out, Dad. Take a picture while you've got the chance. By the look of it, this lot is for the wreckers' ball any day now.'

Millie was right. All along Hugh Street the windows were boarded up. The small, two-bedroomed houses, which had teemed with such large families a century ago, were lifeless. No one would ever live in them again.

They had passed renovated streets of houses that had once been like this, where the old stone setts of the road had been covered with tarmac. Here, he was walking over the original cobblestones.

'It was on the left-hand side. Number sixteen.'

He was few houses away when he stopped. 'That's funny.'

'Looks like it's not all shut up.' Millie said.

Number sixteen had an uncared-for appearance. The paint was peeling. There was a dark curtain across the sash window beside the door. But here there were no boards over the glass. He looked up. The upper windows were uncovered too.

Nick stepped back across the road to take a photograph. As he lowered the camera, he had the fleeting impression of a flash of movement at an upstairs window.

He smiled at the others, trying to sound more confident than he felt. 'It's worth a try. I'm going to ring the bell and see if there's anyone in. With luck, they might even let us see inside.'

'I'm not sure there can be anyone living here,' Suzie said. 'The whole street looks due for demolition. And even if there is someone refusing to move, they're not likely to welcome visitors. Even under normal circumstances, they'd probably like some warning, so they could get the place tidied up a bit. I would.'

'Mum!' Millie snorted. 'It's not as if our house looks like something out of *Ideal Homes* even when you've done the housework.'

'It would look a lot better if you helped with some of it,' Suzie shot back.

Nick thought about their four-bedroomed, detached house in its large garden, on the outskirts of the cathedral city. In two generations, the Fewings and the Bootles had come a dizzying long way from a millworker's two-up-two-down, with a tiny back yard.

All the more reason to be proud of his roots. The people who had made him.

He nerved himself to press the bell.

At first he thought no one was going to answer. Had he been wrong about that movement upstairs?

After a while, the door opened halfway.

The man who held it reluctantly ajar peered round it at Nick. He was a short, fleshy figure with dark, greying hair. Protuberant brown eyes stared at Nick suspiciously.

'What do you want?'

Nick's eye was caught by a flash of colour at the top of the stairs. For a moment, he saw a young woman dressed somewhat like the one who had passed them in Canal Street, towing her small son. This time, it was a salmon-pink kameez, over dark red shalwar trousers.

The man followed his eyes and turned sharply. But the landing was empty.

'I'm sorry,' Nick said. 'It's a bit of a cheek, I know. But my family used to live in this house at the end of the nineteenth century and for most of the twentieth. They worked at Lower Clough Mill. The mill's gone, but you can still see the chimney from the end of the street.'

'Yes? What's that got to do with me?'

Suzie tried her most beguiling voice. 'We were wondering . . . From the look of it, they're going to pull the street down soon. Would it be too much to ask for Nick to come inside and take a last look? Just one for the memory album?'

The man's dark eyes stared back at them. 'No,' he said flatly. 'You're not welcome here.'

Nick swallowed his disappointment. Over the man's shoulder he could just glimpse the front room. There was no entrance hall in these houses. He had a childhood memory of an upright piano, which had been the family's pride. Of lace curtains at the window and an uncomfortably stiff three-piece suite. It had been a room only used on Sundays.

In the dim light through the curtained window he saw that most of the furniture had been cleared. The floor was bare. A bureau had replaced the piano. In the gloom, he saw it was overflowing with papers and cardboard boxes. Before he could take in more, the door was shutting in his face.

There was a commotion behind him in the street.

'Please! Excuse me!' came an unfamiliar woman's voice. It sounded high, distressed.

He turned and found the woman they had met before, in the brown cardigan and the indigo scarf. She was trying to press past Millie to reach the door.

The man's face changed when he saw her. The blank rejection darkened to thunder.

'Please, Mr Harrison. I'm sorry! My little boy . . . They had a party at his school and he was late coming out. I had to take him to his father . . .'

She was gabbling in agitation.

The man looked at her coldly. 'I've no idea what you're talking about, woman. There's no Mr Harrison here. I'm from the council. I'm checking that all this street is empty and the gas and electricity turned off. Don't come back here again.'

The woman gazed back at him in shock. 'But . . . I know you'll cut my money for being late . . .' She wrung her hands.

The door shut on her protests.

The woman covered her eyes with her hands and burst into tears.

Suzie put an arm around her. 'There! It's all right. What are you doing here? Who is he?'

The woman shook her head vehemently. 'No! It's nothing. I made a mistake. I don't know that man. Please let me go!' She was shaking with sobs.

She shrugged off Suzie's sympathetic hands and fled down the street.

Nick looked back up at the house. The windows were blank. But he had not imagined that other woman at the top of the stairs.

# FIVE

'What was all that about?' Millie exclaimed.

'I haven't the faintest idea.'

'She knew him. She was upset about coming late,' Suzie said. 'And yet he denied it. He sent her away.'

'Because we were here. That stuff about being from the council was just for our benefit. He didn't want to let her in while we were watching. He wanted us to think the house was empty.'

'But if she really does work here . . .?' Suzie's voice trailed off. She looked back at number sixteen. 'It doesn't seem likely. The rest of the street is boarded up. It's a pretty small house. What sort of work could she have been doing there? Something secretarial?'

'It's not just her. There was another woman there. Someone dressed like her. I caught sight of her for a moment at the top of the stairs.'

'Perhaps there are loads of them,' Millie said. 'I mean, look at it. The rest of the houses are empty. What's to stop someone knocking a way through all of them? You could have as much space as you liked. Enough for a whole factory.'

Nick stopped dead on the pavement. He looked along the terrace, trying to take in Millie's suggestion.

'I suppose it's possible. The outside's solid stone, but the partition walls are probably just thin brick.'

'See?'

'What are you suggesting? Some sort of sweatshop?'

'Come on now, guys,' Suzie protested. 'Let's not get melodramatic. Somebody would notice, wouldn't they? If dozens of women kept turning up for work?'

'*Who'd* notice?' Millie asked. She turned slowly, taking in the vast square of open ground where the houses had been demolished, the boarded-up streets surrounding it. 'Can you see a single person here except us?'

'But they're obviously intending to knock Hugh Street down, like all the rest,' Nick argued.

'So? When?'

'She's right,' Suzie said. 'Thelma told us this morning the council have had to cut back on their plans. It could be years now before they redevelop this area. Nobody wants to spend money nowadays.'

'What will happen to that woman?' Millie wondered. 'Has she lost her job? Because of us?'

'It may have only earned her a pittance, if it's what we think it is. But it was all she had.' Suzie shook her head. 'There's no work in this town any more.'

They walked on in a gloomy silence. Nick's enjoyment of the working museum, the excitement of their trespass on the derelict mill, his joy at finding his ancestral home at Hugh Street still standing, had evaporated.

'Come on,' he said. 'Let's go back and see if there's any news of Uncle Martin. I think I know a short cut back to the car.'

They wove their way diagonally through the streets, back to the textile museum where they had left the car. They only rejoined the canal at the last moment.

They were still subdued as Nick drove them back to High Bank.

The first thing they saw was Thelma's red Nissan parked outside the house. This afternoon, she greeted them with a brighter face.

'He's conscious, thank the Lord. Pretty tired, though. It's taken all the sap out of him. And one side of his face is stiff. He had trouble speaking to me. But he *can* talk, even if I had a job to understand him. He's still got his wits about him, praise be.'

'I'm so glad.' Nick hugged her. 'I've been kicking myself that I've waited all these years before coming to see you both. Then you see the opportunity slipping away from you, and you think of all the chances you've missed.'

'Go on with you, lad,' Thelma said. 'You've got your own life to live. An architect! We've never had anything as grand as that in the family. Your great-uncle was right proud of you.'

She was leading the way into the living room at the back of the house. It was a small shock to find that Geoffrey Banks was sitting there at the table, a cup of tea in front of him. Nick told himself he should not have been surprised. Geoffrey was a cousin and lived next door. He would have wanted to hear about Thelma's father.

The out-of-work chemist turned his pale blue eyes up to Nick. 'You've been seeing the sights, have you? Such as they are. No doubt you'll have finer places where you come from.'

'We've been to Thorncliffe Mill. The textile museum. And after seeing it –' he turned back to Thelma – 'I'm proud of your dad. And my grandparents. I'd never really been able to imagine their lives till now. It's helped me picture all the generations before them. Kids working with those machines as young as eight.'

'One of them was Millie,' Millie said. 'Millicent Bootle.'

'I've heard my dad mention her,' Thelma said. 'One of your grandmother's family. They were all good friends at chapel, the Fewings and Bootles.'

'Dad crawled under one of the looms to show us what it was like if you were a kid working in the mill.'

'You never! They let you do that? I'd have thought there were all sorts of health-and-safety rules these days.'

'It wasn't there,' Nick said, suddenly discomfited. 'That was later. A different mill. And the loom wasn't working.'

He didn't want to tell his cousin about their adventure at the canalside, the broken grille, their illicit entry.

But it had not escaped the keen ears of Geoffrey Banks. 'Where was this, then? You haven't been getting into places you shouldn't, have you?'

Nick decided to pretend he hadn't heard. 'Well,' he said brightly to Thelma. 'Any news about how soon we might be able to visit Uncle Martin?'

'They said tomorrow, if he doesn't have another setback. Just for a short while at first. He'll be glad to see you. It's a pity he's not here to show you that suitcase he had me chasing up to the loft for. Look at me! Standing here nattering when you'll be parched for a cup of tea. I'll put the kettle on.'

Reluctantly, Geoffrey Banks got to his feet.

'I'll see you later, Thelma.' As he passed Nick he said pointedly, 'You be careful what you get up to. *Their feet run to evil. Wasting and destruction are in their paths.*'

'Cheerful character, isn't he,' said Nick when he was gone.

'Don't be too hard on him,' Thelma told him. 'He's got a lot to put up with.'

Nick and Suzie were sitting on the bench outside Thelma's house. The early advance of evening shrouded the town below with grey. Lights were pricking out along the roads.

Suzie got up and strolled over to Thelma's bed of sunset-coloured dahlias. 'I've been thinking . . . That business in Hugh Street. The Bangladeshi woman, or whatever she was. I'm wondering if we ought to report it to the police. There was something strange going on in that house. I'm sure of it.'

'I know what you mean. I had a bad feeling about it myself. Only Thelma's good news about Uncle Martin put it out of my head. But it's not much to go on. It's true, that man didn't want me to see past the front door. But there's no law that says someone can't refuse to let you into their home.'

'But it can't be his home. No one should be living in that

street. And what about pretending he wasn't Mr Harrison and
that the woman we met didn't work there? He was obviously
lying.'

'And not a very good liar. He made it look a lot more suspicious than it probably was.'

'A sweatshop, if that's what it is? In a street of boarded-up
houses where he probably isn't even paying rent? And it'll be
a whole lot worse than just not paying them the minimum
wage. I shouldn't think he cares a hoot about health and safety.
Goodness knows what conditions those women are working
under.'

Nick's mind was jolted back to the textile museum. The
clatter and whirr of hundreds of looms. The darting machinery
hungry to grab a loose fold of clothing or a lock of hair. It
hardly bore thinking about. Surely nothing in the twenty-first
century could be as bad as that? Or was he trying to reassure
himself?

'I don't like to think about it,' he said darkly. 'I wonder
what would happen if one of them had an accident? I somehow
don't think our Mr Harrison would be calling 999 and getting
the emergency services involved. Imagine it. Police. Medics.
Factory inspectors. All wanting to know what happened and
how. He wouldn't want to take the lid off that particular can
of worms.'

'But he'd have to, wouldn't he? What else could he do?'

Nick got up and began to pace restlessly. 'I know it sounds
a bit melodramatic, but . . . dispose of the evidence?'

'How?'

'How would I know? Drop the body in the canal? Bury it
out on the moors?'

'And if she wasn't dead?'

There was a long silence.

Suzie shuddered. 'We're letting our imaginations run away
with us. There's probably a quite ordinary explanation. But I
still think we should report it and let the police decide.'

Millie opened the front door behind them. 'Tea's up. Thelma
let me do fancy decorations with the leftover pastry for the
meat-and-potato pie.'

'I can't wait,' said Nick, jumping to his feet.

His mobile rang.

'Go ahead,' he told Millie and Suzie. 'I'll join you in a minute. I remember Thelma's meat-and-potato pies.'

He glanced down at the phone. Number withheld. That always rang a little alarm bell.

'Hello?'

'Is that Mr Nicholas Fewings, B.Arch., RIBA, AABC?'

It was strangely put question. The voice was disquieting. Harsh. Demanding.

Still . . . He shrugged. A potential client?

'Speaking.'

'Well, Mr Nicholas Fewings. I would strongly advise you not to tell anyone else about what you saw today. It would be particularly foolish to report it to the police. Accidents can happen. To any of your family.'

The call ceased abruptly.

Nick had scarcely had time to take in the startling message, let alone to ask questions. He was left staring stupidly down at the phone in his hand. The screen was normal. There was no trace of the life-threatening message.

*To any of your family.*

His heart was thudding as he made his way back indoors. He saw Millie facing him across the table, the long swing of Suzie's brown hair from behind. Thelma's comfortably welcoming face. He hardly remembered to say thank you as she passed him a generously loaded plate.

The phone was back in his inside jacket pocket. He was aware of its pressure scarily over his heart.

Nick hardly noticed what he ate. He was aware that he was not joining in the account of their day as enthusiastically as he should. He was grateful to Suzie, who kept up the discussion with Thelma about his mill-working ancestors, as though these older generations of Fewings and Bootles were her family, not his. Once or twice he caught her looking across at him with curiosity. Nick cursed himself that he was not making a better show of hiding his anxiety.

Mercifully, by the time they had cleared away the meal, it was just past the start of one of Thelma's favourite television programmes. The conversation came to an abrupt halt. They settled down to watch.

It was impossible for Nick to concentrate. If he left the room, would Suzie follow? He badly needed to talk to her. But it would look strange if they both absented themselves. He sat through a documentary on Buckingham Palace, hardly taking in what he was seeing.

'Look at this.' Suzie's voice called him out of his troubled thoughts.

Belatedly, he realized that the programme had finished. He looked across at the book in her hand, without real interest.

'I found it on that bookshelf. *A Childhood in Belldale.*'

Thelma looked round from the television screen. 'That old thing! I seem to remember Dad picking it up in a second-hand bookshop when we were off in the dales one day. We've got family buried at Briershaw Chapel out that way.'

'It's got some wonderful pictures,' Suzie said. 'Prints of watercolours. They give you a good idea of what it must have been like growing up in these dales nearly two hundred years ago. Look. There's a little girl jumping across the stepping stones over the beck. And that one of the village school. But this is the one that really intrigues me.'

She found the page and turned the book round to show Nick.

A lean, bespectacled figure with a long beard sat leaning over a workbench in front of a window. He was holding a glass flask of yellow liquid. Strewn around the bench were bundles of herbs. More hung from the beams. The shelves behind him were lined with books and with stoppered bottles of many colours.

'Do you see what it says underneath?' There was excitement in Suzie's voice. '*The Herbalist.*'

Nick stared at it stupidly. He could tell that she was expecting him to respond with surprise and delight. But his anxious mind could make no sense of the picture in front of him.

'The herbalist?' Suzie persisted. 'James Bootle? Handloom weaver and medical botanist?'

The little piece of family history fell into place. Suzie's work on the censuses of 1851 and 1861. The self-employed weaver put out of work by the Industrial Revolution and reinventing himself as a herbalist.

Against the background of the sinister goings-on in Hugh Street and the threatening phone call, it seemed far away and unimportant now.

But he made an effort. 'That's great. I couldn't really picture him before.'

Millie leaned over the sofa to see. 'Looks just like Geoffrey Banks to me. Take away the beard.'

She was right. The bony figure, the head slightly too large for the body, the spectacles slipping forward on his nose, the pale, slightly bulging eyes in the hollow face.

Suzie looked up in surprise. 'I never thought of that. And in a way, I suppose it's the same sort of thing, give or take a century or two. I don't know exactly what an industrial chemist does, but I suppose it has to do with brewing concoctions of some sort. Just on a bigger scale. The only difference is that James Bootle took up herbalism when his work as a weaver was taken away from him. Poor Geoffrey was a chemist, but there's no work for him now.'

'And not likely to be, I'm afraid,' Thelma said. 'He's taken it hard.'

At last they were alone in the small back bedroom. Nick closed the door.

'Right.' Suzie turned to face him. 'Are you going to tell me what this is all about? It was that phone call, wasn't it? You came back indoors looking like death.'

It was on the tip of Nick's tongue to deny it. But he took one look at the determination in her hazel eyes and gave in.

'You're right.' He told her the threatening message. The order not to contact the police about what they had seen. The warning that accidents could happen to his family.

Suzie sat down on the bed, as though her legs no longer felt strong enough to support her.

'It was that man, wasn't it? The one in Hugh Street. The woman we met was clearly terrified of him. And you saw enough to make it clear that something illegal was going on.'

'Enough to resort to death threats?'

'We were only guessing about the sweatshop. Maybe it's something worse. I don't know. And even if it is, if he's that sort of controlling bully, exposing an illegal workshop and getting it closed down would make him really angry. He'd certainly be fined heavily. He might even end up in prison. He's not going to take that lightly.'

'Of course, it could be a bluff. Just to scare us off.'

'And will it?' She raised her eyes to his. 'Nick, we have to decide. Either we report this to the police, both what we saw in Hugh Street and this phone call, or we let cowardice get the upper hand and say nothing.'

Fear crawled through Nick. He had known all along that telling the police was a clear duty. That Suzie's sense of justice would demand it. It was another thing to steel his courage to defy that threat. It had not just been levelled at him. It was the danger to his family. To Suzie. Millie.

He heard again that harsh voice in his ear. *Accidents can happen.*

Suzie got up and walked to the window. It was dark outside. Their room faced up the hill, away from the town. Only a few lights glowed in houses higher up.

Her fingers fiddled with the edge of the curtain. 'Nick. Don't you see? There's something not quite right. This man rang your mobile. He knew your phone number, your name, your architect's qualifications. How could he find all that out? He only saw us for a couple of minutes. *Who is he?*'

He stared at her, speechless. It was not just the shock of what she had said. It was the realization that not once this evening had it occurred to him. The threat had been so immediate, so convincing. He had not dared to ask those questions.

His mouth felt dry. His voice was like the rustle of paper. 'I could kick myself. Why didn't I think of that?'

Suzie turned back to face him. Her normally rosy face seemed paler than usual. 'We didn't have the car with us in Hugh Street. He couldn't have traced us through the number plate, even if he had access to that information. So how did he learn about you? About us?'

Nick concentrated on the memory of that unexpected voice. Just half a dozen sentences. There had been something chilling in its harshness in that first question about Nick's identity, even before he issued his warning.

'I think . . . it may have been someone else. It was a very short call, but I'm not sure it was the same voice as our Mr Harrison. The one who shut the door in my face.'

'So there's a gang of them. This is getting seriously scary. Ring the police now.'

Nick hesitated. 'It's half past ten. There'll only be the night staff at the police station. We need to get there first thing in the morning, to talk to someone with sufficient clout.'

Her eyes were darker now, troubled. 'I don't like this. You don't think he can really know our movements? Where we are now? Whether we do go to the police? I might have thought he was just saying that. Talking big to frighten us. But if he knows so much already, what else does he know about us?'

They slept that night with Nick's arm protectively across Suzie.

# SIX

Nick told Thelma only that they would be going into town in the morning.

'We'll be up at the hospital to visit Uncle Martin at half past two.'

'I've rung the ward. They say he had a good night. He's looking forward to seeing you.'

Nick breathed a sigh of relief. In spite of the disturbing events of yesterday evening, he had still found time to worry about his great-uncle. Ninety-three. A major stroke. There was still the possibility – to put it no stronger than that – that another cerebral haemorrhage would put an end to that long life before Nick could get to his bedside.

'I don't like hospitals,' Millie said. 'They smell funny. And there are all those people, like, at death's door. It just makes me want to turn and run out again.'

'There's nothing to be afraid of,' Suzie told her. 'At least, not if you use their disinfectant washes. But that's more about you not bringing bugs into the hospital as picking them up there. And they put curtains round anyone who's poorly.'

'Dad is so looking forward to seeing you,' Thelma said. 'He'll be that disappointed if you don't show up.'

Millie said nothing more. But Nick had seen the obstinate set of her mouth.

I hope she isn't going to play up about it, he thought. I don't want to leave her behind. After that phone call, I want to keep all my family under my eye. Besides, there's Uncle Martin. It sounds as though this is really important to him as well.

'Tom's coming over as well at the end of the week. We'll have the whole family then,' Suzie said. 'I rang him to put him in the picture about Uncle Martin. He says his last lecture finishes at twelve on Fridays. He wasn't sure which train he'll be getting, but the station's near the hospital, so we've arranged that he'll meet us there.'

'Little Tom!' Thelma exclaimed. 'I remember him from when I came down for your grandfather's funeral. My Uncle David, as was. It seemed a long way to travel down south in those days. Tom must have been about five. But he had that lovely wavy black hair and blue eyes, just like his dad.' She smiled across at Nick. 'I don't remember Millie, though. She would have been a baby.'

'Yes. We didn't think it would be a good idea to bring her to the funeral. A neighbour looked after her.'

'I get to miss out on all the exciting things,' said Millie. 'Just because I'm the youngest.'

'A funeral's not exactly what I'd call exciting,' Thelma reproved her. 'Especially for someone who's just said she's scared of hospitals.'

'It's not the same,' Millie muttered.

She hunched over her toast. This morning she looked more like a moody schoolgirl than the glamorous platinum-blonde young woman Nick was becoming used to. Teenagers. They lived on a roller-coaster of emotions, still discovering hourly who they were, or wanted to be. He smiled across at her, but got no response.

*   *   *

Nick had his leather jacket in his hand. He was staring out of the back bedroom window, without really noticing what he saw.

'Nick!' There was a little edge to Suzie's voice, as though this was not the first time she had said it. 'We said we'd go to the police station first thing.'

The present came rushing back to him. He had almost been afraid to leave his phone switched on, in case there was another unsettling call.

In the clear light of a sunny autumn morning, he began to have doubts. He tried to imagine himself recounting the bizarre events of yesterday to a sceptical police officer. Did they have a stream of nutters coming through the doors with stories as improbable as this? He wondered now how seriously he should have taken that tearful woman, the one occupied house in the boarded-up street, the enigmatic Mr Harrison.

But it had not just been what had happened in Hugh Street. *Accidents can happen. To any of your family.*

It was that phone call which had turned a suspicion of lawbreaking, in which the Fewings would be public-spirited people reporting the irregular goings-on they had witnessed, into a far more menacing scenario.

He heard again that harsh voice and shivered.

'Right!' he said, sounding brighter than he felt. 'Let's get on with it.'

They drove down the precipitously steep hill from High Bank into the town centre. Nick had not wanted to ask Thelma where the police headquarters was. There was no point in alarming her unnecessarily. She had enough on her mind.

He glanced in the rear-view mirror at Millie. For all her glamorously blonde haircut, the face beneath looked small and childish this morning. He had not warned her about last night's phone call. Should he?

Suzie had said, 'Let's tell the police first, and see what they advise. If they take it seriously, we'll probably need to tell Millie. Just so that she's careful.'

Neither of them had wanted to discuss just what they imagined might happen.

Nick drove into an almost empty car park. The town had a

dead feel. Too many people who had no jobs to get up for. He saw another man getting out of his car and went across to him.

'Excuse me. Can you tell me where I can find the police station?'

'It's out of town a bit. Follow the Halifax road and it's on your right, about half a mile up.' He pointed.

'So, no friendly blue light in the middle of town,' Nick said, getting back into the car.

They found it without difficulty. Modern buildings, with a magistrates' court. The morning sun lit up the slopes of Skygill Hill beyond it. Nick looked up at it wistfully. 'We have to find a time to climb that when Tom's here.'

'It looks a long way up,' Millie said gloomily. 'And steep.'

'We can drive up some of the way, and then take the footpath.' Nick ruffled her hair.

She squirmed away. 'Dad! Do you know how long it took to get my hair right this morning?'

'Sorry.' He sensed the vibes were not right today. He hoped desperately that Millie was not going to be difficult about visiting Uncle Martin in hospital. He told himself it was just a teenage thing. A super-sensitivity, perhaps. She'd be all right when they got there.

'Well then,' he tried. 'Let's get this over.'

There was a sergeant at the reception desk. Nick cast a questioning look at Suzie. His head jerked fractionally towards Millie.

Suzie took the hint. 'Come on,' she said to Millie. 'Let's find a seat over by the window. Dad can tell them about the queer goings-on at Hugh Street.'

Nick kept his voice low as he addressed the sergeant. 'I've got two things to report. I assume they're related.'

He gave a brief account of their visit to his grandparents' old address, the agitated woman, the glimpse of another in the boarded-up house, the strange behaviour of the man she had called Mr Harrison.

'And then last evening, I got this phone call.'

'Was it the same man, sir?'

'Hard to be certain. It was a very short call before he rang off. But I'd say not.'

He tried to keep his voice level as he detailed the words of the call as accurately as he could remember them. They still had the power to scare him. 'How the heck did he get my phone number? How did he know who I was?'

'So he threatened you and your family, if you came to us? But you're here.'

'It seemed like the right thing to do. Whoever it is, I want him caught and stopped. I couldn't go around with a threat like that hanging over me and not do anything about it.'

'Quite right, sir. Not everyone is as public spirited. Probably it's nothing. Just some petty felon trying to sound big. But you did right to report it. I'll put you through to Inspector Heap. If you wouldn't mind taking a seat.'

They were kept waiting long enough for some of Nick's hard-won certainty to seep away. For a while this morning, he had wondered whether the whole thing had been too trivial to take to the police. Now he had other reasons for questioning whether he had really done the right thing. It was not just his own safety at stake.

Was it possible that something worse was going on at Hugh Street than the illegal sweatshop they had imagined? He struggled to think what. His imagination showed him the closed face of Mr Harrison, barring to the door to the frantic woman.

But it was the memory of the voice on his mobile that really chilled him. He took the phone out and glanced down at it. No calls, no messages, since then. He put it away again.

At last the duty sergeant called to them. 'Inspector Heap will see you now. Down that corridor. Second on the right.'

Suzie rose to join him. Millie made a movement too, but Suzie put a hand on her shoulder, restraining her.

'Stay here, sweetie. Two's enough.'

Nick saw the rebellious jut of Millie's lip. Too late he wondered again whether they should have taken her into their confidence about the menacing phone call. Still, he could imagine her explosive reaction if he told the inspector about it while she was present. It was better that she stayed where she was until they knew how seriously the police would take it.

'But I'm a witness too!' she was protesting. 'I was there when we met that woman with the little boy, wasn't I? And when that man told her he didn't know her and practically slammed the door in your face. How do you know I didn't notice something you two didn't?'

'If the inspector wants to talk to you as well, I'll come and fetch you. Promise.'

He could feel the indignation seething inside her. For a moment, he was afraid it would erupt into a violent scene of teenage tantrums there in the police station foyer. But she glared at both of them and flounced back into her seat.

They made their way down the corridor the sergeant had indicated. A backward glance showed Nick only Millie's hunched shoulders and short-cropped blonde hair.

Detective Inspector Heap's door was half open. Nick tapped on it.

'Come in.' She was already rising from behind the desk.

Mary Heap was a tall, angular woman. She wore a black skirt with a white blouse. Only the red scarf at her neck counteracted the initial impression that she was in police uniform. Her fair hair was drawn back into a chignon.

'Please. Sit down,' she said when they had introduced themselves.

She stared at them steadily across the desk. There was something chilling about the light blue eyes. Nick sensed no warm curiosity in her smile. A businesslike woman.

'Sergeant Manners tells me you had a strange encounter yesterday in the Canal Street area. Would you like to tell me about it?'

Although it had been Nick who had reported it at the desk, the question seemed addressed to Suzie. Nick noticed the little start she gave. She, too, had assumed that he would take the lead.

She told the detective inspector about their family history quest and their reasons for wanting to find if Hugh Street was still standing. About the unsettling meeting in Canal Street with the woman in the shalwar kameez, who was so visibly upset. How the woman had handed over the little boy and then disappeared down a side street. Finally, she told the detective inspector about the demolished area and then finding Hugh Street still standing but boarded-up, with just this one house that seemed accessible.

'It was the house we were looking for. The one where Nick's grandmother had lived, before they came south.'

Inspector Heap's voice was clipped. 'It's not the past I'm interested in, but what's going on there now.'

'Nick rang the bell, to see if they'd let us look inside. We thought no one was going to answer. Then this man appeared. Sort of peering round the half-open door.'

'Describe him.'

Suzie looked for help to Nick. He had been the one standing on the doorstep with the closest view.

'Shorter than me. And fleshier. Dark hair, going grey, slicked back. Big brown eyes.'

'Asian?'

'I couldn't be sure. There wasn't much light in the room, and he didn't come out into the daylight. His voice sounded typically northern. No foreign accent. He wasn't obviously from the sub-continent.'

He told her how he had explained his reason for coming, and his hope that they might be allowed to have a look at the house he barely remembered from his boyhood.

'Then something caught my eye, and when I looked up there was another woman in a shalwar kameez, standing at the top of the stairs. As soon as she saw me looking at her, she vanished. And then the first woman arrived. The one we'd met in Canal Street after she'd collected her son from playschool.'

He went over the tearful encounter. The fact that the woman had arrived apologetic for being late and obviously expecting to begin work. The man's denial that he knew her.

'I'm sure he was lying. The woman just looked bewildered. And she was devastated when he told her not to come back. It all seemed very strange,' he finished. 'We thought there must be something illegal going on. An unregistered workshop, perhaps. The house is quite small, but if they managed to open a way into other houses in the street, they'd have any amount of work-space to play with.'

The detective inspector's fingernails drummed on the desk. 'Describe this woman.' Again she turned back to Suzie.

'Hard to say. She wasn't wearing a burka, or anything like that. But she had a scarf around her face. She was quite tall. A little more than me. Slim. She had beautiful dark eyes.'

'Young?'

'I'd guess in her twenties. The boy looked about four. But, of course, she may have older children.'

'Attractive?'

Suzie seemed taken by surprise by the question. 'It didn't occur to me to think of her like that. She was so obviously upset. I just wanted to know if there was anything we could do to help.'

'But cast your mind back. Take away the tears. Try to imagine her smiling. Would you say she was an attractive young woman?'

'Well, yes. In ordinary circumstances.'

Mary Heap turned sharply to Nick. 'You say you were the only one who saw the second woman. The one at the top of the stairs. Was she attractive too?'

Nick had a vivid picture of the young Asian woman. The slim figure in the close-fitting pink kameez. Raven hair escaping from her headscarf. The delicate features that had looked in the dim light to be the palest shade of brown.

'Yes, frankly,' he admitted. 'She was. But what's that got to do with working at a sewing machine, or whatever they do, probably for far less than the minimum wage?'

The light blue eyes became steely. 'Perhaps it would be better if you left the detective work to us, sir. There are more ways an attractive woman could be coerced into earning money than with a sewing machine.'

Nick heard Suzie's little gasp beside him.

'You mean . . . it could be a brothel?'

Nick winced. He had a sudden shocked vision of how his grandmother would have reacted to the suggestion that this was the use to which her childhood home was now being put.

Was it possible?

The inspector looked thoughtful.

'Using women from the sub-continent isn't typical. It's mostly Eastern Europeans who get shipped across, ostensibly to work as maids or something, and then find that the deal isn't what they thought it was. Some things here don't fit. The second woman might be being kept against her will, but the one you met in the street obviously isn't. That doesn't mean the man she called Harrison doesn't have some kind of hold over her. Suppose she's not British born. A dodgy visa, perhaps? A forged work permit?'

Again the nails tapped on the desk. A light was beginning to grow in her face. She picked up a phone.

'Send Nichols through to me.'

'There was something else,' Nick said, suddenly remembering what had changed the whole strange episode into something far more sinister. 'It was after we got back to my cousin's. We're staying with her up at High Bank. It was about five o'clock. My mobile rang.'

He repeated, as carefully as he could, the words of that short but chilling phone call.

Again he saw the light sparkling in the detective's eyes.

'But what I don't understand,' he finished, 'is how he could have got my number. I'd given this Harrison man my name when I introduced myself. But not my phone number. Whoever it was even knew my architectural qualifications.'

She stared at him, momentarily disconcerted.

Then she said carefully, 'There are some very unpleasant, controlling people behind these prostitution rings. There can be big money involved. I can't immediately answer your questions about how your caller knew so much. But there's not much you can't find out on the internet these days.'

Of course. It was something of a relief to Nick that there might be a simple explanation. His firm had a website. It was just possible that the man had traced him from there.

Knowledge is power, and the man's unexpected knowledge of Nick had heightened the scary feeling that he held a dangerous power over him.

'He warned me not to approach you. But I have. He can't really find that out, can he? And where we're staying?'

These were things no website could tell him.

Her eyes were serious now. 'You didn't say anything to this Mr Harrison about staying with your cousin?'

Nick tried to think back. It had been a brief exchange. 'No. I'm pretty sure I didn't. Just that I was tracing my ancestors.'

'Hm. Of course, if he knows your name, and he's been able to find out your profession, it won't take him long to discover your home address.'

The new thought chilled Nick. How stupid of him not to have thought of that. Anyone knowing the cathedral city where his architectural practice was could certainly find his home address in the phone book.

Inspector Heap went on. 'Never mind that. We need to get in first. Pick up the people responsible for whatever is going on in Hugh Street. Once they're behind bars, you'll be safe. And so will the women of this town.'

A uniformed woman police officer knocked on the door and entered.

'You sent for me, ma'am?'

'Yes, Nichols. Get hold of Constable Sutcliffe, if he's around. Take this address.' She pushed a sheet of paper across the desk. 'The street's supposed to be boarded up. It's scheduled for demolition. But we have reason to believe there's an illegal brothel operating there. Not the usual prostitutes. Asian women.'

The constable raised her eyebrows.

'Check out the area. See if anyone's noticed any strange goings-on. There won't be any near neighbours if the street's been emptied, but you never know. I need to get a search warrant. Then we'll see.'

She looked round suddenly at Nick and Suzie, almost as though she had forgotten about them.

'Thank you very much for your information. I appreciate your coming here, in spite of that unpleasant phone call. We'll keep you in touch. With any luck, we may need to call you as witnesses.'

'What about the threats to my family?'

'From what you've told me, there's no reason to believe

anyone here knows where you're staying. By the way, would you like to write down your cousin's address for me?'

She pushed a notepad across to him. Nick entered Thelma's address at High Bank. The inspector read it and nodded.

'There may not be anything behind the threat. But just keep your eyes open. Ring us if you have any cause for alarm.' She got to her feet. 'Goodbye now. Enjoy the rest of your stay. We'll look after this.' She gave Nick a rare smile and held out her hand. 'I've been trying for years to nail this kind of thing. You may just have given us the break we need.'

The door closed behind them. Nick found himself out in the corridor with Suzie.

He felt curiously unreassured by Inspector Heap's reasoning.

'I never thought . . .' Suzie said. 'I mean, we jumped to the conclusion that it must be a sweatshop. Prostitution never even entered my head. It's a sobering thought, though. From what I've heard, some of these vice rings can be seriously scary.'

'It's out of our hands now. We can leave the police to sort it.'

He hoped that was true. Phone calls were one thing, though it still troubled him that the unknown man had found his mobile number. But no one knew that the Fewings were staying with Thelma in that little terrace of three houses of millstone grit up on High Bank. They should be safe.

He turned to Suzie with a smile that was only partly reassuring.

'I'll leave you to explain it all to Millie. I don't think I'm flavour of the month.'

# SEVEN

'A vice ring!' exclaimed Millie.

Suzie was trying to explain as they ushered their teenage daughter down the steps outside the police station.

'You mean like fake passports, and they shut them up in houses and never let them go out? And then the police bust them, and they catch these men with their trousers down, and they're trying not to let the photographers see their faces because people think they're, like, really respectable people, MPs and judges and stuff? And the policewomen are taking these girls away?'

To Nick's surprise, Millie seemed more excited than frightened by Inspector Heap's theory. Suzie struggled to convey to her the conditions of slavery under which such girls worked.

'Are they going to raid that place in Hugh Street? If they catch them, and put them in prison, and let the girls go free, it would be all down to us, wouldn't it? I wish I'd taken a photo on my phone when we were there. I can't wait to put this on Facebook!'

'Steady on,' Nick warned her. 'This is just the start of a police investigation. The last thing they'd want is for you to go spreading it all over the internet before they've had a chance to gather the evidence. You don't want to scare them off, or the police would raid the house and find they've flown.'

'Spoilsport!' Millie grumbled. 'But I can tell them afterwards, can't I? When it's in the papers and they put them on trial? I can tell all my mates, "We did that. We were the ones who shopped them."'

'Yes, of course you can,' Suzie told her. 'It just may take a bit of time. Even if they raid the house and find the evidence, it will take a long time to bring it to court.'

She caught Nick's eye over Millie's blonde head.

He felt an uneasy pang of conscience. Neither of them had yet told Millie about that frightening phone call. They had not had a chance to discuss it. Nick looked down at the slender figure of his fourteen-year-old daughter. Was it really necessary to scare her? As long as they were here, it was unlikely that she would be out of their sight for more than a few minutes. He had so much been looking forward to this excursion. The three of them exploring his family's history. Tom joining them at the weekend. As the children grew older, these times together would become increasingly rare. He didn't want anything to spoil it.

'All the same,' Suzie was saying. 'There's still something about it that doesn't sound right. An illegal sweatshop I could

believe. Goodness knows there's little enough employment
here. Women might work for a fraction of the minimum wage
and still think themselves lucky. Especially if they'd been told
not to declare it. But a brothel? Did that woman look to you
like the sort?'

'How do I know?' Nick defended himself. 'It's not my
scene.'

'She certainly didn't look as though she was being coerced
into working there. She was distraught when he turned her
away.'

'So maybe it's not the sort of brothel Inspector Heap thinks
it is. With illegal immigrants.'

'All the same, it doesn't fit.'

They stepped out into the sunshine of the car park.

'What now?' asked Suzie.

Nick felt a double jolt of surprise. First at the sunlight. He
had felt so chilled at times during that interview that he had
forgotten that outside it was a lovely autumn day. Secondly,
by Suzie's implication that they had free time in front of them.
He looked at his watch and was startled to find it was still
only half past nine. They had arranged to see Uncle Martin
in the hospital at two thirty.

'I hadn't thought,' he said. 'What with coming here this
morning and going to the hospital this afternoon, I didn't plan
for anything else.'

'Since we're in town, couldn't we look round the shops?'
Millie said. 'Or Mum and I could.'

Nick's nerves tensed again. He shot a look around the car
park. Could whoever had made that phone call really know
they had gone to the police? Was it possible that he was
watching them even now? There were a couple of other civil-
ians by their cars. Neither of them seemed to be looking their
way. The magistrates' court on the far side looked busier.
Police officers came and went. Cold crawled up his spine as
a new thought struck him. Could that threat have come from
someone inside the ranks of the police? How much more could
he find out about the Fewings?

He tried to fight down his dismay as he remembered writing
Thelma's address on Inspector Heap's notepad.

'Let's stick together,' he said, trying not to sound too alarmed. 'I don't want you two wandering off on your own in a strange town.'

'Dad!'

He saw the blaze of indignation in his daughter's eyes. He heard his own words repeating in his head. It must have sounded incredibly patronising to a fourteen year old who did not know the reason for such exaggerated caution.

Again the finger of doubt strummed on his conscience. Was this the time to tell Millie about that phone call?

'Look,' Suzie put in hastily. 'There's that other place. The old woollen mill further down the valley. It's on our to-do list. It sounds quite a bit different from Thorncliffe Mill. It's powered by a water wheel and it's more about wool than cotton.

'Great!' Millie groaned. 'Another museum.'

'Don't be like that. You enjoyed the last one,' Suzie told her crisply. 'You're just in a bad mood today.'

'Oh, so it's my fault, is it? I get dragged all the way up here for half term, when I could be with my friends. And then I have to go hospital visiting. You know I hate hospitals.'

'So you said,' Nick sighed. 'But really, we can't let Uncle Martin down. Thelma said he's dying to see us.'

'Come on,' coaxed Suzie. 'It could be fun.'

As they drove down the dale out of town, the high crags closed in above them. Nick kept glancing in his rear-view mirror. Were they being followed, or was he just imagining that that blue car was sitting steadily on their tail? It was just too far back for him to make out the driver.

In twenty minutes they found what they were looking for. The tall mill building was almost screened by trees. The Fewings got out and Nick's ears were immediately filled with the sound of rushing water. The river was narrow here, but racing past. He looked up. There was no mill chimney like Thorncliffe's. No steam engine powering the machinery. Belldale was a watermill.

'There's probably been a mill on this same spot since the middle ages,' Suzie said, looking round.

Nick felt a moment's excitement. This was taking the history of the Fewings and Bootles way back beyond the coming of cotton and the Industrial Revolution.

But his mind switched to the present. Surely it was fanciful to think they had been followed out of town out into the dales?

Again, his eyes were alert as they crossed the car park to the mill entrance. He had feared that the blue car would draw in beside them. But though he scanned the road, he saw no sign of it. It must have turned off, or driven past.

He breathed more easily. He had been letting his imagination run away with him, seeing threats where there were none. The rush of the river was soothing. The cluster of houses around Belldale Mill was no more than a village. They read the board beside the entrance. In the nineteenth century, an industrialist had chosen this site to expand the home-based wool production of the dales on a mechanised scale. It looked as if it had changed little since. But its history was older still.

'I was right,' Suzie said. 'The earliest reference to a mill here was in the fourteenth century.'

'I thought you said these big mills didn't happen till the Industrial Revolution,' Millie pointed out.

'Not *that* sort of mill, for mass-produced weaving or spinning. This used to be a fulling mill. People wove the cloth in their own homes and brought it here to be finished. You'll see all about it inside.'

Nick tried to lock his anxieties away in the car and enjoy the experience.

They wandered through the galleries, which demonstrated the fulling process. Explanatory boards illustrated how, back in Roman times, people had soaked the freshly woven cloth in stale urine and then trampled it underfoot, to make it stronger and thicker.

'Yuck!' cried a childish voice behind them.

Nick looked round. There was a family of four following the same route through the mill. To judge by the ages of his children, the father was probably younger than Nick. But he carried more weight. Black hair was slicked down over a forehead that was already receding. His wife was thin, angular, in a pink cardigan. She had anxious eyes on her children. It was the faces of the children that amused him. The boy, about eight, had creased up his face in exaggerated disgust. The little girl, some two years younger, was laughing as she danced up and down, mimicking the drawing of slaves trampling the cloth.

Nick exchanged a grin with the father. 'Don't they just love things like that?'

'The more disgusting the better,' he laughed back.

Even Millie could not resist her delight at the earthenware pots in which, in later times, the millers had collected urine from the families around, to soak the woollen cloth before fulling.

'A penny a pot, and tuppence if you were a teetotaller,' chuckled the guide who had followed them into the gallery. 'The Methodists did well out of it. Now, if you'll follow me, we're about to demonstrate the wheel.'

'Your family would have been OK, then,' Millie said to Nick. 'All those Methodists and Baptists.'

'They're your family too, remember.'

In the next room, there were giant pivoting wooden hammers.

'The fulling stocks,' Suzie whispered. 'To beat the cloth with, instead of using your feet.'

A small crowd had followed them in response to the guide's invitation. Nick felt a sense of unease as they were herded together into this smaller space. He looked behind him. The boy and girl he had seen before wriggled to the front. Their oddly matched parents stood next to Nick. The plump-faced man with his pale, angular wife. Surely nothing to be concerned about there. A Japanese couple, or were they Korean? Their cameras were busy. It was stretching credulity to think that they could have anything to do with it. Yet how did he know? The women in Hugh Street had roots far afield.

His eyes passed over another couple who were probably in their seventies. The woman had permed grey hair, not unlike Thelma's. Her husband was a taller man, leaning on a stick. They spoke together in a comfortable Lancashire accent. No stretch of Nick's imagination could associate them with a criminal gang.

He twisted his head to the other side for a last look, and

stiffened. The last man in the group was alone. He was of middle age, with a military bearing. He stood a little behind the others. Nick glimpsed a yellowish moustache in a ruddy face. He carried none of the obvious signs of a sightseer. No camera. No leaflet about the exhibition in his hand. Nick met his eye. A shiver ran through him. What was this man doing here?

There was no reason why a man like that should not indulge an interest in industrial history.

Nevertheless, Nick felt unsettled as he turned back to listen to their guide.

At the end of the room, the old waterwheel loomed blackly in its housing. Even as they watched, it began to turn. Water spilled from its buckets, powering the endless cycle. As it lumbered into motion, the great fulling hammers began to lift and fall. With each strike, they pounded the cloth in its troughs.

'It's the original wheel,' their guide explained. 'And still going strong. Though it does sometimes slip from its bearings, and we have a devil of job hoisting it back.'

The turning of the wheel and the pounding of the hammers beat a rhythm in Nick's head. He longed to turn and see if the man behind was still watching him.

'Of course,' explained the guide, 'Health and safety means we can't let you experience the original smell. This place would have been reeking of stale piss.'

This time Millie joined the children in a delighted cry of 'Yuck!'

Suzie caught Nick's eye and smiled. He felt some of the tension ease out of him.

He risked another look behind him. The man with the moustache was staring straight in front of him. It was impossible to tell whether he had been watching Nick or the wheel.

Nick found himself moving closer to Suzie and Millie.

The water wheel slowed to a halt. Water dripped from the buckets. The demonstration was over.

The phone in his inside pocket buzzed. Nick started. Slowly, he drew the mobile out. He held it in his palm for a while. He had a strong reluctance to read the text message.

With a sudden decision he clicked on it.

It was message from his architect partner, Jeremy, wanting Nick to answer a question from one of his clients.

He breathed a deep sigh of relief and slipped the phone back inside his leather jacket.

The guide had left them. The little party dispersed. As they walked away to another part of the mill, Nick looked behind him again. The man was standing at the doorway of the fulling room. His eyes seemed to be following them.

The Asian couple and the elderly pair took a different exit. The family with the two young children followed the same route as the Fewings. Next time Nick looked round, the man with the moustache was no longer with them.

They tried their hands at carding wool with teasels from the hedgerows and with combs. They looked at different sorts of loom.

In one room they came upon a life-size tableau. A girl was combing a hank of wool with a spiky teasel-head. Her mother was turning it into yarn on her spinning wheel and the father was weaving the yarn on his loom.

As he stood regarding the realistic figures, Nick's mind flew back to James Bootle, the handloom weaver. This was the sort of domestic scene, the whole family at work, James and his wife had once assumed would be theirs for a lifetime. It had been taken away from them by the building of mills, like the one the Fewings were standing in.

Unbidden, a thread of thought ran through his mind. Like the illegal sweatshop he thought he had discovered in Hugh Street. Women forced by poverty into working long hours for low wages . . .

That was before Inspector Heap had suggested it might be something worse still.

How many young women like James Bootle's daughters been forced into prostitution as their livelihood was taken away by machines?

And now his own daughter was in a different danger because of what he had unwittingly discovered.

Had the man with the military bearing really been here innocently?

'Are you all right, Dad? You keep looking at me strangely all morning.'

'Yes.' He pulled himself up sharply and put on a smile for her. 'Yes, of course I am. And why wouldn't I want to look at my beautiful daughter?'

They left the fulling mill behind. As the Fewings crossed the yard, Nick was conscious of that other family with children waiting by the doorway. Only when the Fewings had passed them did the round-faced father and his angular wife follow.

In another part of the building, there were demonstrations of spinning. The equipment changed, from the distaffs women hung on their girdles to work with as they walked, to spinning wheels of various sizes and complexities, and finally to a room filled with rows of Crompton's Mules. Here again, the two families paused for a demonstration. At a signal, the machines sprang into motion. The moving carriages shot out and raced back, temporarily opening up a gap between the spindles and the roller beams.

'Scavengers had to get under there to clean up the waste that dropped,' the guide shouted above the noise. 'They used kids for that. Probably the most dangerous work in the mill. You were working your way up to be a piecer, mending broken threads. But even then you were lucky if your spinner would stop the mule for you. The older ones might take pity on you. But the young men with growing families didn't want to lose a penny by slowing down. You had to risk life and limb while it was moving.'

'Don't tell me, Dad,' sighed Millie. 'That's what I'd have been doing a hundred and fifty years ago. It's a wonder you had any ancestors left to grow up and have kids.'

'We're a tough lot, the Fewings,' Nick laughed. 'But yes, the mill was a dangerous place.'

A mobile phone rang. Alarm leaped in Nick's throat. It took a second or two to realize that it was not his own ringtone.

He saw the father of the children step back out of earshot to answer it.

All the same, his heart was thudding. All morning he had been resisting the urge to take out his mobile and check for messages.

He looked at his watch again.

'We ought to be getting back. Thelma's doing lunch for us at one. I told her we could look after ourselves, since she's back at work this morning. But she wouldn't hear of it.'

'I suppose she's always been used to nipping back to see to Uncle Martin at lunchtime,' Suzie said. 'She wouldn't want to leave him alone all day at his age.'

'It'll be lonely for her when he goes. I think she needs someone to look after.'

There was no else around in the car park. Nick breathed a sigh of relaxation.

He drove out of the mill entrance on to the valley road. His stomach lurched sharply. There was a blue Honda parked outside under the trees.

Someone *had* followed them to the mill.

His mind flew back to their tour of the galleries. He checked again the people he could remember. He had lost sight of the man with the moustache after the water wheel. Who else had there been? That family with the boy and girl? Hardly. The pair of Japanese tourists with cameras flashing? Could there have been someone else prowling through the mill behind them? Someone unnoticed among the display cases and the tall machinery? Who else might have tracked them here and heard them talking about their movements for the rest of the day?

He must stop scaring himself. How many blue cars were there, for goodness' sake? This one need not have been anything to do with the car that had followed them down the dale. And even if it had, it could be just another innocent tourist, come by the same road to visit Belldale Mill.

He watched his mirror carefully as he drove back to town. Only once did he think he caught a glimpse of the blue car following. Then he lost it. It must, after all, have been his imagination.

# EIGHT

**M**idday dinner was nearly ready when they got back to High Bank. Thelma looked flushed from hurrying back from work to cook for them, but refused Suzie's help. She set Millie to laying the table.

Nick retired outside, to sit on the bench in the sunshine. There was a slight haze in the valley below, where once it would have been dark with smoke. Riding above it, Skygill Hill stood clear and bright. Nick's legs longed to be climbing it. It would be good to shed the worries of the last twenty-four hours and feel only the light burden of a knapsack.

Had he done the right thing, going to the police? The more he thought about it, the more clearly he realized that they were unlikely to catch the ringleaders of a vice ring straight away – if ever. He was increasingly sure it had not been the plump Mr Harrison who had rung him. The voice had been harder, colder.

And had he done the right thing by not warning Millie to be on her guard? He stirred the gravel at his feet. He and Suzie had not wanted to frighten her. They would make sure that Millie stayed with them, wherever they went.

Yet how could he protect his family, if he didn't know what form the threat might take?

Almost without intending it, he found he had his phone in his hand. It had begun to exercise a horrid fascination over him. On the way home, there had been two more text alerts. He had ignored them. He knew that he was waiting for it to ring. It was the menace in that voice he dreaded.

The silver mobile lay in his hand, silent. He could no longer resist the impulse to open it up.

Yes. Two new text messages. Why was he suddenly reluctant to read them?

But he must.

The first was also work related. That could wait until he got back.

There was no number for the caller on the second. The shock took hold of him as he saw the capital letters.

BAD MOVE.

He sat staring down at it. He felt momentarily paralyzed.

It was true. His worst fear. Whoever had warned him not to approach the police knew that he had. He glanced round in alarm. Was someone watching him, even now? It had seemed so peaceful, sitting here in the autumn sun, on his own. Could anyone know he was here at High Bank, at Thelma's? And had they been followed to the police station? Or had the information come from inside the police? Whatever the answer, someone knew. Someone whose voice had made him feel it was not an idle threat.

Should he take his family home now? Drive back south as fast as he could?

It wouldn't help. But Inspector Heap had made it very clear that anyone who already knew that much about him could find his home address. He felt the sweat on his neck.

He found the detective inspector's card among his own business cards, in his inside jacket pocket. He tried to keep his thumb steady as he dialled her number. Her voicemail came on, inviting him to leave a message. It was hard to order his thoughts sensibly.

'He's just texted me. Sorry! This is Nicholas Fewings. We came to see you this morning. It just says, "bad move". He knows I've been to the police. What do I do?'

It sounded pathetic, helpless. There must be some way he could take the initiative, put a stop to this.

He couldn't think how.

Nick was halfway through his treacle tart when his phone rang. He was alarmed at the physical shock he felt. There was a different jolt of surprise when he looked anxiously at the screen and found not number withheld but a local number. He breathed more easily. Of course. It was probably Inspector Heap's landline from police headquarters.

'Excuse me. Do you mind if I take this in the front room?'

He was right. The inspector's voice calmed his worst fears.

'Mr Fewings? I'm sorry I missed your call. I said I'd get

back to you if there was any news. Look, I've got people
checking out your complaint. We haven't gone into the house
yet. You understand it's important we stake it out to get
more than the small-time players, like your Mr Harrison. But,
if it's any consolation, from the present signs, we're pretty
much satisfied that it's not a brothel. There are certainly women
coming and going. More than you'd expect, even if the house
was legitimately occupied. You could be right about their
having broken through to other houses in the street. I probably
shouldn't be telling you this, but the profile of the women just
doesn't look right for prostitutes.'

'That's what we tried to tell you,' Nick tried to intervene.

The inspector's voice swept on. 'And they seem to be coming
voluntarily. It's just not the way those international vice rings
operate. The girls are usually virtual prisoners. Their passports
are confiscated and they're not allowed out. No, I think your
original guess that this is an undercover sweatshop is probably
right.'

'We never thought it was a brothel. That was your idea. But
it's still illegal, isn't it?'

'It's vice and sex crimes I'm mainly concerned with. I'm
handing this over to one of my colleagues. As I said, I shouldn't
think they'll go in until they've got more evidence. But I think
you can rest easy that it's under control.'

'But this threatening text message? I told you. It said "bad
move". Somebody knows I went to the police. And they're
not pleased about it.'

'Let's keep this in proportion, sir. If I thought we were
dealing with a vice ring, I'd be worried. There can be big
money involved, and some pretty ugly characters with
unpleasant methods of ensuring silence. But I hardly think a
sweatshop owner is going to go over the top to track down a
member of Joe Public and put the frighteners on him. OK,
he's got your number. He just hopes a couple of scary phone
calls will warn you off.'

'But he *knows*. How does he know we went to the police
station? He must be following us. And I'm almost sure there
was a car tailing us this morning. All the way down to
Belldale. A blue Honda. It was parked outside the textile

museum. He must have found out where we're staying. I can't think how.'

'Don't you think you may be jumping to conclusions, sir? What did he say? Bad move? You've assumed he meant coming to us. He could just as easily be referring to your visit to Hugh Street yesterday. I understand you're alarmed. It's an unpleasant experience, an anonymous threatening call. But it's more common than you realize. Emails, Facebook, nowadays. Most of the time it's just words. Cyber bullying.'

'And the rest of the time?'

'Mr Fewings.' The inspector sounded weary. 'My colleagues are getting all the evidence they can to put a stop to this practice. Catch the people behind it, if they can. But I really don't think it calls for twenty-four-hour police protection. You've done your citizen's duty, and I thank you for that. The best thing you can do now is forget those phone calls and enjoy the rest of your holiday.'

The line went dead.

Nick was left with a feeling of anticlimax. He stared out of the window, past the potted plant on the sill.

Was he being over-melodramatic? Would that menacing BAD MOVE have been sent, whether or not he had been to the police station this morning? Was he imagining that the blue Honda had deliberately followed them to Belldale Mill?

He was beginning to feel the comforting temptation to let it all slip from his shoulders. To stop looking around for someone watching them. To accept that the goings-on at Hugh Street did not warrant such a life-threatening reaction. Just let the police get on with it, and turn his attention to the purpose of his visit. And Uncle Martin.

He felt a sharp pang of guilt. He had been so caught up in his own anxieties that he had hardly given a thought to the ninety-three year old lying in hospital.

He checked his watch. No panic. There was still an hour before they needed to leave for the hospital.

And tomorrow they would be meeting Tom. Nick's spirits rose. He suddenly realized how much he was looking forward to seeing his tall, good-looking son again for the first time since he started at university.

He felt a glow of warmth. The whole family together again. And united with the last of that older generation he thought he had lost when his grandmother died.

If nothing went wrong. If Uncle Martin, already debilitated by the stroke, made it until tomorrow afternoon.

When Nick returned to the back room, Thelma was already bustling around, collecting her handbag and car keys, ready to go back to work.

'I'll have to love you and leave you. Leave the washing up. I'll do it when I get back.'

'Don't be silly,' Suzie told her. 'We'll do it, won't we, Millie? We've got plenty of time.'

Millie murmured a non-committal reply. She looked drawn in on herself.

Nick felt a spasm of irritation. She had seemed to be getting on so well with Thelma yesterday. She must be still sulking about the hospital visit this afternoon. But it was no good; she would have to come. He could not imagine himself explaining to Uncle Martin that his great-great-niece had simply not wanted to come and see him.

With the three of them helping, the lunch things were quickly cleared away. Nick checked his watch again.

'Be down here at two o'clock,' he told Millie. 'We need to allow time to find a parking space at the hospital.'

'Whatever,' muttered Millie. She went upstairs to the bedroom she was sharing with Thelma.

'Thelma's putting Tom in Uncle Martin's room tomorrow,' Suzie said when she had gone. 'I think he was going to have to sleep on the sofa otherwise. But it's unlikely Uncle Martin will be out of hospital by then.'

'Tom wouldn't have minded. It will be great to see him again. I hadn't realized how much I'd been missing him.'

Suzie looked at him shrewdly. 'That phone call? It wasn't anything serious, was it?'

'No! No, it was Inspector Heap. She said her team have come to the conclusion our first guess was right. It's probably an illegal sweatshop. It's plausible, isn't it? There's a blight on that area at present, with the downturn in the economy. No one's in a hurry to finish the demolition and build anything new. If we hadn't happened along, they could have carried on undisturbed for who knows how long. The police are not going in, even now. They'd like to catch the brains behind it, if they can. But the downside is that I'm afraid our inspector has lost interest. I gather vice rings and crimes against women are what she's after. Breaking employment laws and health-and-safety regulations doesn't quite cut it for her. She's handed it over to someone else.'

'But these women are still being exploited, even if not as prostitutes! It's a modern form of slavery.'

'I know, I know. But the long and the short of it is, she's downgraded that threatening phone call. Doesn't think the fines for running a sweatshop warrant a death threat – or not carrying it out, at least. She says it's just harassment.'

He knew there was a glaring gap in what he was telling her. He still hadn't shared that frightening text message. BAD MOVE. It still chilled him to think about it. He would rather Suzie and Millie didn't know.

But then . . . perhaps Inspector Heap had been right. Perhaps whoever sent that message really didn't know they'd been to the police. It could have been just a carry-over from yesterday and their unwelcome appearance in Hugh Street.

He thought of the tearful woman arriving late to work and being turned away. His conscience troubled him. The Fewings' arrival had cost her a shift's pay, pitiful though that probably was. It might be worse than that. In a town with soaring unemployment rates, what else could she do if she lost her job?

'I'm going upstairs to get ready,' Suzie said, interrupting his thoughts.

He followed her.

# NINE

Nick was aware of a sense of gladness when he saw Millie coming down the stairs. She still looked unhappy about the prospect of hospital visiting, but at least she was there.

Her thin shoulders were hunched inside her green wool jacket.

'Do I have to?'

'Cheer up,' Suzie told her. 'You visited Tamara when she was in hospital this summer.'

'That was different. Tamara's my best friend.'

'Try thinking about Uncle Martin,' Nick told her. 'From what Thelma's told us, he's been looking forward to seeing all of us. You especially. He's never met you. You're the youngest of the Fewings now. The next generation.'

Millie twirled the brass button on her jacket. 'Did you say he actually knew that other Millie? The one who worked in the cotton mill when she was eight?'

'The daughter of the herbalist,' Suzie said. 'That's right. Millicent Bootle would have been in her sixties when Great-uncle Martin was born, but apparently he remembers her. She was a bit of a character, apparently.'

'All right, then,' Millie said grudgingly. 'If I must.'

Perhaps it will be better than she thinks, Nick thought, walking out to the car. The old millworker of ninety-three, the fourteen-year-old schoolgirl. Uncle Martin had no grandchildren of his own, and never would now. Nick could imagine the old man's eyes lighting up at the sight of the slender blonde teenager who was the latest to carry the family name. He prayed that Millie would get over her sulks. She could be delightful when she chose.

The hospital car park looked different in the sunshine of a bright autumn afternoon. Trees had been planted among the rows of cars and their leaves glowed russet and gold.

Nick led the way. There was no need to stop at the reception desk in the foyer. He knew the way. He followed the signs to Crompton Ward.

He paused in the doorway, letting other visitors sidle past him. His eyes moved down the line of beds. Uncle Martin had been on the left side of the ward, hadn't he? About six beds down.

His gaze scanned along the row of patients, most of them elderly. Some already had visitors. A few rested on their pillows, eyes closed. Most of them were connected to electronic monitors. None of them looked the way he had remembered Uncle Martin on Tuesday evening, sunk in sleep, with that grey cadaverous face.

A cold hand closed round his heart. Was it possible that since Thelma had phoned the hospital this morning the old man had died? He tried to tell himself that there were no closed curtains in that part of the ward. No empty bed. Could they really have shuffled him off to the mortuary and filled his bed already? And surely there would have been a phone call to Thelma?

'Can I help you?' a passing nurse asked.

'Martin Fewings. My great-uncle. We've come to visit him. But I can't seem to see his bed.'

She hurried across to the nurses' station and consulted the papers.

She came back smiling, 'Sorry, we've moved him. We like to keep them in here for twenty-four hours after a stroke. That's the most critical time. But there are always new arrivals wanting the beds. You'll find him on Haworth today. Down the corridor and turn left.'

He thanked her. In the corridor he shrugged at Suzie and Millie. 'Sorry, I've led you astray. It's round the corner.'

As Millie fell behind, he whispered to Suzie, 'Just for a moment, when I couldn't find him where he was before, I thought he'd croaked. Imagine having to explain that to Millie.'

Haworth Ward had a livelier feel. Most of the patients were sitting up, either chatting to their visitors or waiting expectantly. This time Nick went straight to the nurses' station to ask.

'Where will I find Martin Fewings? I gather they've moved him here from Crompton.'

A plump young nurse scanned the names before her. 'This way.'

Another nurse put out her hand to stay her. She whispered in her ear.

The nurse's round face turned up to Nick and Suzie, apologetically. 'I'm sorry. He's had . . . a bit of a setback. The doctor's with him now.'

Nick's eyes flew along the ward. Only one bed had curtains drawn around it.

'Is he . . . Is it serious?'

'I'm sorry. I'm not allowed to say. You'd have to ask the doctor. Are you a relative?'

'His great-nephew. We've come all the way from the south-west to visit him.'

'I'm sorry. But there's nothing I can do. Sister's with the doctor. She may be able to tell you more when they've finished with him. Would you like to wait? The canteen's on the next floor. You could go and have a cup of tea and come back in half an hour.'

'Is he going to die?' Millie's voice came unexpectedly from behind them.

The nurse looked flustered. 'I hope not, love. We're doing everything we can for him. Still, he's an old man. We've all got to go one day, haven't we?'

Millie turned and almost ran out of the ward. Suzie hastened after her.

'Sorry!' Nick said hurriedly to the nurse.

'Was it me? Did I put my foot in it?'

'She's just a bit sensitive about hospitals. It's her age.'

He strode after them. Suzie had caught up Millie at the head of the stairs.

'It's all right, love. These things happen, especially at his age. That's why he's in hospital. So that the doctors can see to him straight away if anything goes wrong. They're looking after him now.'

'You don't know that!' Millie rounded on her. 'They drew the curtains round his bed, didn't they? For all you know, he could be lying there dead. And you made me come here!'

'It's OK.' Nick put his arm around her shoulders. He could feel her trembling. 'It's probably like the nurse said. A bit of a setback. We can come again tomorrow. I expect he'll be sitting up in bed, right as rain. How about that cup of tea? Or a latte? I don't know what the hospital canteen runs to.'

Millie shrugged him off. 'Don't patronize me. And I'm not going into any hospital canteen. It would make me puke.'

'All right, then. City centre? A nice café? Possibly a cream doughnut? And a bit of window shopping?'

She managed a shaky grin. 'Now you're talking.'

Light drifts of clouds had blown across the sky in the short time they had been inside. The bright afternoon sun had been obscured. The red leaves on the trees between the cars looked darker.

Nick felt the oppression on his own spirits. He had so looked forward to this. Rediscovering the land of his grandparents, bringing awake the fragmentary memories of childhood visits. A sense of rootedness that he had never quite managed in the rural south-west. That was Suzie's country. Centuries of her ancestors, from farm labourers to lords of the manor. His own heritage was different. Industrial, non-conformist. Ingrained in his forebears like the grime in the millstone grit of the local houses.

Instead, he had stumbled upon a different darkness. The yet-unfathomed crime that must be going on in Hugh Street. The venom in that voice on his phone, which made him constantly look over his shoulder. Great-uncle Martin, whom he had so much wanted to meet again. A treasure house of information about the past, *his* past, which he had never thought to ask about until now. And instead, a stroke-ridden old man in a hospital bed with the curtains drawn. There was a very real possibility that he had come too late.

A little wind was kicking up the leaves on the car park as they hurried to their car. Nick was uneasy. There had been no further messages since that ominous text at lunchtime. But he could not shake off the feeling that they were being watched. Despite Inspector Heap's reassurance, he felt a conviction that the words BAD MOVE were the result of his visit to the police station.

It was too late to change that now. He had done what he thought was right. Suzie had backed him. They would have to live with the consequences.

He only wished he knew what they were.

With heightened caution he looked all around him as he snapped the car locks open. The large car park was full. Hundreds of friends and relatives hospital visiting. He was about to open the door when his heart constricted. A small blue car was backing out of a bay two rows away.

'Look!' he cried, hearing his voice rise an octave. 'It's that blue Honda again.'

Suzie paused on the other side of the car. 'Are you sure it's the same one? Did you get the number plate?'

'No, but it's not going to be a coincidence. It was following us all the way down to Belldale. It was parked outside the mill, but not in the visitors' car park where we would have seen it. And I'm almost sure I got a glimpse of it once behind us on the way back.'

'So? It's half term. Belldale's a visitor attraction. We can't be the only ones who would want to go and see it for perfectly innocent reasons.'

Millie put her head out from the back seat. 'What's up with you two? Are we going to find this café or not?'

Suzie shot a warning look at Nick. 'Sorry, love. We're coming.'

She slid her legs into the passenger seat. Nick started the ignition and put the car into gear. As he checked over his shoulder before reversing out he saw the blue Honda pause, as though to let Nick out first. He had a glimpse of the driver. Male. Round-faced. Black hair slicked down. There was no one else in the car.

A burst of anger shot through Nick. He was not going to drive out in front of the Honda and endure that feeling of being followed again. He waited.

There were several seconds hesitation. Then the Honda drove past. He watched it turn towards the exit gates.

On a sudden impulse he slammed the car into gear again and shot after it.

He raced along the avenue of cars, praying he would not be too late to see where the blue car went. He dodged around cars already starting to back out.

'Nick!' Suzie exclaimed. 'What's the hurry?'

'If he's going to crash the car, I suppose a hospital car park is the best place to do it.' Millie commented from behind them.

'I want to see where he goes. Who he is,' Nick muttered through gritted teeth.

When they reached the main road, the blue car was already heading down the hill.

Nick turned that way, ignoring the blasts of horns as he shot into the fast-moving traffic.

'Nick! You cannot be serious! Just because it's the same make of car as the one at Belldale. It'll be some perfectly innocent citizen on his way home.'

'Would somebody mind telling me what this is all about?' came a voice from the back seat.

Suzie turned round. 'Your father's got some mad idea that somebody's been following us.'

'Great! Like we're some sort of celebrity? Can we expect the paparazzi outside Thelma's house next?'

Nick swallowed down the guilt that told him he should have explained the situation to Millie. How long could he protect her from the frightening facts?

Nevertheless, he swept past the entrance to the shopping mall in the centre of the town, and the signs pointing to car parks. Some way in front of him he could still see the small blue car heading into the housing estates on the opposite side.

Suzie was tense beside him. He suspected she disapproved of what he was doing. A saner part of himself told him she was probably right. But she was not going to argue in front of Millie.

And Nick was not going to lose this chance of following his pursuer to his base and finding his identity.

Did the driver know that he was the one now being followed?

The car disappeared round the corner of a road in a modern estate. Nick slowed. Was it a ruse? Would the driver lurk there until he had driven past, and then slip out to follow him again?

Cautiously he paused at the turning. There was no blue car in sight.

It was Millie who leaned forward and pointed. 'Up there, Dad. At the top of the drive, third house on the right.'

# TEN

Nick eased the car around the corner and stopped.

'Stay here,' he ordered.

'Nick! What do you think you're going to do?' Suzie exclaimed. 'Just because some perfectly ordinary guy happens to drive a blue Honda, you can't go storming up his garden path and bawl him out.'

'I've had enough.' Nick's face felt stiff, though his limbs were unaccountably trembling. He felt fury that someone had cast him in the role of victim. He wanted to be in charge of events.

He strode up the sloping drive. There was a child's scooter propped against the wall beside the open garage. The offending car was parked outside.

Nick pressed hard on the doorbell.

The door opened more abruptly than he had expected. A thin, sharp-boned woman stood in front of him. A pink cardigan hung loosely from her shoulders. Her face looked angry.

'It's his day off,' she snapped. 'Can't he have a single afternoon with his family? First he gets called out to the hospital, only it seems the woman's not at death's door after all. Then some nutter from the university comes barging round again. Now you . . .' Her tone changed. 'Unless someone really has died?'

An expression of consternation was beginning to replace her indignation. Her face was colouring. She wrapped her cardigan round her thin body. 'I'm sorry. It's awful to talk like that. But you've no idea what it's like being a Baptist minister. People just *use* him. All the time. Sucking the energy out of him. Like he doesn't need a private life like ordinary people.'

Nick found himself staring at her. His jaw had dropped. He recognized this woman. She was part of the family of four who had followed the Fewings round the exhibition of spinning and fulling at Belldale Mill. Sure enough, through the open back door he could glimpse the boy and girl playing on the lawn.

'It's all right, Bethan.'

The door into the sitting room had opened. The same round-faced man with the slicked down hair came out into the hall. He looked Nick up and down with a puzzled smile.

'I'm sorry. Do I know you? I've usually got a good memory for faces, but I don't think I've seen you in the congregation. How can I help you?'

'Harry! I've explained that this is supposed to be your day off. And you've got Dominic again.'

'Ah, yes. Dominic.' The minister's voice dropped low. He gave a weary smile and looked back over his shoulder at the sitting room.'

Past his broad shoulder Nick could see a bespectacled young man on the sofa. He was sitting tensely upright, glaring at them.

The minister held out his hand to Nick. 'Harry Redfern?' There was a hint of enquiry in the introduction.

Nick tried to hold on to his anger. It was what had driven him here.

'Nick Fewings. But you know that, don't you? You've been following me.'

He tried to match the minister's rather deep sonorous voice with the threatening tone of that brief phone call. 'Was it you who rang me to warn me off? Did you send that text message?'

'Shall I ring the police?' He heard the anxious whisper from Harry Redfern's wife beside him. She was quietly backing off towards the kitchen.

'No, love. I'll handle it.' The Reverend Redfern turned a tired smile on Nick. 'I'm sorry, Mr Fewings. There seems to have been a misunderstanding. Whoever's being making nuisance phone calls to you, I can assure you it wasn't me. I've enough problems in my line of work to cope with, without creating new ones. And I'm afraid you're a complete stranger to me . . .' He stiffened suddenly. His round brown eyes creased. 'Hang on a moment. I *have* seen you before. Got it! This morning. Weren't you at Belldale Mill? Wonderful place. The kids loved it. As I remember, you had a lass of your own.'

Nick's certainty was flooding out of him, leaving only embarrassment. But at the mention of Millie he checked. Could this be a coded warning? In spite of all his protestations of innocence could this portly Baptist minister really be the man behind whatever gang was operating in Hugh Street? It seemed impossible to imagine, but it would be a great disguise.

But he looked around the modest semi-detached house, the clutter of toys in the hall, the untidy garden, the harassed look of Redfern's wife. There was no evidence here of the proceeds of crime.

He felt himself colouring. 'I'm sorry. I think I must have made a mistake. I'd had this threatening phone call. I think it's about something I reported to the police. And then I saw your car . . .'

'And you thought I was following you because we'd had the same idea of visiting Belldale Mill.'

'And then I saw you at the hospital.'

'Yes. Mrs Beasley. One of my flock. Fortunately not as near death's door as she thought she was.' He looked keenly at Nick with what might be professional sympathy. 'Nothing wrong, I hope.'

'My great-uncle. Martin Fewings. He had a stroke two days ago. We went to visit him, but he's taken a turn for the worse.'

'Martin? I'm very sorry to hear that. Stoneyham Methodist. We've worked together on a few committees, Martin and I. A grand old-stager. I must look in next time I do my hospital rounds.'

'Harry!' Mrs Redfern's voice was low but scolding.

'Sorry, love.' He turned to Nick. 'Excuse me if I don't invite you in. I've got someone else with me.' He smiled wearily at his wife. 'I'll get rid of him as soon as I can, but the lad needs to talk.'

'And you need a rest day.'

Harry Redfern shrugged. He went back into the sitting room. In the doorway he turned his head. 'I hope you've reported those phone calls to the police. I've had my share of them. They can give you a nasty turn, even the ones that are just talk.'

'Yes, I've told them,' Nick said dully. 'They weren't taking it as seriously as I'd like.'

'So you thought you'd take matters into your own hands. Go carefully.'

Nick glimpsed Dominic, the minister's other, younger visitor. He was on his feet and glaring at this intruder before he reclaimed Harry Redfern's attention.

Nick walked down the steeply sloping drive with the consciousness that he had made a fool of himself. The Reverend Harry Redfern had been courteous and even sympathetic. But Nick was appalled that he had let his obsession with those phone calls lead him into such paranoia. Mrs Redfern might not have been playing the role of the smiling minister's wife, but her indignation had been justified.

A figure shot past him. A small boy on a scooter who checked himself with a spinning turn on the pavement outside the gate.

'Ben!' his mother's exasperated cry came from behind them.

Nick grinned at the boy as he reached the gate. 'She's right, you know. You never know what might come speeding along the road.'

'I can handle it,' said the boy loftily.

Nick climbed into the driver's seat. Suzie turned to him with a belligerent air.

'Well?'

'You were right,' he sighed. 'He's a Baptist minister. Harry Redfern. He's a mate of Uncle Martin's. Yes, he was following us to Belldale Mill, but only because he was taking his kids there. You remember that family that were with us when the guide was explaining about the fulling mill?'

'All those piss pots.' Millie added.

'Apparently it's his day off. I suppose he works all Sunday.'

'And it's half term,' Suzie said. 'A perfectly normal thing for a family to do. Like us.'

'He had a call to the hospital. That's why he was there. One of his congregation. I told him about Uncle Martin. He's going to look in and see him.'

'So. A man of God. A pillar of the community. And you go and accuse him of being a criminal mastermind.'

'But why?' Millie asked. 'Why did you think someone was following you? Is it because you went to the police?'

Nick exchanged glances with Suzie. 'Something like that. Sorry, kid. I seem to be getting paranoid.'

'You've been watching too many cop shows on the telly, Dad.'

He eased the car out on to the road and found a place to turn. Once more he had let the opportunity slip by to explain to Millie just what reason he had to fear for her.

# ELEVEN

Nick drove back towards town. He hardly noticed where he was going. His thoughts were filled with a mixture of anger and embarrassment. He sensed from the way Suzie was looking at him that she thought he had made a fool of himself. The worst thing was that he knew he had. He felt the heat creep up his neck as he realized he had stormed up the garden path of a perfectly innocent Baptist minister on his day off. He had accused him of making abusive phone calls, then tailing the Fewings down the dale with his whole family in tow.

He tried to argue back that *someone* had made those calls. Someone had threatened Nick and his family. The police seemed to have lost interest, or to have downgraded the threat. Surely it was left to Nick now to safeguard Millie and Suzie? He had tried to do that. It was not his fault that it had gone so humiliatingly wrong.

Suddenly he thumped the steering wheel.

'Of course!'

He turned the wheel sharply and shot left into a side street.

'What now?' Suzie snapped.

'Look at the clock! It was just about the same time yesterday that we met that woman. She was collecting her child from nursery school. What do you bet she's doing the same today?'

'So?'

'If anyone can tell us what's going on in Hugh Street, it's *her*. Why didn't I think of it?'

'You don't think that the same idea might just have occurred to the police?'

'But they've never met her. They might go up and ask that group of mums, but they wouldn't be able to tell the woman we met from Madonna.'

'I rather think her clothes might give them a clue.'

'We're the only ones who've seen her face to face.'

He was threading the unfamiliar side streets, hoping against hope that his sense of direction was right and they were heading for Canal Street.

'Dad!' Millie groaned from the back seat. 'You *said* we could find a café.'

'All in good time. This shouldn't take long.'

'Leave it,' Suzie said. 'We've poked in our noses enough. It didn't help her last time, did it?'

'Something very wrong is going on there. I don't know what it is, but I don't think Inspector Heap is right. I shan't rest easy until I get to the bottom of it.'

At the end of the street he could see heavier traffic passing up and down the hill. He paused at the corner. His eyes swept up the road towards the school and down to the bridge.

'There!' It was Suzie who spotted her first. She was walking up the pavement towards them.

Despite his show of confidence, Nick might not have recognized her on his own. Today she wore a navy-blue coat, with a blue-and-white scarf draped over her hair. But as he peered through his window he was almost sure Suzie was right.

He slammed the car into reverse and backed away from the corner to park in the side street. He pulled on the brake and leaped out.

Suzie was still unfastening her seat belt. 'Nick! Wait for me!' she called.

But he was off for the main road, determined not to miss their only witness.

He strode down the pavement towards the approaching woman. Her head was down, her shoulders hunched, but the height and build were familiar.

He had suddenly no idea what he could say to her. For a troubled moment, he wondered whether he should have waited for Suzie. He glanced back. She was not yet in sight.

His momentum had carried him on down the hill. He almost cannoned into the woman. She stopped in sudden alarm.

'Please! Don't be frightened. We met you yesterday.'

'No! I don't know you. Get away from me!' She backed against the wall. He met her large terrified eyes.

'You're the only one who can help us. Just what is it that's going on in Hugh Street?'

'I don't know anything.'

She tried to slip away from him. Nick grabbed her coat.

'Someone's been threatening me because . . .'

A roar of anger made him turn sharply. A man was charging up the pavement towards him. Nick took one look at him and knew he was never going to be able to explain the situation. His grip loosened on the woman and she fled up the hill.

Nick lingered only a moment longer. He thought of apologizing, then saw the rage in the man's face. He sped for the side street where he had parked the car.

At every stride he expected to see Suzie coming towards him. But he had turned the corner before he saw her. She was standing beside the car talking into her mobile.

Hands grabbed him from behind. He was spun round. A second man was facing him, fists raised. Nick struggled against his captor as the blow connected with his chin.

He was knocked sideways. The man behind him let him fall. He hit the kerb bruisingly and rolled into the gutter. He threw up his hands to shield his face. A kick landed in his ribs.

Somewhere at the back of his mind he had heard Suzie cry out. He curled up, helpless to avoid a second kick. But none came. He dared to look up through the fingers protecting his eyes. There was no one near him. Suzie and Millie were running towards him. The two men had gone.

He scrambled to his feet and gasped at the pain in his side. A wave of dizziness made him lean against the wall.

'Are you all right?' Suzie had reached him. 'What did you do?'

'What did *I* do? You saw those thugs. They punched me and then kicked me when I was down.'

'The police are on their way. I was already on the phone to them to tell them we'd seen the woman. You should have waited.'

'Oh, so it's my fault now?' Nick fingered the corner of his jaw tenderly.

'What happened down there? Did you stop her?'

'She didn't want to talk. She's still frightened.'

'And?'

'Well . . .' The foolishness of what he had done came over him. 'She was trying to get away. I guess I did catch hold of the coat-thing she was wearing.'

Nick! And you wonder why two Muslim men come haring after you to teach you a lesson.'

'Is that all the sympathy I get?'

She cupped his head in her hands and leaned forward to kiss his bruised face.

'Idiot!' she said softly.

'Mum! The police are coming.'

The two of them spun round. Two tall uniformed constables were turning the corner of the road. They made straight for Nick and Suzie.

'Are you the lady who put in the call?' one asked.

'That's right. This is my husband. Two men saw him in Canal Street, talking to the woman I was telling your switchboard about. They chased him here.'

'Can you give me a description, sir?'

'They're not the important thing. It's the woman you need to go after. She's wearing a navy-blue coat and trousers and a blue-and-white scarf. She was heading up the hill towards the nursery.'

'And why would we want to talk to her?'

Beside Nick, Suzie sighed with frustration. 'Didn't they tell you that when they put the call out? I was trying to explain to your operator. You must have heard there's something going in Hugh Street. Inspector Heap said they've got police watching the place. Well, this is the woman we saw trying to get in there yesterday, only the man sent her away. She's a key witness.'

Nick saw the two police constables look at each other and shake their heads. He could almost see their eyes roll.

'All we heard was a fight going on in Tennyson Street. Two black guys beating up a white one.'

'That's not how I put it. And that happened when I was in the middle of phoning. It wasn't the reason I made the call.'

The two policemen looked at each other again.

'Stay here,' one said. 'We'll want a statement.'

All the same, Nick was glad to see the speed with which they bounded back to the corner. They disappeared from view.

Millie looked from one parent to another. 'Is this really all because someone's moved into a boarded-up house?'

Nick moved carefully away from the wall. He held his breath, waiting for the sharp pain that would tell him he had a broken rib. But when he put his hand to his side, he could only feel bruising.

'I was just trying to do my citizen's duty. It's bound to be something illegal. And that woman we met knows what.'

The warning messages were reeling through his brain. Had those two men really only been protecting the woman from his advances, or had they more to do with Hugh Street?

The two policemen were coming back.

'Sorry. By the time we got there, the mums and kids had gone. Nobody else has seen a woman matching your description. Or if they have, they're not admitting to it.'

'Now, sir,' said the other, taking out his notebook. 'If you wouldn't mind giving me a full statement of what happened, I'll get you to sign it. If you want to press charges against those two gentlemen, I'll need you to come down to the station.'

Nick felt a deep weariness. 'I didn't get a proper look at them. I only know that woman's a vital witness. It's her you've got to find. What happened to me was . . . incidental.'

He hoped that was true. That the two men were not more deeply involved.

He saw the look that passed between the policemen.

# TWELVE

Millie gave an exaggerated sigh. 'Dad! Look at the time. We're hardly going to have any time in town. Do you have to play Superman and solve all the world's crimes single-handed?'

'Sorry, kid. I guess you think I should leave it to the police. I know that's what your mother thinks.'

He eased himself into the driving seat. 'Still time for that latte.'

They were halfway down the hill to the bridge. The phone in his pocket rang.

It was not the illegality of talking on his mobile while driving that stopped him from reaching for it. He felt a huge reluctance to answer his phone now. Why had he not switched it off?

He told himself it could be a double-glazing salesman, or Tom to talk about meeting them tomorrow, or Thelma with more news about Uncle Martin. He was convinced it was not.

'Do you want me to see who it is?' Suzie asked.

She held out her hand.

'Leave it,' he muttered. 'It's probably nothing important.'

If only.

When he parked the car in town, Millie leaped out of the car before Suzie, with an alacrity she had not shown before.

'Honestly! We could have been here an hour ago.'

Nick waited until Suzie got out. 'You girls go and find a café. I'll catch up with you in a minute.'

He had not fooled Suzie. She gave him a troubled stare. 'There's no hurry. We can wait.'

'Just go on, will you?' he snapped.

She gave him a long look, then reached back into the glove compartment. She drew out what looked like a map of the town.

Nick envied her. She had been troubled by yesterday's

threatening call, but it did not seem to obsess her in the way
it did him. Perhaps she shared the inspector's view that it
needn't be taken too seriously. And, of course, he hadn't told
her about the sinister text message after they'd been to the
police.

He watched Suzie and Millie's retreating backs as he took
the phone from the inside pocket of his leather jacket. There
was no reason to suppose that the caller had left a message.
Probably it would just tell him he had missed a call.

But the screen showed him there was one message on his
voicemail. He punched the key more viciously than he
needed to.

The voice was harsher than the first time. Angrier.

'*What game do you think you're playing at?*'

That was all. The anonymous caller had snapped off.

Nick stared down at the little screen. It was odd. He realized his mood had changed subtly. He had no idea what his
tormentor was talking about, but he sensed a shift in their
power play. Yesterday and this morning, the caller had seemed
totally in control of things. He knew who Nick was, what he
had done. He made it sound as if he was planning sinister
consequences which would flow from those actions.

Now something had made him angry. Not in that cold,
menacing way of the first call. Nick had done something the
man had not expected. There was not just viciousness but
surprise in this latest voice message.

He shook his head in puzzlement. The man already knew
that he had been to the police. All Nick had done since then
was to foul things up by haring up to a housing estate and
accusing the wrong person.

It couldn't really be the Baptist minister, could it? A complicated disguise, involving his wife and children? Nick tried to
remember the voice of Harry Redfern. Yes, it had been deep.
The sort of voice that would resonate well from his chapel
pulpit. But harsh, angry, like that question he had just heard?
No. He resisted the urge to play the message again and try to
compare them.

Suzie and Millie were disappearing through a gap between
rose beds that led into the shopping precinct. On a sudden

decision, he switched his phone off, put it back in his pocket and strode after them.

The pedestrianized street was an incongruous mixture. There were two boutiques, one displaying elegant clothes, the other expensive jewellery. At the far end rose two tall department stores. But for the most part, there were the little chain-store shops that you could see in any high street. Most bore printed stickers or crudely lettered placards proclaiming massive discounts. A significant number of shops were boarded up.

Millie was casting longing eyes at the sales in the shop windows all around her. She turned to greet him eagerly.

'Dad, you couldn't, like, advance me next month's allowance, could you?'

'That depends,' Nick told her, 'on just how ridiculous a purchase you've got your eye on.' He grinned for her. In spite of the violence he had just been subjected to, he was surprised to discover a new buoyancy in his spirits. Something he had done had unsettled the mystery caller. He had no idea what it was, but it felt good to know that he too had the power to startle the other.

But he knows, a chill voice whispered in his heart. He still knows what you've been doing. He's tracking your movements.

Did that mean that Nick's suspicion about the blue Honda had not been paranoia? Innocent or not, the Reverend Harry Redfern *had* been following them, first to Belldale Mill and then to the hospital. But if he was not the caller, somebody else must be trailing them. How likely was that?

Had the two men who had beaten and kicked him only been in Canal Street by coincidence?

He looked around at the faces strung out all along the shopping mall. Elderly couples walking slowly, busy women with shopping bags, dispirited-looking teenagers, probably out of a job.

He glanced round quickly, half expecting to surprise someone behind him. The few people between him and the car park had their backs to him.

Suzie fell back behind Millie to join him. She kept her voice low. 'Well? Was it anything important?'

He switched the phone back to voicemail and handed it over to her.

She listened and gave the mobile back. 'I don't understand what he's talking about? Do you?'

'Not a clue. But we've obviously done something he didn't expect. And he's not pleased about it. Somehow, we've wrong-footed him.'

'He wasn't pleased when we poked our noses into Hugh Street. Do you think this makes him more dangerous? Should we tell Inspector Heap?'

Nick sighed. 'We tried that last time. As long as she thought it was a brothel trafficking foreign women, she was keen as mustard. But now she seems to feel factory laws are someone else's pigeon.'

Suzie swivelled her toe thoughtfully on the cobbles. 'She has a point. But there's something that doesn't feel quite right about all this. Are we missing something?'

'If we are, I can't think what.'

She shrugged. 'If we stick together, he can't do anything, can he?'

He looked ahead for Millie, and found her staring avidly into a shop window.

Suzie glanced down at the map in her hand, and then at the shopping mall around her. Nick looked at what she was holding. It was not the modern street map he expected. It showed the town as it had been, what, 150 years ago? Suzie had drawn a circle round a little side road halfway along one of its central streets. He squinted to read the small print. *Market Street Court.*

'You won't find that. This whole area was demolished to build the new shopping centre.' He cast his architect's eye over the undistinguished buildings around them. 'Well, I suppose they thought it was the latest thing about thirty years ago. It's all looking a bit sad now.'

'All the same . . . Market Street must have run more or less through here. This is where James Bootle had his herbalist's shop in the trade directory for 1865.'

Nick's eyes went up. He found himself looking at a branch of Superdrug. In spite of himself, he laughed at the coincidence.

He caught Suzie looking at him. He thought she had been making light of the attack on him in Tennyson Street, but he saw that she was not.

'Are you really all right?' she asked, too low for Millie to hear.

'Just bruises. I'll mend. Go on. It will do me good to think about something else.'

'It must have been a good location for James Bootle to set up shop.' Suzie raised her voice again, to reassure Millie. 'Before we found that trade directory, I somehow imagined him selling homemade remedies from his back door. If it was really here, off Market Street, he must have had quite a successful business.'

Millie turned. 'Herbs and potions? It doesn't quite fit with the Industrial Revolution, does it?'

'You'd be surprised. Herbalism was quite the thing in the late nineteenth century. They brought in lots of ideas from Native American tradition. Recipes centuries old. But, of course, the medical establishment tried to stamp them out.'

Nick pictured the little medical botanist's shop, in an alley off the main street. In spite of himself, he was warming to the idea.

'James Bootle must have been a creative person. He grows up learning to weave by hand – well, by foot, too – at his father's knee. Intricate patterns the early mills couldn't turn out by mass production. Quality handwork. But it cost more. So the bottom falls out of his world. The mills take over, and it's all cheap, mass-produced stuff he can't compete with. But he can't bear not to create something. So he seizes on another skill that's been passed down in his family.'

Is it that creative streak which made me an architect? he wondered.

'It might have been his wife,' Suzie suggested. 'That happened a lot. It was the man's name you put over the door, but she ran the business.'

'More likely they did it together. Like that family scene at Belldale Mill. Even the children helping.'

Nick went suddenly quiet. Belldale Mill brought back uncomfortable memories. Were Harry Redfern and his wife and children really just enjoying a day off?

'Except that the kids weren't helping,' Millie put in unexpectedly. 'While he was having fun running his herbalist's shop, the children got sent to the mill.'

Nick and Suzie looked at each other, absorbing the truth of this. Would they have sent Millie and Tom to work twelve hours a day in the noise and heat of the mill, doing the tiring and dangerous work young children were employed for?

'*Mum*!' Millie gave an exasperated groan. 'You weren't listening, were you? Can we have a look round this beauty shop? It's great. They're offering two for one on everything.'

Suzie shook off the spell of the past. 'Sorry, love! Didn't I hear something about coffee and cake?'

'We'll come back tomorrow,' Nick promised her. 'We shan't be able to stay too long with Uncle Martin, even when we do see him. He's an old man, and it's only three days since he had a major stroke. We won't want to tire him.'

'Dad!' Millie spun round from the shop window in sudden alarm. 'I don't have to go back there, do I? I told you I didn't want to go this afternoon. And look what happened.'

'Millie!' It was Nick's turn to sound exasperated. 'Don't be so selfish. Uncle Martin's been looking forward to seeing us all. And that includes you.'

Millie thrust her hands in the pockets of her green wool jacket and stalked ahead. The almost-white of her dyed hair stood out in the crowd.

Suzie slipped her hand through Nick's arm. 'Don't be too hard on her. She's really not as selfish as she seems. In a way, it's because she cares too much. It really upset her this afternoon, seeing those curtains round Uncle Martin's bed and imagining what might have happened.

Nick passed his hand over his face. 'I'm sorry. It's getting to me. First those women in Hugh Street, then the phone call. Making a fool of myself over Harry Redfern following us – if he really does have nothing to do with it. Getting beaten up for talking to a witness. And now, on top of everything else, Uncle Martin at death's door. This was meant to be a fun family holiday. Me discovering my roots.'

She squeezed his arm. 'Look, the police are sorting it out. Let them deal with it.'

Millie had stopped and was waiting for them.

'Sorry, love,' Nick said as they caught her up. 'I didn't mean to be crabby.'

'I wouldn't call it crabby.' She rolled her eyes. 'Weird! I don't know what's got into you.'

Nick felt his conscience troubling him again. He had not told Millie the full truth. Yes, it was certainly important that the whole family was there tomorrow to see Uncle Martin. But there was another, darker, reason why he did not want to let Millie out of his sight.

His daughter was looking up at the first-floor window above a shop.

'Will this do? You said something about cream doughnuts. Remember?'

The entrance to the Banana Tree Café was up a staircase beside a shoe shop. Nick paused to study the menu in the side window.

After a moment, he realized that it was not the list of drinks, sandwiches and cakes he was looking at. The glass acted as a mirror. Behind his own dark head, he could dimly see passers-by walking along the precinct. His senses sharpened. Was it his imagination, or had one of them paused longer than was necessary? He strained to make out who it was without turning round.

A middle-aged woman in a raincoat. She was carrying an Asda shopping bag in one hand and a capacious handbag in the other.

He scolded himself for being foolishly alarmed. It had been a man's voice on his mobile, hadn't it? Was it possible a woman could produce that deep, harsh tone? Even as he turned, the woman moved on. She had simply been examining the display of shoes in the sale beneath the café.

He let his gaze circle the shopping mall. There was another stationary figure looking his way. A cyclist who had been wheeling his bike through the precinct. He had a scruffy, student look. A fair-isle jumper, ragged at the elbows. Hair the colour of marmalade that flopped over his bespectacled face. Not exactly a crime boss, Nick comforted himself.

His eyes moved on. And now he stiffened. There was a

figure who stood out among shoppers and those simply filling time. A man, in his fifties Nick guessed, in a dark suit. He had paused under the canopy of the shop opposite. One shoulder was turned to Nick as he talked into his phone. Even as Nick watched, the man swivelled his head in the Fewings' direction.

Nick tried to still the excitement in his blood. There was money there. The formal suit, the carefully styled hair. They stood out amongst the window shoppers whose very faces spoke of hardship.

Then a voice of common sense told him that such a man might very well head whatever criminal activity went on in Hugh Street, but he would be hardly be tailing the Fewings himself. He would pay henchmen to do that.

All the same, Nick swept the family up the shelter of the café stairs.

He chose a table in the corner, where he could get a sidelong view of the precinct below, but not be seen.

Millie was studying the display of cakes on the counter. Then she rounded on Nick and Suzie.

'Is Great-uncle Martin going to die?'

Nick was jolted back into the different danger he had been pushing to the back of his mind.

'He's being well looked after,' Suzie assured Millie. 'He's in the best place. It was probably nothing serious this afternoon. Just a little setback. I expect he'll be as right as rain when we go tomorrow.'

'You don't know that. That nurse practically said he could pop his clogs any time. I *told* you I didn't want to go.'

'That's enough,' Nick said more harshly than he intended. 'It's not about what you, or any of us want. Think of him.'

It was the one thing he had not been doing himself. Immediately he was overcome with remorse that he had not even thought to phone Thelma to tell her what had happened. Had the hospital contacted her? Surely they would have done if it had been anything serious?

Suddenly the anonymous phone calls no longer seemed all important. Another crisis, this time certainly of life and death, was playing itself out.

'Let's get those coffees,' he said. 'Then we need to get back to Thelma. We ought to be there when she gets home from work.'

Or from the hospital, he thought. If something worse has happened.

'Can't we do just a little bit of shopping?' Millie pleaded.

# THIRTEEN

The town fell away behind them as the car climbed the hill. Nick felt some of the burden of anxiety slip from his shoulders with it. It had been foolish to let himself get into such a stew over what was probably just a crude attempt at harassment. It was unsettling that whoever was doing this had found his mobile number, but that was all. Inspector Heap was right. It was just some petty criminal trying to bully him, pretending he could punish the Fewings.

'She's not here.'

Suzie's voice alerted him as he turned into the drive. Thelma's red Nissan was not parked outside the house.

Nick looked at his watch. They had given Millie a brief half hour in the shops. 'Ten past five. She's hardly had time to get home from work yet. And she may have looked in at the hospital.'

But even as he spoke, the little car swung on to the gravel behind him. Suzie and Nick were swiftly out of their own car to meet Thelma.

She came briskly towards them with a welcoming smile and her house key ready.

'Did you have a good afternoon? How was Dad?'

Nick felt an enormous relief. If anything really bad had happened, the hospital would have called her.

Cautiously he said, 'When we got there, the doctor was seeing him. We said we'd come back another time.'

'What a shame! And after you've come all this way to see him.'

He waited for some reaction of alarm. But she unlocked the door and ushered them inside.

Nick hung back. Now that one crisis had passed, the other was reasserting itself.

He could no longer resist the uneasy temptation. He switched his phone back on.

There were no new messages. He stared down at the little screen, unable to decide whether he felt relieved or frustrated.

He had not realized how tense he had been until he walked into the house to join the others. The knowledge brought a spurt of anger. He had allowed whoever was making these calls to gain power over him. He was a puppet, jerked about and manipulated. He needed to regain control of his life. But when he had tried to do so, and stormed up to the Reverend Harry Redfern's house, he had made a fool of himself. The attempt to pin down the Asian woman as a witness had backfired, too.

All the same, in the last voice message, the caller had sounded unexpectedly angry. Something Nick had done had unsettled him. But what? Still, Nick allowed himself a little grin of triumph.

Thelma was just putting down the phone. She gave him a broad smile.

'I've rung the hospital, after what you said. They say it's true he was a little bit poorly this afternoon but he's doing well now.'

'I'm so glad! I have to confess, when we saw the curtains round his bed we were worried.'

'Cheer up. We're a tough lot, we Fewings. We'll have Dad back on his feet by the weekend. They've already had him out of bed to go to the toilet.'

Nick spirits lifted. Uncle Martin was on the mend. They really would be able to see him before they left. Tom was joining them for the weekend. They would climb Skygill together.

All he wanted now was news that the police had moved in on Hugh Street, and that whoever was responsible for what went on there was safely locked up. He needed to be able to switch on his phone without that sense of dread.

He might even be able to turn his interest back to family history before they left.

He had a feeling of inevitability when he heard the doorbell ring. The door opened even as Thelma hurried to answer it. Geoffrey Banks, the cousin from next door, walked into the house as though he owned it. His pale blue eyes were hungry for information.

'Any news?'

'He's doing all right. I'll be down to see him this evening, as soon as I've got these people a meal . . . Nick's driving me,' she added.

The out-of-work chemist's face fell. He looked past Thelma at Nick with a stare that was almost hostile.

'Well, if you're sure? You've only got to ask, you know. And you won't always have your fine southern friends around.'

'They're family.'

'So am I.'

'Sorry, Geoff. I'd ask you in, but I really ought to be in the kitchen if I'm going to make it for visiting time.'

'I can tell when I'm not wanted. *He weakened my strength in the way; he shortened my days.*'

'Get along with you!'

As Geoffrey turned to go, Nick was aware of Suzie standing in the doorway to the kitchen staring at the odd man's face.

'There's a police car outside!' Millie came bounding down the stairs.

Thelma looked uncertainly at Nick and Suzie. 'That'll be for you, I suppose?'

As he strode towards the front door, Nick felt a rush of hope. Something positive had happened. The police must have made a breakthrough in Hugh Street. They'd made arrests. He felt a weight lifting from him.

He had the door open before the burly police officer had time to ring the bell.

'Mr Nicholas Fewings?'

'That's me. Have you caught them? The guys behind the racket in Hugh Street?'

'If we could have a word in private, sir.'

Nick led the way into Thelma's sitting room. The officer seemed to fill the small space.

'Inspector Harland.' He did not smile.

'Won't you sit down?'

The inspector took a seat on the edge of the settee, holding his cap in his hand. The usually stiff cushions buckled under his bulk.

'Have you caught them? Did you find out what's going on in that house? Who's been making those phone calls?'

The inspector ignored him. 'It has come to my attention that you have accosted a key witness in a police investigation . . .'

'Accosted!'

Nick's hand flew instinctively to the bruise on his jaw.

'It is my duty to inform you that if there is a repetition of this behaviour you may find yourself charged with obstructing the police.'

'But we were the only ones who could identify her. I was trying to *help*.'

Inspector Harland rose. 'I am not at liberty to discuss the matter further.'

Nick watched with disbelief as the burly officer strode to the front door.

From the window, he watched the inspector get into his car and reverse. A movement in the corner of his eye caught his attention. Geoffrey Banks was standing on his doorstep, watching the inspector's departure. From this angle, Nick could not tell whether his expression was triumph or gloom.

The hospital corridors were becoming familiar. He and Thelma threaded their way along to Haworth Ward.

To Nick's joy, the flowered curtains had been drawn back around Uncle Martin's bed. Even from the door he could see the old man's white head resting on the propped-up pillows.

Thelma hurried to greet her father.

A tall, grey-haired sister stopped her. 'He had a little bit of a do this afternoon. But he's come round well. He's looking forward to seeing you. Don't tire him, though, will you?'

'I won't.'

She almost tiptoed up to the bed. 'What's this I've heard?

They tell me you've been a naughty boy. And just when Nick and Suzie and Millie have come all this way to see you.'

'Lot of fuss about nothing. I'm feeling grand.'

The words came out slurred. One half of his mouth was not moving.

Nick saw the man in the bed with a feeling of half recognition. Great-uncle Martin had been a big man. Above the bedclothes, the same large skeletal frame jutted from his striped pyjamas. But the flesh had collapsed on it. The old face had somewhat the air of a skull. One side of his face drooped.

But it was relief to find no tubes or wires connected to him.

Nick saw him struggle to form the mobile half of his face into a smile as his eyes sought Nick's.

'You made it, then.' The voice was hoarse, but stronger now, the speech a little clearer. 'Thelma said you were coming. And the children. Tom, is it? And . . .'

'Millie. Yes. She came with us this afternoon, but the doctor was with you. We thought it best not to overload you with visitors this evening, after your little setback. But you'll meet the whole clan tomorrow. Tom's coming over from uni.'

Uncle Martin lay back. The eyes were sharply intelligent.

'You're the last of the Fewings. Do you know that? It's not a common name round here, and I've no son to carry it on.' He patted his daughter's hand. 'Thelma's a good girl, but I'm looking to you and your Tom. You're the future, when I'm gone.'

'Dad! There's no call to talk like that,' Thelma protested.' You're good for a few years yet. We'll have you back home in no time.'

'No point in fooling ourselves. I'm ninety-three. I've had a good innings.' Then the half smile broke through, twisting the living side of his face into cheerful wrinkles. 'But I'm not giving up yet. I've told the doctor, I want to be sitting down to Thelma's Sunday dinner in my own house, come the end of this week.'

'And you usually get what you want. You're a tough old bird.'

'I didn't do twenty years as shop steward for nothing.'

They chatted for a while. Despite the old man's initial brightness, Nick could see that his energy was waning. He was sinking deeper into his pillows. The eyes were beginning to close.

Nick got to his feet. 'I think we've tired you enough for tonight. We'll be back tomorrow, all four of us.'

The skeletal hand shot out and gripped his with surprising force.

'There's something that's been on my mind. Before you came, I got Thelma to go up in the loft and bring me down a suitcase. There's a lot of old stuff in there. Things I haven't looked at in years. Family things.'

'I know. We've seen it. But we haven't opened it,' he added hastily.

'No good me hanging on to it, at my age. I was planning to give it to you when you came. But the way things are . . . I've told them I want to be home by Sunday. But, to tell you the truth, Sister pulled a bit of a face. I'm fighting, but I reckon it'll be touch and go. You go ahead and unpack it.'

'Are you sure? Don't you want to wait and see if they let you home?'

'Sunday's your last day, so Thelma tells me. You've a long drive south, so you'll not want to be setting off late. No, you have a good look at it now. I don't doubt you'll have things you want to ask me about the stuff inside. Best do it while you've got the chance. Likely I won't be here next time you come.'

'Dad!'

Uncle Martin patted Thelma's hand. 'The good Lord knows I've had my time and more. I'm ready.'

The half smile faded. The eyelids closed.

Nick stood looking down at the old man's quiet face for several moments. He closed his own hand over Uncle Martin's. 'Goodnight,' he said softly. 'We'll come again tomorrow. All of us. I promise.'

# FOURTEEN

B ack at the house, Nick felt the emotional impact of the day hit him. He felt suddenly weary. The confrontation with the Reverend Redfern, which now embarrassed him, his disastrous attempt to get the answers to his questions from the woman in Canal Street, Inspector Harland's warning.

Yet there had been one glimmer of hope. Today, he had rattled the anonymous caller.

He resisted the temptation to look at his phone again. He told himself he was being strong-minded.

'Well, now,' Thelma said, 'I don't know what you'll find in this old thing.'

The suitcase had once been a dark red. It was scuffed now, so that the buff papier-mâché from which it was made showed through in many places. The locks were tarnished. Nick eyed it with a hunger that surprised him. He thought the bizarre events of the last few days had driven the quest for his ancestors out of his head.

But, in spite of everything, there were reasons for optimism. Uncle Martin was improving. There had been an innocent explanation for that blue car. The police were definitely on the case. And he sensed a subtle shift of power between him and the menacing caller.

Thelma threw back the lid. 'There you are! Goodness knows what you'll find in there. As far as I ever knew, it was just a lot of old papers.'

The first thing Nick's eye fell on was a wedding photograph. He paused on it. A bride with a veil fitting closely round her head, holding an enormous bouquet of chrysanthemums, her arm through that of a proud bridegroom with a moustache.

'I recognize that. That's Granddad Fewings and Grandma. She used to work as a weaver. Must have been taken in – what – the twenties or thirties? My parents have got a copy on the sideboard.'

'And there's *my* Dad.' Thelma pointed. 'My, doesn't he look a handsome guy with a carnation in his buttonhole?'

Nick studied the faces of the family group. Great-uncle Martin had been a tall man, like Nick's own father. All these years, he had been insufficiently curious about these people. It had been just an old photograph in a silver frame in his parents' sitting room.

'Do you know who all these people are?'

'Some of them. That's your Great-aunt Ruth. You remember her. She was still alive when you used to come here as a boy.'

'And you were a teenager riding a bicycle.'

'Do you remember that time I'd lost my front teeth? My brakes failed and I ended up smashing into a stone wall at the bottom of the hill. I was more upset about the bike than my teeth at the time. But then, I grew up thinking everybody had false teeth by the time they were middle-aged.'

Beneath the photograph was a bundle of letters, tied with pink tape. They had an older look. The paper was soft, as if it might crumble at his touch.

He lifted them out carefully and eased the knot free. The first letter bore a single name in the top corner for an address.

'Briershaw.'

'Now that's real Fewings country,' Thelma exclaimed. 'Before the family moved into town. You'll have passed the turning when you came up the dale on your way here. The old chapel at Briershaw, that's what they used to talk about. They were Baptists, our family, in those days. It's mainly been Methodists since. I've heard our Dad telling about Elijah Fewings who used to preach from his doorstep, with a Bible in his hand, before the chapel was built.'

Just for a moment, the image of the Baptist minister, Harry Redfern, flitted through Nick's mind. He pushed it aside.

'How long ago was that?'

'Search me. I'm not into this family history business. Just some old story got handed down.'

Nick examined the date on the first letter. 'This says 1852. The Bootles, my grandmother's family, were already in town by then. But James was still a handloom weaver, and none of the children were in the mills.'

Suzie rustled through her family history files. 'Here they are. I've got the 1851 census for the Fewings of Briershaw. Hey, look at this list of names! Enoch, Jephthah, Noah, Gideon, Esther.'

'They were strong on the Old Testament, then.'

'Like that man next door who keeps quoting the Bible at us,' Millie muttered.

Suzie read on. 'They may not have moved into town yet, but they were cotton spinners and calico printers. The Industrial Revolution seems to have caught up with them, too, even out in the dales.'

'Oh, yes,' Thelma said. 'It wasn't just the towns. There was hardly a village round here that didn't have at least one mill. And where are they now?'

Nick turned the letter over. He felt a start of recognition. 'This one is from Jephthah. Didn't you read out his name in the census?'

'The cotton spinner?' Suzie asked.

'It gives you a sort of shiver, doesn't it? He's down there in the statistics, along with the lists of all the other families in Briershaw. And I'm holding in my hand a letter he actually wrote. Suddenly he comes alive. He was a real person.'

'So were they all, Dad,' Millie pointed out.

For a moment, Nick sat feeling the physicality of the paper in his hand, looking down at the rather large and scrawling signature of Jephthah Fewings.

Then he shook himself. 'Well, we'd better have a look at what he says. It's addressed to . . .' he turned over to the first page, 'Moses.'

'He's not in this Briershaw census,' Suzie said, scanning the list.

'He wouldn't be, would he, if Jephthah is writing to him?' Millie put in.

'Good point. But I'm sure I've read his name somewhere.' Suzie ruffled through her papers. 'Here it is. Yes, He was Jephthah's elder brother. He's down in the Briershaw Baptist Chapel records as born on sixteenth April 1825. They're not like the parish registers, which just tell you when the baby was baptized. This gives the exact date of birth.'

'Well, they had to, didn't they?' Thelma pointed out. 'Baptists don't baptize people till they're old enough to speak for themselves. It's generally when they're teenagers. But they still want to keep a record of the babies.'

'So Moses left home.' Nick looked down at the letter in his hand. 'The lure of the big town must have got to him.'

'We can chase him up on the census lists for here. But I'll need to get on my laptop, if I can get a Wi-Fi link.'

Nick read through the first page of Jephthah's letter. 'He starts with the usual exchanges. He hopes Moses' family are in good health, and gives news of the folks at home. He says Father is failing. Still getting about, but not as sharp as he used to be. *He wanders sometimes, though Mother, thanks be to the Lord, is in good heart.*'

'So they had senile dementia in those days,' Suzie said.

'Well, why wouldn't they?' Millie asked.

Nick turned the page. His attention sharpened. 'Here, listen to this. *The bailiffs came yesterday because we had not paid our Easter dues. I think it shameful that half of Briershaw are godly Baptists, yet we must still pay tithes to the parish church. We refused, as did several other families. The bailiffs came when only Mother was at home. But they were mistaken if they thought she was a weak woman. She would not let them in nor take their writ. They were still on the doorstep when Esther came home from school. You know what a firebrand she is. She seized the writ out of the bailiff's hand and stuffed it down the back of his shirt.*'

'Yay!' Millie cried. 'Good for Esther!'

'Hold on,' Nick said. 'There's more. *But they came back that evening and found Father in the garden. He had not the wit to say no to them. He took their writ. So now we must face the expense of going to court, and if we do not they will seize our furniture and sell it to pay the dues, which causes me much indignation.*'

Millie broke into song. '*It's the sime the 'ole world over, It's the poor wot gits the blame. It's the rich wot gits the gravy. Ain't it all a blooming shame?* But you've got to give it to Esther. How old was she, Mum?'

'Let's see. She was ten in 1851. So eleven. She wasn't in the mills like Millie Bootle, but still at school.'

'I think she's terrific,' Millie said. 'I'd like to have seen that bailiff's face when she stuffed his writ down his shirt.'

Nick warmed to the sudden enthusiasm in Millie's face. He shared a grin with her. 'I'd always thought of this part of my family as straightforward working class. Toiling in the mills. Doing what other people told them. Making the best of what little they had. I didn't know there was a more radical streak to them.'

'Now I know where it comes from,' Suzie said. 'That propensity for lawlessness. Breaking and entering someone else's property.'

Nick looked up, startled. There was a momentary pause before he had a picture of a broken grille over the window of a derelict mill. Climbing in.

Thelma looked confused.

'Come on, Suzie,' he defended himself. We didn't do any harm. I was just curious.'

'Anyway,' Millie said. 'I'm with Esther.'

'You would be. As far as I remember, breaking and entering was your idea.'

Nick lifted the rest of the letters out. He thumbed through the mementos beneath.

'My head's reeling. There's so much stuff here. Photographs, obituaries, letters. I can't take it all in.' He put down the letters and closed the suitcase. 'That's as much as I can handle for tonight. We'll do some more tomorrow.'

Thelma had gone back to recounting stories of her girlhood. Nick had childhood memories of hearing them before.

'I used to love taking that bike out. It only took us fifteen minutes to get to the foot of Skygill Hill. Then we'd leave our bikes at the café and set out to climb it on foot. Will you be going up it while you're here? You ought to show Suzie and Millie.'

'Oh?' Nick shook himself back to the present. 'We certainly will. I'm saving that for Saturday, when Tom's here.'

'What about tomorrow, then?'

'We've arranged to meet Tom at the hospital in the afternoon. We haven't made plans for the morning.'

'I have,' Millie said eagerly. 'More shopping. You promised.'

'Or we could drive out to Briershaw. Look for this chapel Jephthah writes about.'

'Dad!'

'You can go shopping any time. And even after half an hour, you seemed to come home with half the shopping mall this afternoon. You don't have to waste the rest of the holiday on it.'

He could not decide whether her pout was pretended or real.

It had been a fascinating evening. His whole perception of his family had shifted. It was not until he was climbing the stairs some time later that the cloud of apprehension descended again.

Suzie was already in the bedroom. Nick hung his leather jacket in the wardrobe. He was about to shut the door when he hesitated.

Suzie's voice came from behind him. 'Go on, then. Get it over with. You've got to switch it back on sometime.'

'I didn't know you'd been reading my thoughts.'

'You've been like a cat on hot bricks. Every time I think you've got carried away with family history, you'd go suddenly quiet. I could feel you twitching.'

'It was all that talk about the Baptist chapel. Then I'd remember Harry Redfern. The Baptist Rev. It may not have been him following us, but somebody must be.'

'Switch it on, for goodness' sake. Then we can both get a good night's sleep.'

He reached into the wardrobe for the mobile in his jacket pocket. For a moment he stood staring down at it. Then, with sudden resolution, he snapped it on.

There was one new text message.

'VENGEANCE IS MINE. I WILL REPAY.'

In silence, he passed it to Suzie.

She frowned. 'It's a pity he's forgotten the last bit.'

'What?'

'It's in the Bible. *Vengeance is mine. I will repay, says the Lord.* We're not supposed to take matters into our own hands.'

'Do you think that by vengeance he means us? Or is he talking about the punishing the world in general?'

'Are you going to tell Inspector Heap now?'

Nick shrugged. 'What's the point? She's already decided this isn't big-time crime. Just somebody who's annoyed we've shopped him and has decided to harass us to get his own back. And now Inspector Harland's warned me off . . . But that still doesn't explain the first call. How did he know so much about me?'

Suzie sat down on the bed. 'There's something else bugging me. That quote. Where have I heard something like that before?'

Nick went to the bathroom. When he came back, Suzie had changed into her nightdress. But she still sat up on the bed with her knees hunched before her.

Suddenly her head shot up. Her face was alive with discovery. 'I know what that biblical stuff reminds me of! Millie spotted it first with those old family names.'

'Yes?'

'Geoffrey Banks. The cousin from next door. He keeps coming out with sayings like that. What was it this evening? *He weakened my strength in the way; he shortened my days.*'

Nick stared at her uneasily. 'Geoffrey? You're not serious! I can't believe he has anything to do with those women in Hugh Street.'

'He may not be a crime boss, but he has a supersize chip on his shoulder. I mean, I know it's tough being thrown out of work at his age, but to hear him talk, you'd think it was part of some apocalyptic endgame. God will get his own back on a sinful world.'

She wriggled down under the bedclothes. As Nick got in beside her she said, 'There's something else. He's in and out of this house all the time. He must know more about our movements than anyone else in this town. What if the phone calls have nothing to do with Hugh Street? What if it's just because you're a soft southerner with an architect's practice and a nice car?'

She snapped off the light. Nick lay in the darkness staring up at the faint glimmer of the ceiling. Could she be right? Had he allowed himself to be obsessed with anxiety for nothing?

Then he rolled over and said quietly against her back, 'You're forgetting something. That first phone call told us not to go to the police. Why would Geoffrey do that?'

# FIFTEEN

N ick stretched and yawned. He was standing at the window in his pyjamas. Sunlight was already gilding the crags above him. He had a feeling that there was something special about today. He struggled to remember what it was.

Tom! At last. This was the day when they would meet up with their eighteen-year-old son. It was a month since they had waved him off to university on the train. Nick had offered to drive him, but Tom had insisted that he didn't want to be taken there in his parent's car. Even as he gave him a last hug, Nick had known that his son was putting down a marker. He was leaving home.

But today he could push that thought behind him. Tom would catch a local train after his last lecture of the week. He would meet the rest of the family in the hospital foyer. They would have the weekend together, while Nick took pride in showing the next generation to carry the Fewings name what he had discovered about his family.

The pleasure lasted only a few moments before reality caught up with his sleepy brain.

Someone was threatening to harm his family.

He turned to see Suzie's sleep-softened face just coming round into wakefulness. Already he could feel the tightening in his throat. If the threat *was* real, and not just phone-bullying, how could he keep them safe?

As Suzie opened her eyes, he thought about her theory that it might have been nothing to do with Hugh Street. That the caller was Geoffrey Banks, bitter against a world that had thrown him on the scrapheap, and wanting to get his own back on a successful architect from the south. But even if she was right, Geoffrey wouldn't really hurt the Fewings, would he?

He shivered a little, and made for the bathroom to shower. Whatever was going on, he would keep a close eye on his family.

'We're taking you out to supper tonight,' Nick told Thelma at breakfast. 'And you needn't bother rushing home to get lunch for us. I don't know what we're doing this morning yet, but we'll get our own.'

'It's no trouble. I've been coming home to cook something for Dad ever since he retired. I wouldn't know what to do with myself if I stayed in town.'

'Go shopping?' said Millie hopefully. 'That's what *I* want to do this morning.'

Suzie sighed. 'Love, we've got the same sort of shops back home. We don't want to waste a whole morning on that, when we've got this once-only chance to find out as much about Dad's ancestors as we can. *Your* ancestors,' she corrected herself.

'It may surprise you to know that there are some people in this world who are not nuts about genealogy.'

'You were interested in Millie Bootle, scavenging under the machines. And Esther Fewings, shoving the bailiff's writ down his collar. And anyway, we shan't be able to stay all afternoon with Uncle Martin. Why don't we go down into town after that?'

'I suppose so,' Millie muttered reluctantly.

'Right!' Nick exclaimed with a show of brightness, as he and Suzie readied themselves for the day. 'Briershaw Chapel. Where all those Fewings brothers with biblical names lived, before the family moved into town. '

'And Esther,' Suzie reminded him. 'The firebrand who had a run-in with the bailiffs.'

'Whatever Millie may say, I think she's taken to Esther as a role model.'

'How far is it?'

'Not too far. About ten miles at a guess. We'll be back in time for lunch.'

'I know it seems a lot of work for Thelma to come home and cook it, but, honestly, I think she needs it. Someone to look after, I mean. She's missing her father more than she lets on.'

'Right, then. After you.'

Suzie went ahead of him down the stairs. She walked out on to the gravelled drive.

Geoffrey Banks was bending over as if to inspect the Fewings' car.

Nick's first instinct of shock was overtaken by Suzie's reaction. He was startled by the speed with which she hurled herself across the drive to confront him. Yesterday, she had been embarrassed by his verbal onslaught on the Reverend Redfern. She had no such inhibitions now.

'What do you think you're doing? Get away from our car!'

The scrawny chemist with the dirty yellowish hair backed away in alarm.

Suzie's flow of rage went on. 'Isn't it enough that you've been harassing Nick with phone messages practically ever since we've been here? Were you trying to sabotage our car as well? I'm very sorry you're out of work, but it's not our fault!'

Nick was out on the drive behind her now. Geoffrey's watery blue eyes were darting from one to the other.

'Suzie!' Nick said, trying to keep his voice reasonable. Despite the suspicions that chased each other round his mind, he could not believe that this rather pitiful figure had anything to do with it.

Geoffrey had recovered from his initial shock. His eyes narrowed. He almost spat the words at Suzie.

'*He that trusteth in his riches shall fall, but the righteous shall flourish as a branch.*'

'Hang on,' Nick protested. 'It's just a Mazda Six. It's a nice car, but it's not exactly the coronation coach.'

Even as he spoke, his eyes went along the drive. For the first time he realized. There was no car parked outside Geoffrey's house. Not even a battered old runabout. Was that something he had had to give up when the redundancy money ran out? Nick felt an uneasy squirm of conscience. His own car was not ostentatious, but it was almost new. Was that enough to explain the look of near hatred in those pale blue eyes?

He moved protectively beside the car. Suzie couldn't be right, could she? Could Geoffrey have been trying to tamper with the car in full of view of Thelma's house?

The man turned on him now. '*The wicked in his pride doth persecute the poor; let them be taken in the devices that they have imagined.*'

'We haven't imagined any *devices*,' Suzie countered. 'But you have.'

Through the open door behind her, Thelma came hurrying out. She was dressed for work in a lime green suit. Her kindly face creased now with anxiety.

'What's up with you lot? I could hear voices from inside. Was that you, Suzie? Shouting at Geoffrey? And what's got *you* all steamed up?' she said to her older cousin.

'It's nothing,' Nick put in hurriedly. 'Geoffrey was having a look at our car. It was just a misunderstanding.'

Someone else had appeared on the doorstep behind Thelma. Millie's small face looked mystified and, more than that, alarmed.

'Would someone mind telling me just what's going on?'

Her eyes went accusingly from Nick to Suzie and back.

Nick felt a sense of betrayal. Perhaps they should have told her more. But he could not explain it all now, especially in front of Thelma.

'We're going to Briershaw,' he told his cousin. 'We'll be back for lunch. And then we'll introduce the kids to Uncle Martin.'

With Suzie and Millie on board, he put the car into neutral. He found he was oddly nervous. He had been quick to dismiss the idea that Geoffrey Banks could have done something to the car. But the man had been an industrial chemist. He probably understood more about the workings of a car than Nick did. He saw again the hatred in the watery blue eyes.

He might even . . . There was a sudden catch in Nick's breath. But it was too late now. He had turned the key. The ignition fired. His mouth opened to yell at Suzie and Millie to get out.

The engine settled to a steady purr. Nick relaxed somewhat. He had nearly made a fool of himself again. It was ridiculous to think of Geoffrey Banks, the disappointed chemist, making a car bomb in his garden shed. He was just a rather sad man whose life had been taken away from him.

All the same, he drove rather more carefully than usual to the end of the drive. He negotiated an unexpected pedestrian on the corner and turned up the steep hill out of town.

There was another moment when he tensed. As they crested the hill the road dropped down the dale in front of them. It wouldn't need anything as dramatic as a car bomb. Just a severed brake cable. Too late now to test it. They were already heading down the long slope.

He tried the brakes, cautiously. To his relief they responded. Suzie looked at him oddly as the car slowed.

'Something wrong?'

'No,' he said, with what he found was a genuine cheerfulness. 'Everything's OK.'

For the first time his eyes took in the broad sweep of the country in front of him. The massive hills, moulded over aeons into flat-topped fells with steep valleys cut by sparkling becks. Out here, too, the houses were solid stone, blackened by mill chimneys that had gone cold long ago. This was a tough country that bred tough folk. Not like the softer cob-and-thatch cottages of Suzie's native south-west. He felt a slightly ridiculous surge of pride. He had, after all, never lived here.

Millie's accusing voice came from the back seat.

'And just when are you two planning to tell me why you're behaving like an over-the-top episode of *Coronation Street*, with everybody screaming at everyone else?'

Nick and Suzie glanced at each other in alarm. Suzie recovered first. She turned round to Millie. He could hear the reassuring smile in her voice.

'Sorry, love. I expect we're just a bit edgy because of Great-uncle Martin. And then there was that funny business in Hugh Street, and having to go to the police. Dad's been a bit worried that someone might try to get back at us because of that.'

'Like how?'

'Oh, I don't mean they *are*. The police told us there was nothing for us to be alarmed about.'

'So Dad goes and bawls out some Baptist minister and practically assaults some Asian woman and you were shouting your head off at that man next door. And you want me to think you're not worried?'

Nick cut into the conversation. 'Look. I'm sorry if we've been over-cautious. Yes, I know I made a fool of myself with Mr Redfern yesterday. But let's put it all behind us, shall we? It's a glorious day. Fantastic scenery. And we're taking you to see where Esther Fewings used to live. You know, the teenager who told the bailiffs what they could do with their summons.'

'Oh, her. She was great.'

'And this afternoon, we're all meeting up with Tom.'

In the rear-view mirror he glimpsed Millie throwing herself back against the seat. 'Oh, yeah. Tom. Like the sun hasn't shone since *he* left home.'

'Millie!' Suzie protested. 'There's no need to be like that. We shall miss you just as much when you leave home.'

'Sez you.'

She subsided into an offended silence.

Teenagers, was Nick's first exasperated thought. But it had diverted Millie's attention from more difficult questions.

He drove on. Sometimes, when the steep hillsides closed round them, shadows encased the dale. Nick's satnav directed them off the main road into narrower lanes. Sheep grazed the fields on the other side of substantial stone walls.

'You need to watch your steering here,' he said, after he and another car had eased past each other with inches to spare. 'In Devon you'd just scrape the hedge. But here it's solid stone.'

The country road was rising. They came round a bend and Briershaw Chapel rose in front of them. There was no mistaking it. There was no village here. Just a scatter of grey farms and houses among the sheep-dotted fields. But the tall gritstone building dominated the lane.

Suzie jumped out as soon as Nick stopped the car.

'Look at those big windows on the top floor. I bet there's

a gallery up there. And, look, there's a date over the door –'
she went closer – '1760.'

But Nick's eyes were fixed on the two cars already parked
outside the chapel.

One was a blue Honda. He had last seen a car like that
parked outside the Reverend Redfern's house.

# SIXTEEN

'Stay where you are,' Nick ordered, as Millie started to
open her door.

He eased the car quietly along the road and parked
further along in a splay under an elm tree. The car would not
be hidden from the chapel, but it would be less obvious. In
the first second, he had wondered about calling Suzie back
and driving away. But she had opened the gate into the little
graveyard and was wandering through the grass reading the
headstones.

The Reverend Harry Redfern was almost certainly inside.

'Dad! What's wrong with parking in front of the church?
What's got into you?'

'There's more shade here.' He gave her what he hoped was
an unconcerned smile.

His mind was hammering. *Why here? And how could he
get here before we did?* The blue car certainly hadn't followed
them today.

Millie went through the cemetery gate ahead of him.

'Hey! There are two sheep in here. They need to repair their
wall.'

Suzie looked up from the inscription she was reading. 'I've
an idea they're meant to be here. They're cheaper than a
lawnmower and greener.'

The turf was certainly cropped short around the graves.

'Not much good putting an expensive bunch of flowers on
your mother's grave, is it?' Millie was heading for the nearest
sheep, which skipped away from her with surprising agility.

Suzie looked at Nick's face, worry in her hazel eyes.

'You don't have to tell me. You think it's the same car, don't you?'

'I'm fairly sure. The number plate was something like that.'

'But then we know who owns it. And he can't possibly have anything to do with Hugh Street.'

Then why is he *here*? And how did he know we were coming? How can he know so much about us?'

She sighed. 'He's a Baptist minister and this is a Baptist church. You don't think he might have a legitimate reason?'

'OK. So you think I'm getting paranoid. But how about the way you flew off the handle with Geoffrey Banks?'

She flushed. 'I know. That was stupid. But he gets on my nerves. And then he was spouting that biblical stuff. And the last message on your mobile . . . Is it switched on?'

He nodded. 'Nothing since then.'

'What are we going to do? I guess your Harry Redfern must be inside.'

'I'd rather not meet him, after last time.' He strode away from her and stopped. 'I feel so *helpless*. As though somebody's playing with me.'

'I think the inspector's right. Nothing's really going to happen. Just words. It's been two days now. What *could* he do?'

'I wish I knew. All I'm sure of is that we need to stick together. That's probably the reason nothing's happened. Because he hasn't been able to get one of us on our own.'

They heard the sound of the door opening at the front of the church. Nick grabbed Suzie and pulled her to the back of the building, out of sight.

Voices came suddenly loud on the clear air. A man's and a woman's.

'I'll see you on Sunday, then. Thanks for your help. God bless.'

'It's we who should be thanking you. It's been difficult arranging communion services without a minister of our own.'

Nick struggled with his aural memory. Was that Harry Redfern's voice? He regretted now the impulse of panic that had made him hide. With a start he realized that Millie was still standing in the graveyard in full view.

'I have to see,' he hissed at Suzie.

Cautiously he stole round the corner. He was just in time to see the rear view of a man getting into the Honda. Certainly on the large side. But he needed to see the man's face to be sure.

Too late. The engine sprang to life. The little car turned in the splay outside the chapel and sped off down the road. Now he would never be sure. Unless . . . The woman had not appeared. Had she gone back inside the chapel?

Nick was just starting towards the front entrance, which was still hidden from him, when Millie's voice hailed him from across the graves.

'Dad! Come and look at this!'

He paused, torn between two demands. Then he started across the cropped turf towards Millie.

Her face was beaming with pride. 'It's them, isn't it?'

He looked at the gravestone she was pointing to.

In loving memory of
ENOCH FEWINGS
of Briershaw Lane
who died March 6th 1861
aged 57 years
also of HANNAH his wife who died
at High Bank
Feb 7th 1887 aged 77 years

'It's them, isn't it?' Millie cried. 'That family who wrote the letters in the suitcase. And that's Jephthah over there.'

'High Bank.' Suzie had joined them. 'That's where Thelma lives! So when Hannah was a widow, she moved into town where some of her sons had already gone. And the Fewings have been there ever since.'

Suzie's voice had the warmth of enthusiasm. But Nick felt the chill sadness of those words. Before much longer, Great-uncle Martin would die. Even if he recovered from this stroke, his time was running out. Thelma would be left alone. The last of the Fewings at High Bank, childless.

There was only his own family to carry the name on.

Tom.

From across the graveyard they heard the sound of the heavy door shutting. Suzie turned and started towards the sound. But already they heard the second car starting. They were just in time to see it heading away.

'*Bother*!' said Suzie. 'I was hoping she'd let us see inside the church.'

'I thought they usually left churches open,' Millie said. 'In daylight, anyway.'

'Parish churches, yes. But nonconformist ones are generally locked.'

They hurried across to the front of Briershaw Chapel. It had two heavy doors, symmetrically placed. There was an iron ring on each of them.

Suzie tried them. She had been right. Both doors resisted her efforts to open them.

'It's your fault,' she scolded Nick. 'Playing hide and seek like that. And if you'd warned me we were coming to Briershaw, I could have looked it up on the internet, to see who keeps the key.'

Nick fought down the instinct to argue in front of Millie. Yes, he had jumped to the conclusion that the blue Honda must be Harry Redfern's. It had brought all his first suspicions flooding back: that the round-faced Baptist minister was not as innocent as he appeared; that in some inexplicable way he must be linked to what was going on in Hugh Street. And it was surely too much of a coincidence that another Baptist minister would be out here at Briershaw in the same type of car.

But he had to admit that it made no kind of sense. Might Harry Redfern really have come just to arrange a service on Sunday?

There were too many question marks. That chill feeling of someone looking over his shoulder would not go away.

Suzie was peering through the small-paned windows, shading her eyes against the reflected light. Nick joined her.

'It hardly looks as though it's changed since 1760. Look at all those box pews.'

The interior of the chapel was filled with wooden enclosures

like cattle pens, panelled in brown and white. Similar panel-
ling surrounded the gallery, which ran round the building at
first-floor level.

'I bet the musicians played from that gallery,' Suzie
exclaimed. 'Don't you remember? When they first built
Briershaw, they used to carry their instruments over the fells
from villages ten miles away. That must have been quite a
sight.'

Nick felt a burst of anger. This was what he had come to
Lancashire to find. Yet he was being cheated of it. He felt as
if he was looking at it through the wrong end of a telescope.
It was too small and faraway to be of real interest. There were
other concerns filling his mind.

He was acutely conscious of the mobile in his pocket. Today,
he had deliberately left it switched on. He was not going to
run away from whoever was sending those messages. He would
track him down and confront him. All he needed was for the
caller to make one mistake and leave him a clue.

But the phone had stayed ominously silent. Had the anonymous caller given up?

All the same . . . He took a deep breath of clean air. What
work was it that Jephthah and his brothers had done? Calico
printing? He looked round at the pastures surrounding the
handful of farms. There was not a sign of Briershaw's industrial
past.

And there in the distance rose Skygill Hill. In spite of
himself, his spirits rose. Tom was meeting them this afternoon.
Tomorrow, all four of them would climb it.

All he had to do was keep his family together and they
should be safe.

They were driving back down the winding lane when Nick
saw the cyclist in front of him. He was hunched awkwardly
over the handlebars. The hood of his grey sweatshirt was pulled
up over his head. He was pedalling furiously, as if to outstrip
the car.

Twice Nick tried to overtake him. Both times, the cyclist
beat him to a bend. Nick held back, in growing irritation. The
road was straightening out a little. This time he should get

past. He swung out. The cyclist wobbled in his attempt to stay ahead. Nick touched his brakes fractionally, then put his foot on the accelerator and swung past.

The next bend was racing towards him faster than he expected. He had lost precious seconds in overtaking the bike. He was already swinging back to the left-hand side of the road, when round the bend came another car, too fast.

He heard Suzie cry out.

The wheel jerked in Nick's hands. Desperately he fought to find the slender gap between the stone wall and the oncoming car.

He almost made it. He felt the impact, heard the smash of metal against stone. Too late, he braked hard.

The other car shot past without stopping.

Nick sat, heart pounding, too shocked to take in the damage yet.

The hooded cyclist overtook him. As he pedalled past, he turned round to stare at the Fewings' car from shadowed eyes.

# SEVENTEEN

Slowly Nick turned to look at Suzie. She was holding the side of her head, looking dazed.

'Are you all right?'

'I took a bit of a bump on the side window. It's just a bruise. The car's taken more damage.'

He turned round to Millie.

'I'm OK, thanks very much. I don't know about gangsters running sweatshops. You're doing a pretty good job of trying to kill us yourself.'

'Sorry. I thought I had time to get round the bend.'

He got out of the car and went round to inspect the damage. There was that sickening feeling of having made a mistake he would do anything to take back.

The left wing was crumpled and there was a long scrape across the door. Nick grieved for it. He had rejected indignantly

Geoffrey's insinuation that he was flaunting his wealth with such a car. It wasn't in that sort of bracket. But it was nearly new. He had been proud of it.

But the damage was irrevocably done. It had been his fault. There had been that infuriating cyclist who didn't want to let him past. But he should have controlled his impatience and waited until it was safe.

But that silver-grey car? It had been coming round the bend far too fast. Could it possibly have known Nick would be there? Could the driver have *wanted* to force him off the road? He looked back up the lane, but the car had long since gone. He had not had time to note the make or number.

He got back into the driver's seat. 'The headlamps are OK, thank goodness. But the bodywork's a mess. I only hope it hasn't twisted the chassis.'

He tried the ignition. It sounded normal. Before he put the car into gear he turned to Suzie.

'I don't suppose you got a look at who was driving that car?'

'Male, I think. There were two of them. But don't ask me to describe them. I had more important things to think about.'

'I thought those airbag thingies were supposed to pop up if you had a crash.' Millie's voice came from the back of the car.

'Not for a side impact.' He turned back to Suzie. 'They didn't stop.'

'No, well, the speed they were going they'd have been round the next bend before they even noticed.'

He felt a little mollified. Suzie didn't think it was all his fault, even if Millie did.

Gingerly he eased the car back on to the road. There was a scraping noise as it freed itself from the wall. It was going to be an expensive repair. But the car appeared to be in working order. Would it get them home on Sunday? Or would he have to find a local garage? Get his insurance to provide a courtesy car?

He drove slowly on, his senses alert. Was the steering responding as normal? Slowly his breathing steadied as he decided that it was.

He still had no idea whether it had been an accident or deliberate.

They had almost reached the main road at the bottom of the dale when his phone rang. His tense nerves told him immediately who it would be. He could already hear in his mind that harsh, deep voice.

For seconds he did nothing. Then he was aware of Suzie holding out her hand. He took the phone out of his inside pocket and handed it to her.

He heard her gasp as she looked at it, and then the delight in her voice. 'Tom!'

The name seemed to come to Nick from a long way away. Of course. There was another world beyond the shadow that had fallen over him. This afternoon they would be meeting Tom at the hospital. Uncle Martin was recovering. They would be sharing his reminiscences. Even the reluctant Millie.

'That's great. We'll see you there.' Suzie put the phone on her lap. 'Tom says he's out of his lecture. He's on his way to the station. He should be with us at the hospital. Before half past two.'

Nick turned on to the road that led back into town. The car appeared to be behaving itself. The sun shone golden on the oak trees along the dale. It was becoming increasingly ridiculous to think that the occupants of that silver-grey car could have known he would be driving down from Briershaw Chapel just then. Just a speed merchant who took no account of winding country lanes.

Yes, he'd taken a risk himself, and paid for it. But he hadn't been driving that fast, had he?

They were nearing the top of the hill that would take them down to High Bank when Suzie turned to him.

'Would you mind driving on into town? Or at least to a corner shop? My head's hurting a bit. I'd like to get some paracetamol.'

He was instantly anxious. 'You said it was just a bruise. Are you sure? We ought to get a doctor to look at it.'

'I'm all right. There's no need to make a fuss. But you know how it is. You have a fall, or something, and you don't think you've hurt yourself much. Then when the shock wears off, all the aches and pains come to the fore.'

Millie piped up from the back. 'You're going to the hospital this afternoon. You ought to take her into A and E.'

'*We're* going to the hospital,' he corrected her.

'Do I have to? It's scary. Those beds with curtains round them. You don't know whether it's somebody having a bedpan or if they're dead.'

'Thelma rang the hospital this morning.' Suzie told her. 'Uncle Martin's fine. He's had a good night. And he's looking forward to seeing us. And that includes you.'

There was an ominous silence from the back seat.

Nick came down the hill past High Bank, without turning in to the house. He was halfway down the hill into town when he spotted a small row of shops.

'There!' Suzie said at the same moment. 'That one's a chemist's.'

There was parking at the roadside for half a dozen cars. Nick waited for the traffic to ease and backed into the only empty space.

'Bother,' Millie said. 'I thought we were going back to that shopping mall.'

Suzie was swiftly out of the car. 'I'll only be five minutes.'

Nick turned round to Millie. 'We'll take you into town again after the hospital. Promise. Here, I think you're due for some extra holiday money.'

He slipped a note from his wallet and passed it back to her.

'Thanks, Dad! You're a star!'

'You and Mum can go off and do girl stuff, while Tom and I have a coffee and talk about football.'

'But, Dad, you don't really like football.'

'No, but it's what blokes do. Talk about footie as though it really matters.'

'Men!'

Nick looked at his watch. 'I hope there's not a queue at the chemist's. We need to get back. Thelma wouldn't have it when I told her we'd stay out to lunch. And she only gets an hour off work. We mustn't be late.'

He peered out at the row of shops. This was different from the shopping precinct, with its brand names and chain stores. The shops here were individual. They looked as if they were locally owned. There was a newsagent, Asian by the look of it. A butcher with fresh meat laid out in the window, not plastic-wrapped. A bakery with home-made cakes. His eye travelled along the row to the chemist's shop where Suzie had disappeared.

For a moment, there was a catch in his breath. It was a small shop, but its window display caught him with an unexpected familiarity. There were glass shelves arrayed with flasks and phials in striking colours of blue, yellow and green. It was like the sort of chemist's shop so old that he had no personal memory of it. Yet it was printed on his imagination as the iconic picture of how such shops once looked.

Was this how James Bootle, medical botanist, would have displayed his homemade wares?

He stared at the coloured flasks. They were only there for decoration. Today, the shop was selling modern medicines, baby goods, cosmetics, perfumes. But there was still something about it that fitted an older pattern.

He got out and walked towards it. After a moment, Millie joined him. He turned to smile at her.

'I didn't find what I was looking for in the shopping mall where Market Street used to be. James Bootle's herbalist shop. Not that there was ever a chance it would still be there. But I wonder if it looked a bit like this.'

'Is this what that Geoffrey bloke next to Thelma did, before he lost his job?'

'No. He was an industrial chemist. He'd be working in a factory, probably turning out tons of the stuff, whatever it was. The sort of thing they take round the country in tanker-loads. Seriously scary stuff, to a non-scientific sort like me, if you don't handle it right. Pollutants, inflammables, that sort of thing.'

He couldn't identify the pulse of fear that quivered deep inside him as he spoke these words.

'Still, I guess they had something in common, James Bootle, the weaver turned herbalist, and our out-of-work chemist. Only when James was put out of job by the cotton mills, he didn't just sit around feeling sorry for himself and quoting vengeful bits of the Bible at people. He reinvented himself and set up a shop like this.'

'Is that what you think Geoffrey Banks should have done?'

'I don't know. It's hard to make money when everybody around you is out of work too.'

He watched an Asian women in a long coat and headscarf coming out of the shop. His mind flew back to that first encounter in Canal Street, and the woman in tears. Her terrified eyes when he caught her next day. A frightening recall of the two men beating him up.

What had happened to her? He felt a sharp regret when he remembered how his curiosity about the house in Hugh Street might have cost her her job.

But he had been right to report it, he argued with himself. Hadn't he? What was happening there now? Were the police still keeping it under surveillance? Had Inspector Heap been right to dismiss it as no more than a breach of employment and factory laws? It must surely be linked to the phone calls.

And those two men who had chased him into Tennyson Street. Had they really just been members of her community protecting her? Or did they play a darker role in this? Was that why an inspector had visited Thelma's house to warn him off?

He was suddenly conscious of the mobile in his jacket pocket. No call today. No text message. Had the caller given up?

He did not know whether he was relieved, or whether it made him more on edge.

He turned away from the window, with its brightly coloured flasks.

There was a scatter of people on the other side of the road. Most were walking up or down the hill. Many had their heads bent, as though the familiar grey street held nothing of interest. There were no shops over there. Nothing to stop for.

Just one figure stood on the pavement with his arms crossed over the handlebars of his bicycle. The slight figure of a teenager in a grey hooded top. He was staring across at the chemist's shop.

Nick felt himself go still. Don't be ridiculous, he told himself. Half the teenage boys in town wear a hoodie like that.

All the same, he saw the cyclist weaving his erratic way down the hill from Briershaw, denying Nick the chance to overtake until he reached that fateful bend. And then that moment of shock after the car hit the wall. Watching the cyclist suddenly fill his windscreen as he pedalled past. The thin face turning to stare at him from under that hood.

Just as that hooded figure was staring at him now.

His foot had left the kerb, hardly stopping to notice the traffic speeding downhill, when Suzie's bright voice arrested him.

'That's that done. And it's only ten to one. We'll still make it before Thelma gets home.'

When he swung round, he was startled to see the bruise that was turning blue-black on the side of her temple.

'Are you sure you're all right?'

'Yes,' she smiled at him. 'I bruise easily. It probably looks worse than it is.'

He looked from her face back to the crumpled wing of the car. Suzie had been sitting on that side. Another foot and . . .

Nick shot a look of anger at the youth on the other side of the street. He was still leaning on his bicycle. He might have been watching the Fewings. He might have been lost in a world of his own. There was no way Nick could tell whether it was the same teenager on a bike ten miles away.

'Come on, Nick,' Suzie chivvied him. 'Wakey, wakey.'

He climbed back into the car, found a place to turn, and drove back up the hill to High Bank.

Nick was at the front door, tapping his car keys impatiently against his thigh. Thelma had hurried back to work. It was five past two. Suzie was getting into the front passenger seat. Only Millie was missing.

He sighed. Over lunch she had still been looking sulky about the hospital visit. But it was important that she be there. She was the fourth generation from Uncle Martin, his great-great-niece. He had never had grandchildren of his own. Now there was just Millie to carry on the family. And Tom.

Nick's blood quickened with pleasure. By now, Tom must already be on the train bringing him from his university town for the weekend. It was a month since he had left home. Nick remembered his son passing through the barrier at the station. Turning to wave one last time. The laughter in his blue eyes. Tom had never been away from them this long before. How much would the experience have changed him?

It would fall to Tom now, not Millie, to carry on the family name. In a few years' time, he would be marrying and having children of his own. Nick pulled himself up short. In these days, he might be having children, but not marrying. Maybe, after all, it might be Millie's children who carried on the Fewings name . . .

He cut this alarming thought off short.

'Millie!' he shouted up the stairs.

No answer.

'Millie! We have to leave now . . . What is she doing?' he said crossly to Suzie, through the open car door. 'She went upstairs before you did. Surely she must be ready by now?'

'It's her age. Probably having a bad hair day.' Suzie slammed her door.

Nick waited for a few more moments, then strode upstairs. He rapped on the bedroom door.

Silence within. He threw it open, scarcely able to restrain his impatience. He was in no mood to deal with a difficult teenager. Tom's train would be arriving soon. Uncle Martin would be waiting.

The bedroom was empty. There was a pink satin cover on Thelma's bed, a tartan travelling rug over the folding bed in the corner where Millie slept. His eyes raked the bottles of cosmetics on the dressing table, Millie's open holdall on the floor. He turned in exasperation and ran down the stairs.

There was no one in the living room or the front room.

He rushed outside, half expecting to find her already on the gravel path, getting into the car. Only Suzie was there.

Nick flung open the car door. 'She's not upstairs, or downstairs either.'

'Did you try the bathroom?'

He flew upstairs and bounded down again. 'No. There's no one there.'

Suzie frowned. 'She didn't want to come to the hospital, did she?'

She got out of the car. He watched her go back indoors. She was wasting time. He had looked everywhere. Millie definitely wasn't in the house.

A fear was beginning to grow inside him. He looked wildly around him, as though she might be somewhere in the steeply sloping garden, among the gooseberry and currant buses. He had sworn that he wouldn't let her out of his sight. Inspector Heap might discount those phone calls, but she hadn't heard the cold menace in that voice.

*VENGEANCE IS MINE. I WILL REPAY.* The words of the last text message came rushing back to haunt him.

But it wasn't possible. How could anyone have got at Millie, up here at High Bank, with her family around her?

# EIGHTEEN

Now Nick was trying to fight back the waves of panic that were telling him Inspector Heap was wrong: that the threats had been real and immediate; that someone had taken Millie from under their noses; that, even now, while they wasted time . . .

Suzie came out of the front door. She was holding a piece of white paper.

'I found this on the dressing table.'

Nick started in shock. How could he have missed it?

She handed it to him. He found that his hand was shaking as he looked at it. It took a moment for his eyes to focus on the writing.

'*Gone shopping. I told you. I hate hospitals. See you later.'*

He swore, uncharacteristically, with a mixture of rage and relief.

Nick read the same emotions in Suzie's face: the terror that the detective inspector had underestimated that warning phone call, now replaced by exasperation that it was simply Millie's unpredictable teenage behaviour.

He tossed the car keys furiously. 'The little idiot! We're going to be late already.'

He was being pulled two ways. He so much wanted to meet again that frail ninety-three year old who was expecting them. But could he really risk leaving Millie alone in a strange town with that threat hanging over the family?

He could have kicked himself now for not sharing with her even the first phone call, let alone the chilling text message that had followed their visit to the police. He hadn't wanted to scare her. Now he wished he had scared her enough to make her want to keep close.

Suzie seemed to read his thoughts. 'I think I know where she'll be. She was very taken with that beauty shop in the shopping mall. We didn't have time to go there when we went shopping after coffee yesterday. You get to the hospital. I'll go and read her the riot act and bring her there on the bus as soon as I can. It shouldn't take me too long. And, anyway, hospitals sometimes have rules about not allowing more than two visitors at a time. So if you and Tom go in and see him first, Millie and I can follow you. After all, you're his great-nephew. You're the one who's been following up the Fewings and Bootles. You'll have far more to talk to him about than Millie and I will.'

He knew it wasn't true. Suzie was the true family historian. She got just as much pleasure from helping him to follow up his own roots as she did in pursuing hers.

But he realized suddenly how much he had been looking forward to introducing Uncle Martin to Millie. Astonishingly, his great-uncle was old enough to remember that other Millicent Bootle who had scavenged under the looms as a child. The child from the 1861 census. It was an astonishing thought.

He came to with a start.

'Right. I'll drop you off in the town centre. It's not much out of my way. I hope Tom got his train all right. He should be at the hospital any time now. He'll be wondering what's happened to us.'

'Come on, then.' Suzie hurried back into the car. 'I'll give that young lady a piece of my mind when I find her.'

Suzie had her phone on her knee, as Nick threaded his way down to the town centre.

'I keep wondering whether I should ring her. Arrange to meet her somewhere. But I'm afraid it will be too easy for her to put the phone down on me, if I sound like I'm coming across as the heavy parent. If she thinks I'm on her track, she could take off to somewhere less predictable than the precinct.'

'She's out of order. It's downright rude to Uncle Martin.'

'Some people do have a thing about hospitals. Scared to be reminded of their own mortality. I've got a friend like that. She didn't even visit her own father.'

'Well, it's a new one on me as far as Millie's concerned. When her friend Tamara was in hospital last summer, she went to see *her*.'

'They change so fast at that age. She hardly knows who she is from one day to the next. Remember that day she came home from the hairdresser's a platinum blonde? But another day, she's just a little girl.'

'I don't remember Tom being like that at her age.'

'No. Tom was always just Tom.'

They fell silent. Nick thought about this afternoon's meeting with apprehension. It was only a few weeks since they had said goodbye to Tom. Was it possible that life as a university student could have changed their son to someone they no longer quite recognized? No longer the charismatic schoolboy whose blue eyes had cast a spell of enchantment over just about everyone he met? He felt a stab of jealousy that others were sharing these new experiences with Tom, and Nick, his father, was, for the first time, shut out.

He saw a splay in the pavement where he could pull over and headed for it.

'Look. I've been thinking. Maybe we were wrong not to tell Millie about that phone call. It worries me to think of her wandering round town, not realizing that someone could be watching her.'

'You really think that? I thought Inspector Heap wasn't taking that threat too seriously.'

'There was something else. I'm sorry. I should have told you. Yesterday's message with the biblical text wasn't the only one I had. After we'd been to the police, I got a text message. All it said was "bad move". Number withheld.' He halted the car at the kerbside.

Suzie gasped. 'Nick! Why ever didn't you tell me? So he knew? He's been watching us. He may still be.'

Her hand was on the door handle, but she did not open it. She stared at him in disbelief.

'I've said I'm sorry. I didn't want to frighten you. I told the inspector and she shrugged it off. She seems fixated on tracking down vice rings. I got the impression that a sweatshop is too much like small fry for her. She's passed it on to someone else. And she pointed out that it could be just a follow-up to the first call. "Bad move" might simply mean ringing the doorbell at sixteen Hugh Street. He didn't have to know we'd been to the police.'

A car honked behind them.

'Look, I've got to go.'

Suzie got out. It hurt him to see how scared she looked now. There was no time to put it right. This was the wrong situation, the wrong place.

'Try not to worry. Just get Millie and bring her back as soon as you can.'

She slammed the door.

There was nothing to do but seize a gap in the traffic and drive off. Through his wing mirror he saw her standing on the pavement irresolute with shock.

Nick cruised the hospital car park for a frustratingly long time. Then he spotted a car pulling out and darted into the space. He almost ran across to the hospital entrance.

Tom came striding across the foyer to meet him. His spirits soared instantly at the sight of his son. Tom was a younger version of the self Nick saw in the mirror every day. A shock of black, waving hair. A lean, mobile face. Unusually vivid blue eyes.

He felt his face flower into a smile more spontaneous than anything he had managed today. Words of greeting were on his lips. But Tom surprised him by enfolding him in a warm hug. It was not something they had felt they needed to do when Tom lived at home. It confirmed the difference in their situation now. Tom had become a separate person, to be reunited with his family only occasionally. Nick felt a sharp sorrow for his son's new experiences he had already missed.

'Hi, Dad! Where's Mum and Millie?' Tom was looking around eagerly. It was not only Nick he had missed.

'It's a long story. I'll fill you in later. Mum's gone to fetch Millie from town. They'll be here soon. Right now, we're late for Uncle Martin. It's Haworth Ward.'

Tom checked the multiple routes from the foyer. 'Yup. Follow the red signs.'

'How are you doing?'

'Great. Wait till I tell you about our history lecturer. He's a scream.'

They were almost at the door of the ward when Tom's phone rang. A slip of a nurse, who looked hardly older than he was, reproved him. 'Switch your mobiles off, please. They're not allowed on the ward.'

'Sorry!' Tom favoured her with his dazzling smile.

Nick fished his own phone out reluctantly. He looked down at the screen, wondering if he dare check for messages, and decided not. He switched it off and watched the screen go blank.

It felt like a betrayal. It was the slender link between him and Suzie, who by now would be searching the shopping precinct for Millie. This was her only way of contacting him if she needed to.

Why did he think she might? The sort of shops that interested Millie were concentrated in a fairly small area. It shouldn't take Suzie long to locate her. Millie might protest, but he could hardly imagine she would defy her mother face to face and refuse to come.

They would be here quite soon. Wouldn't they?

'What's up, Dad? Text from a girlfriend?'

Tom was already inside the ward door, grinning back at him.

Nick gave him a startled look and thrust the mobile back in his pocket.

Tom was ahead of him, scanning the beds on either side. Nick followed his eyes. Alarm caught hold of his heart. Uncle Martin's bed was empty. For a moment, he tried to convince himself he had got the wrong one. But there were visitors already at the bedside of the other patients. And surely that was where he had seen the old man lying on his pillows last night?

Then his eyes registered the figure in the dark-blue dressing gown, sitting in an armchair on the far side of the empty bed

As he started towards his great-uncle, the nurse hurried past them. She shot them an attractive smile.

'He's amazing, isn't he? He gave us a bit of a fright yesterday, but he's doing fine now. Aren't you, Mr Fewings?'

She twitched the pillow behind the old man and helped him sit up straighter.

'Here are your visitors, love. Would you like a cup of tea?'

Uncle Martin beamed at them as well as he could with his lop-sided face. 'Eh, lad, it's grand to see you again. And this'll be Tom. He's the spitting image of you.'

Tom grasped his hand. 'Good to see you. I've been hearing all sorts of things about you.'

'No scandal, I hope.' The eyes twinkled.

Then he looked past Nick, as Tom had done. 'Where's Suzie, then? And little Millie? I can't remember as I've ever seen her. How old would she be?'

'Fourteen.' It came out more sharply than Nick intended. Old enough to know better, his tone suggested. But he knew that anxiety for her was sharpening his anger. 'They'll be here soon. We thought you wouldn't want the whole clan descending on you at once.'

He felt, rather than saw, Tom's eyebrows rise at the white lie.

'How are you, then?' he asked. Too late, he realized that he had meant to stop off at the hospital shop and buy a small present.

'Fair to middling. I can't complain.'

To Nick's surprise, Tom drew a packet from the pocket of his fleece. 'Old-fashioned humbugs. I hope that's OK.'

The old eyes sparkled. 'Thelma's been telling you my little secrets. Thank you, lad.'

Again, Nick had that feeling of being cheated out of something. Tom and Thelma had obviously had conversations on the phone he knew nothing about.

'Well, then.' Uncle Martin pointed Nick to a chair on the other side of the bed and patted the mattress at his side for Tom to sit down. 'So,' he said to Nick. 'You've come all the way north to talk to me about the family, after all these years?'

It was true, Nick thought wryly. It had only occurred to him to visit his northern relatives once he had been bitten by the family history bug. Before then, it had just been the annual Christmas letter exchanged with Thelma. For years, he had been the passive supporter of Suzie's enthusiasm for tracing her roots. Only this year had his interest in his own origins been quickened. And suddenly he had realized what a precious asset he had in Great-uncle Martin, the last survivor of his generation, and how little time there was left to tap his memories.

He felt an uncomfortable guilt that he was using this frail old man for his own ends. That he was in danger of failing to see him as a real person, facing his imminent mortality, and not just as an irreplaceable resource for genealogical information.

'Well,' he tried to excuse himself. 'People like you are important. All over the country, schools are sending out children to interview your generation. I realize that, since Granny Fewings died, you're our last link with the nineteenth century. That's incredible.'

'Hey, up! I'm not that old!'

'Sorry! I don't mean you lived then, but you knew people who did. I hardly know where to start my questions. Anything you can tell us about those people. Your parents, for instance. My great-grandparents . . . But you mustn't let us tire you.'

Uncle Martin managed a crooked smile. 'If Thelma was here, she'd tell you you'd have a hard job stopping me talking, once I get on to the old days. It's a funny thing, as you get older, what happened when you were young comes back as clear as yesterday. But you've a job remembering what you did last week. You saw that suitcase, did you? Thelma got it down from the loft. You might as well have it.' He lay back in the chair looking suddenly tired. 'I've no grandchildren of my own to pass those things on to, more's the pity. She never married, Thelma. But she's a good girl. Looks after me.'

'Yes. She showed us it yesterday. It was terrific. A real treasure trove.' Nick turned to Tom. 'You have to see this. There's this whole suitcase full of old photographs, newspaper cuttings, all sorts. And best of all are the letters. Written by Fewings in the nineteenth century. They're full of things, like your great-great-great-great-grandfather suffering from diabetes, even in those days. And how the family fell out with the bailiffs, because they were solid chapel-goers who wouldn't pay tithes to the Church of England.'

'Great stuff! You mean we've got revolutionaries in the family?'

'We went out to Briershaw this morning. Millie found some graves.'

The enthusiasm in his voice tailed away. The coincidence of Harry Redfern's car parked outside. The nightmare of his foolishness, driving back down the lane. The hooded cyclist who would not let him past. The bend rushing towards him too fast. The silver-grey car. And the irrevocable smash against the wall. The crumpled wing and the bruise on Suzie's head.

'Aye, the chapel,' Uncle Martin murmured. 'That was a big thing in our family. Of course, in my time it wasn't Briershaw Chapel out in the dales. We all went to Stoneyham Methodist on the road into town. Ah, we had some grand times. You young ones won't understand.' He looked at Tom. 'You're all for pubs and getting drunk and beating each other up nowadays. Beats me how you can think that's a good night out.'

'Hang on!' Tom protested. 'We're not all like that. I don't mind a pint of beer, but I don't get blind drunk.'

'No, well. In my day, it was the chapel youth club. There was badminton on Friday nights, and we used to go cycling of a weekend. I remember one Saturday, clear as anything, about forty of us cycling through the Trough of Bowland.

Lovely sunshine, it were, when we set out, and we'd gone ten mile when the heavens opened and we had to get home in a thunderstorm. Like drowned rats, we were. But you don't care, do you, when you're that age? That was the day I fell in love with Netta.'

He looked beyond them with dreaming eyes. Then his expression sharpened.

'Didn't Thelma say you had a girl?'

'Millie,' said Nick.

'That's right . . . I forget things.'

A sudden stab of consciousness brought Nick back to the present. His eyes flew to the ward door. There was still no sign of Suzie and Millie. Where *were* they?

'Ay, Millie. Now there's a name that takes me back. Millie Bootle.'

With an effort, Nick turned his head back to the old man. 'You knew her? The old Millie, I mean? Suzie found her in the census. Millicent Bootle, daughter of James Bootle, the herbalist. She was born in the 1850s.'

Uncle Martin's half-immobilised face registered surprise. 'You know about her? All those years back? Well, isn't it wonderful what they can find out these days? It'll be these computers, I suppose.'

'Yes. What was she like? You must have been born in . . .'

'In 1920.' Tom had done the calculations first.

'So she'd have been in her sixties, seventies, before you met her.'

'You didn't ask a lady's age in them days. But she had white hair. Going deaf she was. Talked at the top of her voice. Of course, if you've spent your working life with hundreds of looms clattering and the steam engine going, it was either shouting your head off or learning to lip-read. Used to tell us how she worked in the mills from when she was a girl. Of course, we all did. I was a beamer. I used to spin the yarn on to rollers for the weavers. But I got to be an underlooker, first, then an overlooker.'

'An underlooker?' Tom seized on the word with relish. 'Is that what you call someone who crawls under the machine to pick up the waste?'

'No, lad. That's a scavenger. Millie Bootle used to do that when she started. No, you've got your underlooker. He's a sort of trainee foreman. And then there's the overlooker. He's the man that inspects every bit of cloth that comes out of the mill. And if it's not good enough, you'll not get paid for it. All the weavers used to fear him. He'd got your day's wage in his power. Time was, when the overlooker used to beat the children, too, to make them work when they were falling asleep on their feet. And he'd have his underlooker helping him. You had to have an eye for it. I know good cloth when I see it. If there's owt wrong with it, it was my job to spot it. But I'm glad to say, we didn't have the young 'uns working in the mills when I were on the job.'

Nick's mind was racing with questions he would love to ask: about Uncle Martin's work, about his parents and grand-parents, and the memories Millicent Bootle carried with her into old age. Questions about life outside the mill, too: their homes, their pastimes, their food, the songs they sang. There was such achingly little time, and so much to tell.

But he could not concentrate. His anxiety was growing. Why wasn't Suzie here to listen to this? Had she found Millie in the shopping centre? Had she persuaded or scolded her into coming to the hospital? Thelma had said there was a bus every fifteen minutes from the town centre. Surely they should be here soon?

He told himself he was panicking unnecessarily. They might be outside in the corridor, waiting their turn to see Uncle Martin.

He was pushing down his worst fear. That Suzie had not been able to find their daughter. That, in the short time between lunch and their finding her note, something had happened to Millie. Millie had left the house alone. Someone had been watching. But surely Suzie would have rung?

He felt the slight weight of his mobile phone in his leather jacket like an unexploded bomb. Of course, he had switched it off in the hospital. If Suzie was trying to get through to him, he wouldn't know. He imagined her growing panic. Suddenly he had to get out of the ward. Somewhere where he could switch on his phone and make contact with her.

'. . . Eh, they were good times.' Uncle Martin was in animated conversation with Tom. 'We never had much money, but you didn't expect it. You learned to do without. Of course, there were the wars. Two of them. I was only a nipper then, but I remember Uncle Harold. He'd come back from the first one, gassed. He never could breathe properly after that. Died before he was forty. And then I got called up for Hitler's one. Twenty-three, I was, and just married.' His face clouded. 'I was away four years. North Africa, mostly. I won't tell you what I saw there. But it's hard coming back to civvie life after that. We only ever had the one girl, Netta and me. Thelma. Still, she's been a good daughter to me.'

His voice was failing. Nick noticed a nurse hovering near. He started to rise.

'It's been lovely seeing you, Uncle. There's so much more we'd like to talk to you about. But we're tiring you. Why don't we come back tomorrow?'

'Suzie. You said she was outside. And your girl. Millie.'

His short-term memory was not so bad, after all. Nick tried to smile. 'I expect they're waiting for us. I can send them in for a few minutes, if you're sure it won't be too much. That nurse is looking anxious.'

'I'd like to see the girl. Millie. That's a good old name. She was a bit of a character, Millie Bootle, as I remember.'

There was no doubt his voice was fading now. Nick glanced at the nurse again. Would she let two more visitors see Uncle Martin? Supposing they *were* there.

He pressed the thin old hand, feeling the knuckles through the loose skin. 'Tomorrow. We'll come and see you tomorrow. All of us.'

He hoped desperately that he could make that promise good.

# NINETEEN

Suzie and Millie were not in the corridor.

A door led out into a gravelled garden with a fishpond. Nick's mobile was in his hand before he stepped through it. Hungrily, he watched the little screen spring to life. He checked for messages. Nothing. No voicemail, no text. He tried to stifle his anxiety by telling himself that this must be good news. Suzie had found Millie. They were on their way. There was nothing untoward to report. At any moment they would be here.

If Suzie arrived now, how would she find him here, in this secluded garden? Would she go straight past to the ward, or wait for him to appear in the hospital concourse?

He was striding back towards the corridor, almost at a run, when a hand gripped his arm. His nerves were so on edge that he gasped.

It took him a moment to realize that it was only Tom.

His son stood looking at him with concern.

'What's up, Dad? Your nerves are shot to pieces. You've come all this way up here to see him, but half the time Uncle Martin was talking, you weren't really paying attention. And what was all that about Mum and Millie not being here? You said it was a long story. Shoot.'

It would be a relief to share it with someone else. Nick rubbed his hand over his face, trying to order his teeming thoughts.

'It was our first day here. We had this queer experience. I thought I'd go over to Hugh Street, where my grandparents lived. Thelma said they had plans to demolish it, but she thought it was still there. And it was, but all the houses were empty and boarded up. At least, that's what it looked like. Only . . . Oh, I forgot. Something happened before that. We met this woman. I guess she was from Pakistan or Bangladesh. Muslim dress. She'd collected her little boy from nursery school, and she was crying, but she wouldn't tell us why. And then we got to Hugh Street, and I was just going to take a photograph and go away, when we saw a movement. Like there was someone inside. So I rang the bell. And the guy that answered looked at me suspiciously around the door, like he didn't want me to see inside.'

He could see Tom's eyes brightening with excitement. Nick rushed on. 'I'd been hoping he'd let us in for a last look round. But he clearly wanted to get rid of us. And then I saw another woman at the top of the stairs. Dressed like the first. The one we met in the street. And then *she* came along. The one who was crying. I could swear she was turning up to work because she was apologizing for being late. But the guy pretended he didn't know her and sent her away. Then he shut the door in my face.'

'Great stuff!' Tom cried. 'What did you think was going on there? A bomb factory?'

'You watch too many thrillers. No, my guess is it's something more prosaic. But still illegal. Probably a sweatshop, using vulnerable women on starvation wages. Unemployment's rocketing here. That's what the police think, anyway.'

'Hang on, Dad. You've got a stereotype about downtrodden Asian women. They could be more proactive, couldn't they? A terrorist cell?'

'If it was, you'd expect the man at the door to be lot more subtle. And the woman we talked to didn't look nearly as hard-bitten as that. She had a little boy. But here comes the really scary bit. Even before we had time to report it to anyone, I got this call on my mobile. A man's voice. No number. He warned me not to go to the police. He didn't just know my name, which I'd told to the guy at the door. There was a whole lot more. He'd got my mobile number, my architect's qualifications. He was threatening not just me but my family.'

Tom whistled. 'But you *did* tell the police. Right?'

'Of course I did. We went to the police station next morning. And at first the inspector seemed really interested. She had her own theory. It was a brothel, run by an international vice ring. I think she's holding a brief for that sort of thing. You could tell she was really keen to catch them. Then, later that morning, I got a text message. All it said was "bad move". Like he knew we'd been to the police. And there have been two more threatening messages since then.'

He started down the corridor towards the hospital concourse. He would not be easy until he saw that Millie was safe. Tom's long legs almost had to run to keep up with him.

'So the guy knew you'd reported him?'

'It looks like that. Of course, I got back to the inspector. But she's gone cool on the whole thing. Seems they've got the house under covert surveillance but she's ruled out the brothel thing. Handed it over to someone else. She didn't think that text message meant what I thought it did. Just a follow-up to the first call. "Bad move" meaning our calling at the house, not going to the police. But I'm convinced someone's following us.'

'See? I wasn't exaggerating. Who's going to be that scary about a sweatshop? It's got to be something worse.'

'Millie was nervous about hospital visiting and when we came here yesterday, there were curtains round his bed. She thought he'd died. She didn't want to come today. I thought we'd talked her round, but when it was time to leave this afternoon we found a note. She's gone into town on her own. Mum's gone to fetch her and bring her up here.'

Tom gave a low whistle. 'And they haven't shown up?'

They came in sight of the hospital concourse, with the reception desk and shop and the colour-coded trails to different departments.

Nick scanned it eagerly. People were sitting near the doors, waiting for transport. Others were arriving, looking around for where to go.

No sign of Suzie and Millie.

Nick stopped dead. He felt the blood leave his face.

'They should be here.' He turned his troubled face to Tom, as if his teenage son could have the answer. 'When Millie went AWOL after lunch, Suzie thought she knew where she'd be. There was a shop Millie had her eye on down in the shopping mall. Suzie said she'd find her and bring her here on the bus. That was more than an hour ago.'

Tom tried to smile. 'You know Millie. Perhaps she wasn't

where Mum thought. Or they've had a row and Millie is digging her heels in. Some people do get paranoid about hospital visiting, you know.'

'But Suzie would have rung me. There's nothing; no voice-mail, no text.'

He got his phone out again and speed-dialled her number. The wait seemed endless.

'It's switched off.'

Tom took his elbow and steered him towards the coffee shop. 'There's got to be a simple explanation. This isn't South America. People don't snatch teenagers off the street. Mum knows you were in the ward with Uncle Martin. She'll have guessed you'd have to switch your phone off. Why don't we have a coffee while we wait for them? We can watch the door.'

'She could have texted me.'

'Probably in too much of a spin. Black coffee for you? If's she's chasing around town worried about Millie, she won't be thinking too much about anybody else. She just wants to find my crack-brained sister and bring her up here to fly the family flag before visiting hours are over. Come to think of it, my sympathies for Millie are cooling. Uncle Martin was such a great old guy. Time she grew up.'

He found seats for them at a table, facing the door. He fished his own phone out.

'I just tried,' Nick said. 'She's not answering.'

'It's not Mum I'm ringing. It's Millie. I'm going to give the brat a piece of my mind.'

Nick held his breath.

Tom sighed and clicked his phone shut. 'No joy. She's switched off too.'

Nick pushed his coffee cup aside. 'I've got the car outside. I'm going down to look for them.'

Outside the hospital, Tom stopped short when he saw the crumpled wing of his father's car.

'What happened? Had an argument with a stone wall?'

'There's a whole lot more I haven't told you yet. I was convinced this Honda was following us. Turned out to be the local Baptist minister. But then we went out to Briershaw this morning, and there he was again. I have this nasty feeling that he's mixed up in it somehow.'

'And he tried to drive you off the road?'

Nick flushed. 'Not exactly. He left before we did. But I guess my nerves were shot to pieces. Let's just say I misjudged a bend. There was this other car coming fast towards me. I didn't quite make it.'

He had a vision of that hooded cyclist turning to stare back at him through the windscreen. In triumph?

He had hardly begun to tell Tom all his suspicions.

They were halfway down the hill that led to the town centre beside the river and the canal. Nick was driving faster than he should.

Tom glanced sideways at him. 'Steady on, Dad. One crash a day is enough.'

Nick's phone rang. He snatched it out of his inner pocket. He was about to snap it open, on tenterhooks to know who was ringing.

A car braked sharply in front of him. Nick just had the presence of mind to clamp both hands on the steering wheel and stamp on the brakes.

Tom grabbed the phone from him. Out of the corner of his eye, Nick was aware of the look of alarm his son was giving him. For the next few moments, he tried to concentrate on the thickening traffic and remember his way to the central car park. The other half of his mind was all too alert to the conversation going on beside him.

'No, it's Tom . . . Never mind that. Where are you . . .? How long ago was that . . .? Look, stay where you are. We're heading into the car park. We'll be with you in a few minutes . . . Try not to worry. It's probably nothing serious. We'll sort it. *Ciao.*'

Tom put the phone down on his knee. He looked at his father more gravely, as Nick manoeuvred into a parking space.

'That was Millie.'

'*Millie?*' The car came to an abrupt halt. 'Where is she?'

'In a café in the shopping mall. The Banana Tree? She says Mum rang her to say she was in the precinct and they agreed to meet there. That was forty minutes ago. Mum hasn't shown up and she's not answering her phone.'

The two stared at each other in silence.

At last Nick found his voice. 'But I dropped her off here about twenty past two. Well, not actually in this car park. At the side of the road, at the other end of the precinct. She was going to check out that beauty shop where she thought Millie would be. If she was already in this area before she rang Millie, she would only have been a few minutes away from this café. How could she *not* turn up?'

Tom's voice was low, strained. 'You've been worrying what might have been happening to Millie, on her own, after those threatening calls. Did neither of you think that Mum might be in just as much danger?'

# TWENTY

The precinct seemed full of slow-moving people, with too much time and not enough money to make window shopping a real pleasure. Nick struggled to hurry through them, sometimes bumping shoulders in his haste. Tom seemed more agile, almost dancing through the shifting gaps.

'Where's this café?' he panted, as their paths converged.

'The Banana Tree. Over that shoe shop.'

They found the narrow entrance and pounded up the stairs. Millie was sitting at a table by the window. Her head was turned away from them. The elfin face was silhouetted against the glass, with its crop of unnaturally blonde hair.

Nick felt a rush of relief and anger. He had been so afraid for this vulnerable fourteen year old. Even now he found himself casting around the café to see if anyone was sitting at a table alone, watching her. They looked like unremarkable shoppers, filling out the long hours over a cup of tea.

But it was Millie's folly that had led her mother into a trap.

Tom got to the table first. Millie's coffee cup was empty.

She turned her head towards him with an almost wilful attempt to appear unsurprised.

'Hi, there.' She smiled at Tom. 'How's uni?'

'Never mind the small talk. Where's Mum? You said she told you to meet her here?'

'She said she was in the precinct. She should have been here in five minutes, max.' Her eyes went past him to her father. 'Would somebody mind telling me what's going on?'

Nick slumped into the empty chair facing the window. 'Sorry. It's a long story. I have a nasty feeling someone's following up on whatever was going on in that house in Hugh Street. I had a phone call warning me off.'

'You never told me!'

'No, well. I didn't want to worry you.'

'Dad, is that true?' Tom exploded. 'Millie didn't know? You let her come down here alone . . .'

'I didn't *let* her. She was supposed to be coming to the hospital with us.'

Millie looked from one to the other in growing alarm. 'You and Mum went to the police, didn't you? You wouldn't let me come in with you. That was it, wasn't it? It wasn't just that creepy man in the boarded-up house. You were going to tell them you'd had this threatening phone call. And you didn't tell *me*!'

'I'm sorry, sweetheart. It never occurred to me you'd take off on your own.'

Millie's grey-blue eyes grew wider. 'And you think Mum . . . She came here to get me and . . . she's just, like, vanished?' He watched the last blood leave her already pale face. 'You think somebody's got her, don't you? *Who*?'

'I wish I knew. I've no idea what all this is about. And I don't believe the police do, either. They'd pretty well written Hugh Street off as some kind of illegal factory, breaking all sorts of laws, I don't doubt, but it hardly seems to fit anything as melodramatic as kidnapping.'

His eyes were intent on the precinct below the window. He was searching for any sign of Suzie hurrying towards the café. He knew it was a vain hope. She should have been here nearly an hour ago. A cold numbness was creeping over him. He didn't know what to do next. Everything in him wanted to put the clock back. To keep a close watch on Millie, so that she could not have crept out of the house unseen. To forbid Suzie to go off into town alone to find her. Another part of his mind wrestled with the problem of how he could have come with her and left Uncle Martin waiting in vain.

He should have sent Suzie to the hospital and come here himself. But was he invulnerable? Were any of them? Whoever was behind those phone calls might have missed Millie slipping out of the house. But they must have followed Suzie. Seen the point at which Nick left her on the pavement. Walked behind her the short distance into the precinct. And then . . .

The shutters came down on his imagination. He had no idea how they could have seized her in broad daylight with so many witnesses.

He rubbed his hands over his eyes to clear the unsettling vision.

'We're wasting time,' Tom said. 'She's been missing for an hour, and we still haven't told the police.' He had his phone out. 'You've got a number? I don't just mean 999. Who did you talk to?'

Nick retrieved some slips of paper from his inside pocket where he kept his phone. His own business cards, some handwritten memos. He selected Inspector Heap's card and put the rest back. 'I'm not sure she's the right person now. She'd gone cool on Hugh Street.'

'She's not going to stay cool about a kidnapping, is she?'

Tom dialled the number. Nick realized the state of shock he must be in to let his son take the initiative. But when the call connected, Tom pushed the phone across to him. 'You'd better do this. She knows you.'

Nick felt a numb certainty that she would not answer. But he was startled into action by the sound of her voice.

'Inspector Heap.'

'It's me. Nicholas Fewings. My wife and I came to see you about a threatening phone call.'

'I told you to leave it to us, Mr Fewings. I know these things are unpleasant, but we don't think there's any substance behind it. Just a nuisance call to warn you off.'

'There have been three more calls since. And my wife's missing.'

There was silence at the other end of the phone.

'Just a moment. I'm copying someone else in on this. Right. Go ahead.'

Wearily he went over the events of the afternoon. Millie's absence. Suzie's belief that she could find her. The hospital visit. Millie's call. A sense of futility stalked over him. He knew already that the police would have no more idea where Suzie was than he did.

He closed Tom's phone and handed it back. 'They're coming. At least she believes me now. She's taking it seriously this time.'

Millie had gone quiet. They were all watching the shifting patterns of humanity in the shopping mall below them.

Nick was watching for the trim female figure of Inspector Heap. Another part of his mind was alert for something less reassuring. He was not sure what he expected. The teenager in the grey hoodie? The seemingly innocent Reverend Redfern?

His eye caught the two men striding along the shopping precinct immediately. Amongst the drifting window shoppers and the harassed young mothers with toddlers and pushchairs they stood out. Their middle age and masculinity; the speed and purposefulness with which they walked. The way their eyes were scanning the shops around them, on the lookout for something.

He caught his breath.

One was taller than normal, with something burly about his build. From above, Nick could see his bald head within a ring of black hair. He wore a dark suit, but the jacket was unfastened casually. The other was shorter, younger, a shock head of golden-brown hair above square shoulders. A tweed jacket and grey trousers. Nick had had a stereotyped suspicion that there would be something foreign about whoever was behind what was going on. Asian? East European? Russian? There were too many fantastic scenarios whirling through his brain.

This pair looked uncompromisingly white British. He would not know until he heard them speak.

The eyes of the shorter one went up to the café window.

There were only moments left.

He shot a look around the café. The only exit seemed to be the stairs they had come by. There must be another through the kitchen. In a few seconds the men would reach the door.

Tom had caught his alarm. He half rose to his feet. Millie looked scared.

None of them had put their thoughts into words, but it was obvious to all of them that the two men had come looking for them.

Tom had his phone out. He's got quicker reactions than I have, thought Nick.

'Are you dialling 999?'

Tom nodded.

'They can't do anything, can they?' breathed Millie. 'Not here in front of everybody.'

Everybody. Nick looked round at the two women behind the counter. An elderly couple drinking tea. A younger woman with an older one who was probably her mother. A couple of teenagers not much older than Millie, drinking milkshakes. The men had looked powerful, fit. They had vanished from sight below the window.

As Tom lifted his mobile to his ear, there were footsteps pounding up the stairs.

The tall man paused in the doorway momentarily. It took only a second for him to identify the Fewings at their window table, made all the more conspicuous by the fact that all three of them were on their feet. He strode across to them, with the shorter man in his wake. One of the women behind the counter gave an audible gasp. The other customers stopped drinking to watch.

The leading man's hand went to his inside pocket. Is he going to draw a gun? Here? Nick thought incredulously.

Tom was already making contact. 'Police. I'm in the Banana Tree Café, in the shopping precinct. Two men . . .'

The taller man thrust a warrant card at them. Nick saw the multi-pointed police star surmounted by a crown.

'Detective Superintendent Mason. And this is Inspector Collinge.'

The younger man flashed a brief smile as he offered his own card.

For moments, the shattered pieces of Nick's interpretation of the scene whirled through his mind. Tom's mouth was open. His phone had dropped away from his face.

'Are you the *police*?' Millie asked unnecessarily.

Mason's eyes narrowed as his glance went quickly round their fearful faces.

'You called us. You reported your wife was missing. And you said you'd had threatening messages.'

'I was expecting Inspector Heap.'

'Sorry to disappoint you, sir. You'll have to make do with us.'

Nick's mind was making rapid calculations. A detective superintendent must be two ranks above an inspector. And he had his own inspector in tow. Did that mean the police were suddenly taking this more seriously than the theories of an illegal workshop or even forcible prostitution had warranted? For the first time, he felt the warmth of hope.

Superintendent Mason cast a rapid glance around the small café. The tables were close together. Everyone in the room was listening avidly.

'I think, sir, we'd be better doing this somewhere more private.'

He turned and led the way briskly downstairs.

The Fewings followed dumbly in his wake, with Inspector Collinge bringing up the rear like a vigilant sheepdog.

The precinct had an air of unreality. The shoppers moved past Nick like fish seen from the other side of a glass tank. He was no longer one of them. He inhabited a different sphere of existence.

In spite of his anxiety, he felt something of the burden of responsibility lifted away from him. Detective Superintendent Mason exuded an air of authority. Nick even began to hope that he might have an answer to the strange events that had engulfed the Fewings. That he might actually know where Suzie was.

Mason turned into a walled garden. The flowerbeds were mostly bare, but a few purple and pink petunias blazed a late farewell to summer. There was a roofed shelter in the centre, with benches. The detective led the way to it and motioned them to sit down.

'Now, sir. Let's hear it from you. Start at the top.'

Inspector Collinge had his notebook out. A flicker of Nick's mind wondered why he didn't simply record the interview.

He took a deep breath, and tried to steady his thoughts.

'It began two days ago.' Even as he said it, he was struck with incredulity that so much could have happened in forty-eight hours. 'My family came from here, a couple of generations ago. So I wanted to see if the house where my grandparents lived was still standing.'

Hugh Street. Such an ordinary row of millworkers cottages. It seemed an unlikely setting for the drama that was now being played out.

The Superintendent heard the rest of Nick's story in watchful silence.

'And then I got Millie's phone call, asking where Suzie was. She hadn't shown up. She was supposed to be here over an hour ago.'

Mason turned swiftly to his inspector. 'Get some uniforms down here, fast. There may still be people around who saw her. What was she wearing?' he asked Nick.

For a stupid moment, Nick stared back at him. He had a vivid impression of Suzie's heart-shaped face. The intelligent hazel eyes. The way the soft brown curls framed her face. The rosy lips that hardly needed make-up.

But what was she wearing today? He had no idea.

'White jeans,' Millie said firmly. 'And a sort of soft woolly jumper. Angora, or something. Sky blue.'

Nick smiled at her thankfully.

'Any coat?' the DSI asked.

'I wasn't there, was I?' Millie retorted. 'She's had a sort of pinky-purply quilted jacket she's been wearing here.'

'Mr Fewings?'

'Um. I can't remember if she put it on. Yes. Probably.'

DI Collinge nodded. 'Do you want me to cordon off the shopping mall? Question everyone inside it, before they leave?'

'You've got two multi-storey department stores. I'm not

sure we've got the manpower to cover every exit and question half the town. Just do what you can.'

Nick realized the horror that the whole world would not come to a stop because Suzie was missing. There were finite resources to search for her. The police were taking him seriously now, but there were limits to what they could do.

It was not as if they were investigating a murder.

He prayed desperately that this was true.

'But I don't understand,' he protested. 'I left her on the edge of the precinct. The mall was full of people, like now. How could someone kidnap her in front of them?'

'You'd be surprised, sir. People don't like to get involved. And perhaps it didn't need to be strong-arm stuff. Your man might have said something to her to persuade her to go quietly.'

'Threatened her, you mean?'

'Put a gun in her back?' Tom chimed in, almost eagerly.

'Or threatened someone she cared about.'

Nick's eyes, like Mason's and Tom's, swung round on Millie.

Colour flamed in her cheeks. 'Don't blame it on me! I didn't know, did I? Nobody told me.'

'There's no need to go blaming yourself, lass,' Mason told her. 'I don't know what's going on at the back of this. But I'm getting the feeling of some nasty customers. You just happened to stumble along at the wrong time. Try not to worry. Inspector Collinge will have got half the force on the look-out by now.'

'Do you think she's at Hugh Street? Are you going to search it now?'

The Superintendent thought for a moment. 'There's something not quite right about this. He was warning you off reporting the goings-on there. But if he knows you've already been to us, why carry on? Like they say, if you're in a hole, stop digging. I gather we've got officers staking out the premises. Hoping to catch more than the small fry. They should have seen if he took your good wife there. But yes, I think we'll have to go in now, make sure. If you'll excuse me, I'll get on to it right away.'

'What can we do?'

'You, sir? Stay out of trouble. I'll send a police officer to keep an eye on you. If you have any change of plan, tell her.'

'Can't we help?' Millie said. 'Ask people if they've seen her?'

'Kind of you to offer, but best leave it to the professionals, lass.'

Nick looked at his watch. 'We ought to be getting back. Thelma will be home from work soon. Or was she going to drop in on Uncle Martin first?' He rubbed his forehead. 'I can't remember. But what are we going to tell her when she gets home?'

'How about the truth?' Tom suggested. 'She's got to know.'

It was at that moment that the reality struck home to Nick. This was not just a bad dream, like the sense of disconnection he had felt among the shoppers unaware of his catastrophe. Once they told Thelma, it would become fact. Someone from the sane, ordinary world would become involved. The Fewings' frightening secret would become public property. He would be acknowledging that it had actually happened. Someone really had kidnapped Suzie.

He thought of the cold harsh voice of that telephone call.

As though his thought had triggered an electronic response, his mobile buzzed.

For a moment, he went cold, rigid. He was suddenly aware of the others staring at him. Tom, Millie, the Detective Superintendent who had been on the point of leaving.

He tried to control his hand as he drew the phone out and pressed the key to retrieve the message. He glanced down at the screen.

'AREN'T YOU GOING TO CUM AND GET HER?'

# TWENTY-ONE

The Superintendent snatched it out of his hand.

'What does it say?' Millie demanded. 'Tell us!'

Tom read it out over the Superintendent's shoulder.

'He's taunting us,' Mason fumed. 'He's not even trying to keep it secret. He's assuming you know where she is.'

'But we don't know,' Nick protested. 'At least, I'd taken it for granted that it wouldn't be Hugh Street, because he'd know that was the first place we'd think of. But maybe it is. It doesn't make sense. He warned us not to tell you about it. So why would he lead us there, if it's supposed to be some undercover operation?'

'Perhaps he doesn't care now,' Millie said. 'If you've blown his cover, he'll empty out his factory stuff, won't he? Leave Mum tied up in some horrible, boarded-up room.' She spun round aggressively to the Superintendent. 'What are you waiting for? Aren't you going to get her?'

'Hold your horses, young lady. There's something about this that doesn't smell right. We've got officers watching those premises. If they'd tried to move their stuff out, we'd have seen it, and gone in fast. I've told them to alert me if anything happens there, and nothing has. Still, the waiting game's over. We're going in.'

'I want to be there,' Nick claimed. 'She's my wife.'

Detective Superintendent Mason was making for the exit from the park. 'I understand your feelings, sir. But the best thing you can do is stay out of the way and go home. We'll tell you as soon as we've found her. I gather you're staying in the area.'

'With my cousin. Up at High Bank. Yes.' He scribbled Thelma's address on a business card and passed it over. But an unspoken rebellion was telling him he would not go straight there. How could he not be around when the police broke into Hugh Street and brought Suzie out?

If they did. If she was there. If it all went according to plan.

The mocking tone of that message haunted him. Why would her kidnapper want them to come? Why had he kidnapped her in the first place? What good would it do him? A colder thought was quelling his first excitement. What trick had that unknown abductor got up his sleeve?

Was he even sane?

He wanted desperately to be in Hugh Street when the police went in. But he was increasingly, chillingly afraid of what they might find waiting for them.

*       *       *

DSI Mason was already striding ahead across the precinct in the direction of his car. Inspector Collinge had disappeared, but he had not been idle.

'They're out in force,' Tom remarked. 'If you'll excuse the pun.'

The shopping mall bristled with police officers. Black-and-white uniforms, chequered hat bands, some fluorescent jackets. They were stopping everyone at the exits from the pedestrian precinct. In spite of DSI Mason's pessimism it looked like a fairly comprehensive coverage.

Nick suddenly felt the futility of it. What if someone remembered seeing Suzie with an unknown man? How would it help the police find where he had taken her? What he intended to do with her, and why?

The taunting text message echoed in his brain. *Aren't you going to come and get her?*

The caller knew that the Fewings had been to the police, but the message had been sent to Nick, not the constabulary. He felt that he, and he alone, was being dangled on a string for the macabre amusement of a man whose motives he had no way of understanding.

This couldn't be all about a sordid sweatshop in a back street, could it?

'You're not really going back to Thelma's, are you?' There was a belligerent tone in Millie's voice.

'Too right, I'm not. Tom, will you take Millie back? It's over the bridge and straight up the hill.'

'No way!' Tom cried. 'If you're going up to Hugh Street, I'm coming too.'

'And don't think I'm going back on my own,' Millie protested. 'It would be a whole lot more scary than coming with you. From the sound of it, there's going to be half the Lancashire police force there. It'll be much safer than Thelma's.'

Nick felt an odd sense of relief. He should never have let Suzie go off alone. He would feel much safer keeping Millie and Tom within sight. And Millie was right. The police wouldn't let them do any more than watch the raid on Hugh Street from a safe distance. But he would be there to comfort Suzie when they rescued her.

If they did. If she was there.

An unease sneaked across his thoughts. Could the threat to the Fewings family extend to Thelma? Was she safe on her own? He ought to have put this to Superintendent Mason.

'What I don't understand,' he said at last, 'is that whoever did this must have been watching us. I can see how they might have found my home address. But how could they know we were staying at Thelma's?'

'Easy. Same surname,' Tom said. 'They'd only have to look in the phone book.'

'But there must be dozens of Fewings. They couldn't stake them all out.'

'Actually no. I checked it out a couple of weeks ago when I wanted to ring Thelma. There are several Ewings here, but only one Fewings. In fact, I remember now. Isn't that what Uncle Martin said? About me being the only one to carry on the name?'

Nick digested this. A piece of the jigsaw fell into place. Anyone who wanted to track them down and follow them could have found Thelma's address. Of course, the Fewings could have been staying in a hotel, but the man who made those phone calls might have found the single name match too much of a coincidence to ignore.

A flicker of memory snatched his attention. Turning out of High Bank this morning, he had had to avoid a pedestrian standing just round the corner. He tried frantically to remember more details. Male? Young? Could it have been that teenager in the grey hoodie? He didn't think so, but infuriatingly he could not be sure.

'It scares me,' he said. 'He's gone to a lot of trouble to track us down. He's been spying on us, following us. Looking for a chance to get one of us alone.'

Millie shivered. 'Why wasn't it me?'

'How do we know it's a he?' Tom said. 'There might be a whole gang of them. I haven't a clue what's going on, but it's hard to think that it's just one guy on his own. But you seem to have got under his skin. When you sussed their operation in Hugh Street, the sensible thing would have been to keep quiet and get out fast. Leave as few clues as possible. But here's this guy flaunting it. Snatching Mum off the street and taunting you to come and get her.'

'Why?' Nick glanced at Millie and wished he hadn't spoken. It was in his mind that if he turned up as the text message challenged him to, he might not find Suzie. He might be walking into a trap. He was thankful that the police were dealing with it. He knew himself well enough to be sure that, if things had been different, he would have gone alone.

'Let's go,' he said abruptly.

Tom matched his stride to Nick's. 'You know something that's bugging me? I bet they don't usually put a detective superintendent in charge of a hunt for a missing woman. The police think they're on to something big.'

'Inspector Heap pretty well ruled out a vice ring. And whatever it is, why is that text message inviting me to walk in on it? None of it makes sense.'

Another horrid thought occurred to him. Was the text message luring him to a place that would be empty, except for Suzie . . . dead?

They were stopped at the exit from the shopping precinct, like everyone else. Two uniformed constables started to go through the routine questions. Had they seen a woman: white jeans, blue jumper, a pink-and-purple jacket . . .?

'She's my wife,' Nick said curtly. 'And no, I haven't seen her.'

The three of them walked past the speechless constables towards the car park and the battered Mazda.

The car lurched forward and stalled, as Nick attempted to put it into reverse and missed.

'I'm driving.' Tom got out of the passenger seat. He walked round and opened the driver's door, and stood back with an authoritative air.

Nick stared gloomily at the steering wheel, then reluctantly stepped out to change places.

'Sorry. I'm not myself.'

'Shock,' Tom said. 'It's natural.'

He swung the car expertly out of its parking space and headed for the exit.

What it is to be young, Nick thought. To have that self-confidence, even when things are going disastrously wrong. It was unfair to say that Tom was enjoying it, but he was excited by the crisis. He wasn't paralyzed with nerves and shocking fears as Nick was.

'Which way?'

Nick was recalled to reality sufficiently to give Tom directions to Hugh Street. It seemed like tracing a route he had walked with Suzie and Millie in a dream, not two days ago in real life. The bridge over the canal, where they had emerged from the towpath. The hill up to the nursery school, where they had met the tearful woman with her little boy. The derelict space where row upon row of millworkers' terraced houses had been demolished.

But something had changed dramatically. The entrance to Hugh Street was barred by police tape. Vehicles, most with police markings, were parked there.

'Where do you want me to go?' Tom asked. 'Something tells me we're not going to get past that lot.'

'Pull over here. I'll walk across. They'll have to let me through.'

'You wish,' said Millie, unfolding herself from the rear seat.

'You two stay here.'

'Not a chance,' protested Tom. 'She's our mum too.'

Nick was intensely aware of being watched as the three of them picked their way across the scattered bricks from the demolition. The one remaining mill chimney pointed upwards like a warning finger.

There were a pair of uniformed constables guarding the police tape, one male, one female.

'Sorry, sir,' said the taller, male one. 'I'm afraid we're not letting anyone through for the moment.'

Belatedly Nick became conscious of two young women with toddlers, waiting uneasily to one side of the barrier. They must have come from collecting their children from the nursery school, along a route which normally took them through the boarded-up Hugh Street.

How many people passed along that way? Did they not notice the comings and goings to a house that was supposed to be empty? Had none of them reported it, as Nick had done after a single encounter? Or was there a conspiracy of those down on their luck against authority, including the police? What difficult encounters might there be between the relatives of these tired-looking women and the forces of law and order?

If any of them had seen Suzie dragged here against her will, would they have said anything?

The woman police constable was urging him to move. 'Come along, sir. We've got a police operation going on here. It's no place for spectators.'

'My wife,' he said, though his tongue felt thick and hard to move. 'They've got my wife.'

'You just leave it to us, sir. If she's in that house, I'm sure they'll bring her out soon. There's nothing to worry about.'

Her soothing words were belied by the sight of the pavements of Hugh Street crowded with police officers in riot gear. Helmets with visors, stab vests, truncheons. His blood ran cold as he thought that some of them might have guns.

Would they knock on the door first or ring the bell, as he had? Would the suspicious Mr Harrison open it a fraction to peer round? But surely someone inside must already have seen the police presence blocking the street.

Was Suzie inside?

What would happen to her in the few seconds before the police broke the door down. If they had to?

Millie's cry came a split second after the crash that sent the raiding party hurtling into the house.

She clutched his arm. 'Is she going to be all right?'

He put his arm round her, hardly conscious of what he did.

'Yes, love. They've got it under control now.'

He desperately hoped he was right.

It seemed an age that the three of them waited.

Nick sprang forward as the first figures began to emerge from the door. He was suddenly conscious that the tall constable had his arm out across his face, barring his path.

'Keep back, sir, if you don't mind. You'll only be in the way.'

Between the black-clad, anonymous figures of the police squad, there were colourful dresses now. Women, some in shalwar kameez, like the two he had seen before. Others looked European. A portly man in a brown suit, who might be Mr Harrison, was handcuffed to an officer. His head was turned so Nick could not see his face. They were bundled away towards two police vans waiting at the other end of the street.

The movement in the road was thinning. Nick could make out plain-clothes officers now. DSI Mason and DI Collinge, he thought. One of the helmeted officers came out of the house some time after the others. He shook his head.

Nick ducked suddenly under the constable's arm. He broke through the plastic tape and ran down the street, heedless of the shouted order behind him. He raced up to the detective superintendent.

'Suzie! What's happened? Is she in there?'

The detective turned his grave face. 'I told you to go home and wait, sir. I said we'd keep you informed. I'm afraid, sir, we haven't found your wife. You were certainly right about this place. There's been illegal activity here but no evidence yet that it involves kidnapping. We've got some questioning to do. Like I said, we'll keep you informed. Unless you have some other reason to suggest why your wife might have disappeared?'

It was almost an accusation. Nick felt himself go hot and then cold. Did the superintendent really think that Suzie had walked out on him? That his story about the threatening phone calls meant nothing? It didn't make sense. Mason had seen the last text message for himself.

Tom was at his elbow. 'Come on, Dad. There's nothing here. Leave it. Let's go back to Thelma's and figure out what to do next.'

'It doesn't mean they haven't got her, because she's not here,' Millie said. 'They might have other places. They'd expect the police to bust this one, wouldn't they? After you told them about the calls.'

'I'm well aware of the evidence you've given us, sir. Leave it to us. Now do as your son says, and go home.'

There was nothing for it but to turn back, along the eyeless street, to where they had left the car, isolated in a desert of demolition.

# TWENTY-TWO

'**I**'ll do it.' Nick held out his hand for the car keys.

'You sure?'

'Yes.'

Tom handed over the keys reluctantly. Millie had already installed herself in the front passenger seat. She was asserting her right not always to be relegated to the back row, just because she was younger.

As he slid the car into gear, Nick felt surprisingly calm. No. Not calm. Numb. He had been so sure that those taunting messages were luring him back to the boarded-up house in Hugh Street. That Suzie must be there. That the police would find her. Alive or dead.

Now the bottom had dropped out of his certainties. He was left in a dark void. If Suzie was not in Hugh Street, where was she? Why had the mystery caller seemed so keen for Nick to come and find her? Why did he assume he knew where she was? Nothing made sense any more.

He drove mechanically. There seemed to be a distant, detached part of his mind which watched out for traffic lights, signposts, other vehicles and pedestrians. He did not think he was driving dangerously. If anything, he was more careful than usual. He did not consciously remember the route to Thelma's house, but the car was taking them there.

'Do you think those police guys have got another theory?' Tom's voice came from the back seat. 'I mean, that sweatshop, or whatever it is, was top of their hit list. But they may have ideas about who was running it. They could have other addresses.'

'There's someone following us,' Millie said.

The car swerved momentarily. Both children gasped. Nick brought it back under control.

'Sorry, folks. Which one, Millie?'

'The white one.'

Nick looked in his rear-view mirror. Two cars back, he saw a white Polo. As the road swung round a bend he glanced back. He had a glimpse of a young woman driving. He made out the head and shoulders of a taller man beside her.

He corrected his steering. 'Are you sure?'

'Yup. They've been there almost since we started. They must have been watching us at Hugh Street. They know exactly where we are, what we're doing. It's creepy.'

The numbness that had fallen over Nick was shattered. His breath was coming fast now. Fear. Anger. He was conscious of the two people he loved most after Suzie in the car with him. His son and daughter. Was there anything he could do to shield them from whoever had got the Fewings firmly in their sights?

It had been such a small, innocent thing. A quest for family history. Taking Suzie and Millie to the house where his grandmother had grown up. To relive the days of clogs on cobbles, of whirring looms, of streets begrimed with the smoke of a hundred mill chimneys. Surely nothing they had stumbled upon, or suspected, could warrant the abduction of Suzie and the all-too-present threat to the rest of them?

'Have you got your mobile, Tom?'

'Of course.'

'Ring the police. Describe the car. See if you can get the number plate.'

'Difficult. The car behind us is in the way.'

Again he sensed that Tom was relishing the excitement and importance of making the 999 call; detailing the car and its occupants, the route they were taking.

Nick swung off the main road on to the bridge and up the hill that led to High Bank. The car immediately behind them drove on. The white Polo followed them across the bridge.

Tom read out the number plate.

'They're not taking much trouble to disguise themselves, are they?' Millie twisted round to watch.

'It's like that phone call,' Nick said, through gritted teeth. 'Practically goading us to come and get Suzie. But what was the *point* if she wasn't there?' He slammed his hand on the steering wheel and was shocked by the blast of the horn.

He was struggling to maintain control now. He swung the car on to the gravel path in front of the terraced houses on High Bank. Thelma's red Nissan was already there.

Suddenly a wider reality flooded in. Thelma. He had involved her in this danger too. Great-uncle Martin, lying in hospital, looking forward to the family's next visit. To meeting Suzie and Millie. Hoping to come home on Sunday. How could he possibly explain to them?

He saw in the mirror the Polo make the same turn on to the gravel behind them. He leapt out and strode towards it as it slowed to a halt. The fair-haired young woman and the taller man got out. Brazenly open. Nothing furtive or disguised. His anger exploded.

'What the hell do you think you're playing at? *Where's Suzie?*'

He was aware of the physical presence of Tom close behind him.

The woman in the suede skirt and brown jacket flipped a warrant card open.

'Detective Sergeant Candy Bray. And this is DC William Riley. The Super has detailed us to keep an eye on you, under the circumstances. I'll be inside the house, if that's all right. My constable will be keeping watch outside. I gather you think that whoever took your wife has been keeping you under surveillance since you stumbled across them.'

Nick was left speechless. His anger evaporated. He was conscious of a strange regret as he looked at the detective constable. For a heady moment, he had thought he was facing the man who had made those phone calls. But he was wrong. He had not, after all, discovered the only people who knew where Suzie was. He felt more lost than ever.

It was left to Millie again to ask the obvious, unnecessary question.

'You're the *police*?'

Thelma met them in the hall. It was the moment Nick had dreaded.

Her face was bright with welcome. 'Have you had a good day? I dropped in on Dad after work. He was right chuffed that he'd had a chance to talk to you. Tom! Look how you've grown! I've put you in Dad's room instead of on the sofa, seeing as he's not here. It won't take me long to change the sheets if they let him come home on Sunday.'

The warmth of her voice was dying. Her eyes were going over the little group. Puzzlement, then an anxious questioning.

'Where's Suzie? Dad did say she and Millie hadn't come to the hospital. I couldn't explain to him why. And who's this?'

'Detective Sergeant Bray.' The policewoman took over. 'I'm sorry, Miss Fewings. There's been a problem. I don't want to alarm you, but Mrs Fewings is missing. We're putting out a search for her and in the meantime I'm keeping an eye on the family. Don't worry about me. I shan't need a bed or anything. One of my colleagues will relieve me later. And in case you wonder, that's a police constable you'll see outside. Nothing to worry about. Just belt and braces.'

Thelma stared at the young woman, astonished. 'Well I never! Suzie missing? And you say there's nothing to worry about? I'm not as daft as I look, you know. But I dare say somebody will tell me what this is all about.' Then she rallied. 'Well, from the sound of it, you'll all be glad of a cup of tea.'

Nick felt a rush of relief. Thelma was not the woman for histrionics. He hugged her warmly and kissed her powdered cheek.

'Thanks, Thelma. It's all been a bit of a shock.'

Soon they were settled in the front room. Thelma provided not only tea but a fresh lemon cake.

It was Millie who seemed most agitated. 'She was supposed to meet me in town. I waited and waited, and then I phoned Dad. And after that the police came. It wasn't my fault, was it?'

Nick put his hand over hers. 'Of course not, love.'

But he ached with the knowledge that if the three of them had gone to the hospital together, this could not have happened.

He flushed with guilt of his own when he turned to Thelma. 'We thought she might be up at Hugh Street. Do you remember we told you there seemed to be something fishy going on? What I didn't tell you was that I had a phone call warning me not to go to the police. But we did. The police have raided Hugh Street but she wasn't there.'

'There's more than that you haven't told me. Enough to bring a couple of the police back with you. Witness protection, is it? You hear about it. People having to change their name and move elsewhere. Something serious, isn't it?' She looked directly at the detective.

'We don't know what's at the back of it yet.' DS Bray studied her rose-patterned teacup. 'And if we did, I wouldn't be at liberty to tell you. But I'd ask you to keep quiet about this. My colleague outside will try to be discreet, but I'm afraid if the neighbours ask questions, you'll have to stall.'

'I shouldn't want to sound stand-offish. We're good friends here.'

'Do your best.'

It was a second before Nick put down his cup with a shock that rattled the saucer. Geoffrey Banks. Every day since they had arrived, Thelma's cousin next door seemed to be watching out for them. Within minutes, he had opened the door, inviting himself in to hear the latest news. Nick glanced over his shoulder. Where was he?

Stray threads of suspicion were gathering together. The embittered chemist, out of work, unlikely ever to be employed again at his age. His evident jealousy of Nick's work, the new car. Those quotes picked from the Bible that had more to do with punishment than love. He heard an echo in that text message: *VENGEANCE IS MINE.*

Was Geoffrey home? Was the reason he had not come round to Thelma's door because he was holding Suzie somewhere else? Might she even be inside his house next door?

Thelma was busy refilling teacups. 'You can hardly credit it, can you? The way folks carry on nowadays. Even the girls are rolling round drunk at night. And the men would as soon slash you across the face with a bottle as give you the time of day. It wasn't like that when we were teenagers.'

The voice that threatened Nick on the phone had not struck him as a teenager's.

Should he tell DS Bray about Geoffrey Banks? Should he phone the Superintendent? He waited until Sergeant Bray left them to check on the rest of the house. He followed her into the kitchen and watched her test the back-door lock. Her face registered surprise when she turned round and found him watching her.

Even before he spoke, he was aware of the futility of it. 'There's something you ought to know,' he tried. 'There's a man next door. Geoffrey Banks. He's a cousin of Thelma's. Used to be an industrial chemist, but the firm closed down. I found him this morning doing something to my car. At least . . .'

Her expression suddenly sharpened. 'Is that why you smashed up the wing? Why didn't you tell us?'

'Not exactly.' Shamefacedly he went on. 'It was my fault. I was trying to overtake a cyclist and I left it till too near a bend.'

'You're saying there was nothing wrong with your brakes? Or the steering?'

'No. I mean, I don't think Geoffrey Banks actually had time to *do* anything. But he doesn't like us. He keeps quoting biblical texts at us. It made me think of one of the text messages. *Vengeance is mine.*'

'Really?' He read the scepticism in her voice. He should have expected it.

Sergeant Bray sighed. 'I'll tell the boss. Now, if you don't mind, I'll check upstairs.'

Nick turned back to the sitting room. The evening stretched away in front of him like a featureless desert. And then a sleepless night, alone in Thelma's spare bed. He could not rest until he had Suzie back, but he could think of nothing else he could do.

Would it make any difference if he went back to Hugh Street on his own? Would the police have left officers on guard to preserve a crime scene? Could he get in, and crawl all over the house, looking for a detail they might have missed? Even break through into the adjoining houses? Had they searched those?

Even as he imagined it, he knew that the forensic team would be at work, studying the minutiae of the evidence more thoroughly than he would know how to.

He was helpless.

\* \* \*

The children had gone upstairs. Thelma was in the kitchen preparing the evening meal. DS Bray was familiarizing herself with the layout of the house. Nick was left alone in the not-too-comfortable front room. He felt exhausted. He leaned back against the stiff upholstery of the sofa. Should he go upstairs and rest on the bed? He was afraid to close his eyes because of the images he feared would sweep in to haunt him. Better to let his tired gaze rest beyond the window on the soaring bulk of Skygill Hill.

His phone chimed. He could hardly keep his hand steady as he opened it.

'Yes?'

It might be the police. It could be good news.

It was not. That same harsh voice grated out its message.

'Well, well. I'm really surprised you haven't got here yet. How much longer do we have to keep your little lady? You've been a naughty boy. Sending the police on a wild-goose chase. Did you know you can get done for wasting police time? See you.'

The line went dead.

DS Bray was standing in the doorway.

'Don't tell me. That was him, wasn't it? You've gone quite white. What did he say?'

Nick told her.

She held out her hand. 'I'm wondering whether we should pass your phone to the station. If he rings again, they might be able to get a trace on it. But they'd need to keep him talking. Does he know your voice?'

'He never gives me time to answer.'

'Funny, that. He's practically asking you to come and find him. He seems sure you know where he is.'

'Do you, Dad?' Tom appeared behind her. 'You've got to know something. It doesn't make sense otherwise.'

'I thought I did. I told you. They raided Hugh Street, but now he says that was the wrong place. He's laughing at me. *But I don't know where he is!*'

'Easy, Mr Fewings. Why don't you take a rest? Maybe something will come back to you.'

'For heaven's sake! We'd been here less than twenty-four

hours when I got his first call. We hadn't *been* anywhere else. Except Thorncliffe Mill.'

'The working museum place? By the canal?'

'Yes.'

The detective's brow furrowed. 'I don't see how that could be a crime scene. Too many people coming and going. You'd think it would be impossible to cover up anything suspicious there. But I'll let the Super know.'

She had her mobile out and withdrew into the hall, shutting the door. He heard her subdued voice, but not the words.

Tom threw himself into an armchair. 'That would be pretty clever, though, wouldn't it? School parties coming in and out all day. Dressing up in Victorian costume. And all the time, there's this modern crime going on right under their noses.'

'*What* crime?' retorted Nick.

'Search me.'

Nick's mind hunted through the scenes of that first morning. The vast weaving shed with its whirring looms. The shining steam engine thrusting its piston to and fro. Room after room with displays of shuttles, bobbins, raw cotton, woven cloth. The basement boiler room. But there had been other doors marked PRIVATE. How many more rooms might there be not open to the public? Was it possible that in one of them Suzie was being held?

The detective sergeant was telling Superintendent Mason. A faint hope stirred in Nick. Would the police raid the museum as well?

# TWENTY-THREE

Thelma was cooking high tea. She looked up defiantly as Nick stood in the doorway of the kitchen.

'I know you said you were taking me out to supper, but nobody's going to want that now, are they? But you've got to do something, haven't you? It's no good sitting around brooding.'

Nick's eyes took in the iridescent shapes of rainbow trout, the little pile of flaked almonds. Thelma was melting butter in a large frying pan. He shouldn't underrate her. He must adjust his mind to something more than a woman who dealt in the clichés of hotpot and meat-and-potato pie.

There were five plump trout. And only four Fewings now.

He was not going to be able to eat one, however good a cook Thelma was.

Thelma followed his thoughts. 'Do you think that detective would like one? It seems a pity to waste it.'

'I'll ask her.'

He was glad to escape the kitchen. He ran the risk of hysterical laughter, asking DS Bray if she would like to join them in *truite aux amandes.*

The policewoman shook her head. 'Sounds lovely. But I'm on duty. I don't think I should take my eye off the ball. Not that I'm expecting anything to happen.' She added hastily. 'I'm sure you're quite safe here. And we've got Riley outside. If you could rustle up a sandwich, that would be good.'

He had not expected tragedy to interfere with Tom's appetite. But he was surprised to find Millie tucking into high tea with enthusiasm.

He took a few bites of his own fish and pushed it aside. 'Sorry. It's beautiful, Thelma, but I'm not up to it.'

'You're not helping Suzie, you know,' she scolded him. 'I don't know what's going to happen, any more than you do. But when it does, you want to be fit to cope with it.'

He rose from the table and went to stand at the back window. Most of Thelma's garden lay at the front of the house, across the gravelled drive, spilling down the hillside. Here at the back, High Bank rose on up to the skyline. Sheep dotted the higher fields in the late sunlight, though the valley bottom was already in shadow. He felt a sudden longing to be out in the clean air, with the cool autumn breeze bracing him. To have the big distances and the high hills speaking of a power greater than his tangled confusion of thoughts and fears.

'Dad was asking if you'd found those letters about Russia in the suitcase.'

Thelma's words came meaninglessly at first.

'What suitcase?' Tom asked. 'Is that the one Uncle Martin said he was going to give you?'

'We already saw it,' Millie said. 'Before you got here. It's stuffed full of all sorts of family things. And there were these letters. From people with names like Jephthah and Elijah. And how they had to go to court because they were Baptists and wouldn't pay tithes to the parish church. But I don't remember anything about cotton mills in Russia.'

'It's true, though.'

Nick marvelled how they could talk normally about family history at a time like this. He wanted to shout at them that Suzie was missing. She had been kidnapped in broad daylight. They had no idea where she was. She was a prisoner some-where. She might be injured. She might be dead. Could she have been spirited abroad? To Russia?

He fought to control his anger. He ought not to frighten Millie more than he had to. He could see what Thelma was trying to do. Keeping a semblance of normality, to protect the children from the worst of the thoughts that were tormenting him. To take their minds off the appalling reality of what had happened to their mother.

But Tom was an adult now, legally. Eighteen. Nick still found it difficult to accept the new equality this implied. Tom was Tom, his blue-eyed little son. Altered by these few weeks at university, but still a long way from maturity.

And Millie, at fourteen, was still a child, however much her elegantly cropped blonde hair and eye make-up attempted to say otherwise.

He wanted to put his arms around them and keep them safe. The horror was that he had no idea of the nature of the threat that seemed to be hanging over them. It made no sense. What could they possibly have seen or done that could call down such retribution on them, if it was not to do with the goings-on at Hugh Street?

It chilled him to think that the police seemed not to know either. Unless they had information they were not sharing with him. Knowledge which necessitated the presence of DS Bray inside the house and Constable Riley patrolling outside.

What did they suspect?

'Dad showed me those Russian letters, Tom. You've a treat in store,' Thelma was saying. 'Two of those brothers from Briershaw, Gideon and Noah, got picked by the mill owners to go abroad. Gideon was an overlooker and Noah a beamer. The Ruskies were wanting to start up a whole lot of new mills over there, and they sent to Lancashire to find out how to do it. It was our family got picked to go to Kiev to show them how it was done.'

'You're kidding?' Tom exclaimed in spite of himself. His knife and fork clattered on a plate empty of all but fish bones.

'No, I'm not. You'll see. Dad's still kept the envelopes in that suitcase, with the Russian stamps. And those two boys wrote back to tell the family all about how it was like. How they helped them set up the machinery. It all had to be sent out from England in those days. They hadn't got the factories to manufacture their own looms and spinning mules then. So then they had to show the Russians how to use them.'

Even Millie looked up from her half-empty plate. 'So they taught these Russian girls to weave cotton, like Dad's granny used to?'

'That's the size of it,' Thelma sighed. 'And now you look at this town, and all the little places down the dales. And there's hardly a chimney left standing. What mills there are have mostly been turned into museums.'

The word brought Nick's thoughts up short. They were back to that. The only other possibility to explain where Suzie was. What the Fewings might, inadvertently, have stumbled upon. The Thorncliffe Mill Museum.

But he had no idea what they could have seen there that they should not have. His mind raked frantically through his partial memories of their visit. Nothing would come.

The kitchen was too hot. It smelt of fried fish. He had to get out or he would be sick.

'I'm going outside,' he said, making for the door. 'I've got to clear my head.'

'I need a walk.' Nick heard the belligerence in his voice as he informed the detective sergeant. He was challenging her to forbid him.

He saw the alarm in her grey eyes, the need to make a quick decision.

'I'd rather you didn't go out of sight of the house, sir. I can't keep my eyes on both you and your children otherwise.'

'Can't I even take a turn round the garden?' he exploded.

'No problem there, sir. Riley will have you in his sights.'

It heightened the sense of unreality that he could not even step outside Thelma's front door without a detective watching his back.

He saw the tall Constable William Riley straighten instantly from his casual pose against his car. DS Bray came out of the house and exchanged a few words with him. Nick sensed the policeman relax a little. But he was still alert, watchful, as Nick crunched across the gravel path.

He turned his back on the constable and began to walk down the grassy paths of Thelma's garden, between the vegetable beds.

He felt a prickle down his back. He could be watched, not just from Thelma's house, but from Geoffrey Banks'. He turned his head. There were no lights in the next-door windows. He did not know whether that was good news or bad.

He walked on.

Despite the unreality of the situation, everything about the scene that met him struck home with heart-aching clarity. The sun had dropped below the steep fells, but the air still held a pearly clarity before twilight. The solid permanence of Skygill Hill made him long to be climbing it with his family, as he had promised himself. Would that ever happen now?

Neat rows of vegetables patterned Thelma's sloping garden. Leeks, carrots, the ragged heads of Brussels sprouts, their buds barely starting to fatten for Christmas. Street lamps were starting to come on, beading the streets of the town below him. He could pick out the cupola of the town hall. The solitary chimney of Thorncliffe Mill.

The museum. The thought made him draw his breath short, like a fist to his chest. Was it really possible that Suzie was there? He needed to have hope that there was an answer somewhere.

He could hardly restrain himself from jumping into his car and rushing there to see.

Had Superintendent Mason taken the information seriously? That Hugh Street was a red herring and the real threat lay in the museum?

*Why*? He found he was stamping the dew-damp grass between the gooseberry bushes. Why was her abductor taunting him? Surely, if there was something criminal going on, the perpetrator would want above everything else to keep it secret? What was the sense in goading Nick to follow Suzie to wherever he was hiding her?

He? Them? He did not know whether he was dealing with a solitary lunatic or an organized gang. There was something deeply wrong about the whole scenario. It made no sense.

At the bottom of the steep garden, Nick stopped. It was hard to tear his eyes away from Thorncliffe Mill. Every moment, he hoped to see flashing police lights. To know that they were going in to end this.

After a fruitless wait, he made himself turn back.

He saw the front door open. Tom and Millie came out. Both had their jackets on. He watched them look around before they spotted him below them. They crossed the drive and started down the slope towards him. Nick walked up the grassy path to meet them.

They stood in an awkward silence.

'Do you think they've found her?' Millie burst out. 'Are they going to look in the museum?'

'You two really think she's there?' Tom asked. The boyish enthusiasm for adventure had gone out of him. He looked older. His blue eyes went across Millie to his father's. This was no longer a challenging mystery to be solved. His mother might not be coming back.

'I don't *know*,' Nick said, exasperated. 'Nothing in all this makes sense. Why draw attention to himself? Why take Suzie in the first place, still less taunt me to come and get her? But if the reason isn't in Hugh Street, it's got to be the textile museum. We didn't go anywhere else. We spent the morning at Thorncliffe Mill, had lunch in their restaurant, then we set out along the canal path and ended up in Hugh Street. There only *are* those two places where we could have seen something wrong we might have told the police. And we didn't find anything out of the ordinary in the museum. At least, it was all pretty amazing, but certainly above board. There wasn't a single thing I can think of that looked suspicious. If she's there, then they've kidnapped her for nothing.'

'You're wrong, Dad.' Millie said suddenly. 'There *was* something else. Don't you remember? We were walking along the towpath and there were all those empty old mills. I found the grating over the window of one of them was loose, and we broke into it. They had machines, like the ones we'd seen in the museum, only dustier.' Her words were coming rapidly now. 'You wanted me to crawl under one, so I could imagine I was Millie Bootle, but I wouldn't. So you did!'

Nick stared at her, speechless. He was appalled. How *could* he have forgotten? His mind had been a mill race of churning memories, struggling for the cause. But not of this. The scene came back to him in vivid clarity.

'Someone had been there,' he said huskily. 'There were footprints in the dust. They led to a locked door at the end of the weaving shed.'

'There was something else, Dad. On the outside of the mill. All those graffiti. Remember? Out of the Book of Revelation, Mum said. *Their torture was like the torture of a scorpion.* Stuff like that.'

Nick stared at her, wide-eyed with shock.

Tom looked from one to the other. 'Why the hell didn't you say so?'

Millie rounded on him. 'Because we thought it was all to do with Hugh Street, you daft pig. Who wouldn't? There *was* a crime going on there. It was only that last phone call that told Dad we'd got it wrong . . . Dad!' She whirled round to him. Her pointed face blazed with realization. 'That explains it! You know you said you couldn't think how that man at Hugh Street had got your mobile number, when you only told him your name? Well, in the mill you took off your jacket to crawl under the loom and show me. Idiot! Why didn't I remember? When I passed it back to you, some stuff fell out of your pocket. Your mobile. Business cards and stuff. We were scrabbling all over the floor picking them up.'

Nick's hand went slowly to his inside pocket. His phone. And yes, a little sheaf of cards. He drew them out and looked at them. His name and architectural qualifications. Just the information with which that first call had mocked him. His office address. Phone numbers, both landline and mobile. Email address of the firm. Some of them were still smudged with dirt from the abandoned mill floor.

He thumbed through them. There was a piece of paper wedged between them. It seemed to be torn from a small notebook and folded in four. He could not remember what it was.

He unfolded it. There was a list scrawled on it. Words he did not recognize. The writing was not his.

'What's the matter, Dad? Tom asked.

'I don't know this piece of paper. Do you remember picking this up, Millie?'

'Sort of. I suppose it was on the floor with everything else. Some of them had slid under the loom. I fished out everything I could see.'

'It's not mine. I don't even know what half these words mean. I didn't write this.'

Tom took it from him. 'Let's have a look.'

His waving black hair fell across his face as he bent his head to read the words in the paling evening light.

Suddenly he straightened up. There was shock in his face.

'Dad! We have to get there! Straight away!'

'Why? What does it mean?'

'Caesium-137? TNT? At least he doesn't mention uranium. Run!'

# TWENTY-FOUR

Tom's long legs sent him hurtling up the slope, outstripping the others. Nick's mind was reeling. The letters TNT hammered in his brain. A bomb factory? In the derelict mill? Who? Why? The thought of Suzie imprisoned there suddenly galvanized him into action. In a few moments he had caught up Millie's running figure.

They broke out on to the level drive behind Tom. He was making for their car.

'Have you got the keys?' he flung over his shoulder at Nick. 'Yes!'

Constable Riley leaped from the seat of his own car, where he had been keeping surveillance. He started to run towards them, shouting into his radio as he did so. Nick ran round to the driver's seat of the Fewings' car.

Riley had reached them and was grappling with Tom.

'What's the hurry? Wait! You can't go anywhere without telling us.'

'How about a bomb factory?' Tom shouted at him. 'They've got my mother.' He thrust the piece of paper at the constable. 'It's all there. TNT. Caesium-137. Detonators. You know what that means.'

Sergeant Bray was running from the house.

Nick shouted at Millie as she folded her legs into the car. 'No! Stay here.'

'Not likely. Look what happened the last time we split up.'

She leaned out of the window and called to Constable Riley. 'It's a derelict mill beside the canal. About halfway between the weaving museum and Canal Street. You can't miss it. It's painted all over with slogans about the end of the world.'

As Nick put the car into gear, those last words broke over him with renewed meaning.

The end of the world. They had thought the graffiti on the mill was the work of some nutter who had merely used those walls as a convenient backdrop. It had not occurred to him that it might have anything to do with what was going on inside. Had it? Was this some volatile mix between the manufacture of explosive devices and the apocalyptic vision of the end of the world? What madmen were they dealing with?

Sergeant Bray hammered on the window, but the car sprang away, leaving the two police officers helpless in its wake. In the mirror, Nick saw them race for their car. It was the detective sergeant who was now talking rapidly into her radio as she leaped into the car beside Riley.

Then he swung on to the downhill road and lost them. A few moments later, he thought he saw them emerge from the drive, already a long way back up the hill behind him.

Would they see him as he turned the car into the residential streets through which the Fewings had threaded their way back from Hugh Street yesterday?

He tried to damp down the feeling that he was running away from the police, evading capture. They had got away from High Bank before their escort could stop them. But now they would surely need the backup of the police.

All he could think about was the need to find Suzie and be with her. What happened next he could not imagine.

He blessed the accuracy of his memory as the car shot out of a street of terraced houses on to the huge, desolate area where the houses had been demolished. For a moment, he was disorientated. Then his sense of direction reasserted itself and the car roared forward on to Canal Street. Horns blared as he sped across the oncoming traffic into the far lane and turned downhill for the canal bridge.

'Dad!' Millie exclaimed. 'It's not going to help Mum if you get us killed.'

She was right. He steadied his hands on the wheel.

'What's caesium-137?' he asked Tom.

'Radioactive isotope. They use it in university labs and hospitals. Easiest place for radioactive material to go AWOL. Combine it with explosives and you've got yourself a dirty bomb.'

'What's that?' Millie asked. 'Aren't all bombs dirty?'

'Not like this. The aim is not to blow people up, unless they're really close, but to spread contamination over a wide area. Streets, houses, drinking water. You can't see it, so you don't know what's safe and what's not. Result – panic.'

'And you think . . . Inside that mill . . . Where Mum is . . .?

'We don't know for certain she's there,' Tom said grimly. 'But, from what you say, I've a pretty clear idea now what's going on there. It sounds like the perfect place for a clandestine bomb factory.'

They were level with the steps that led down from the bridge to the canal. Nick hesitated. Should he ditch the car and run along the towpath? But it was some distance away that they had found and entered the mill. On a hunch, he turned the car right, being a little more careful this time to find a gap in the traffic. He drove into a narrow side street that seemed to run parallel to the canal.

He was in unknown territory here.

'Keep your eyes open,' he ordered Millie. 'It should be somewhere over there on our right. Shout if you think you see it.'

There were more abandoned mills with lifeless eyes. Would the one they had entered look any different from this direction than the others? Were there graffiti on this side too?

'Got it!' Millie yelled. 'Over there. THE END TIME IS COMING.'

'For them, it is!' Tom said.

Nick stopped the car abruptly. The three of them got out.

'Stay here,' Nick told Millie again.

She threw him a look of exasperated scorn.

The factory was only a block away. They threaded a narrow alley and stood beneath its forbidding bulk. It stood darkly brooding against the grey evening sky. No light showed.

Nick began to feel a chill uncertainty.

Warning letters were painted across the wall in metre-high letters.

PREPARE TO MEET THY DOOM.

'This is evidently the front entrance,' Nick said. 'We got in round the back.'

'Three doors, but all boarded up,' Tom observed.

'There was a thingy on the canal side,' Millie said. 'You know, like where they swing things out and lower them into barges.'

'We went in through a window.' Nick was urgently scanning this side of the building to look for a weak spot. 'But these grilles look pretty secure here.'

'We're wasting time,' Millie urged him. 'Why don't we just go round to the towpath, where we were before?'

'There's a light!' Tom said suddenly.

It was a tiny bud of illumination in an end window. Nick drew his breath in a gasp so sharp it was almost painful. Someone was there. His hunch was becoming reality. No one should be in this derelict mill. And if someone was, it meant almost certainly that Suzie was in there too.

Panic was receding. He felt an almost steely determination. He knew what he had to do now.

'I'm going round the back. Tom, you come with me. Millie, you stay here and wait for the police.'

'Shouldn't we all wait? What if the people inside have got guns?'

'I'm not sure they're that kind of criminal. Religious fanatics, by the sound of it. The sort that want to hurry on the end of the world. But from that paper you found, our guy seems to be more into using chemistry than firearms.'

'You hope. Who's to say he hasn't got both?'

Nick and Tom began to move towards the corner of the mill. An inner voice was telling Nick that Millie was right. The police knew what was happening here. Tom had given them the alarming ingredients scrawled on the piece of paper. Millie had told them how to find the mill. Any moment now, police cars would come racing down this side street, lights flashing, sirens blaring. They would have the manpower, the equipment, the weapons, the experience to deal with this far better than him and Tom unarmed.

But a more urgent voice was telling him that it might not end like that. The police might come and surround the building – from a safe distance. Tom seemed certain that whoever had taken Suzie was constructing a dirty bomb. The police would surely have safety regulations. They wouldn't risk going in unprepared where a bomb might be detonated. Would they send for a specialist unit? The SAS?

How did Tom know about these things? Nick had no idea how big an explosion they were talking about, or how wide an area might be contaminated with radioactivity. He was pretty sure that anyone in the immediate vicinity would be in serious danger.

How powerful was the explosion? How close did you need to be for that itself to blow you apart? The tall mill ahead of him suddenly seemed not nearly big enough.

He reached the wall. Shouldn't he order Tom to stay behind too? He took a sideways glance at his son's set face and knew he would be wasting his time. From close underneath its shuttered walls, the mill loomed huge. They were working along the front wall, away from that bead of light, towards the further corner. They had to climb over a crumbling wall into a patch of waste ground, where the neighbouring mill had been demolished. As they dropped down, a cat fled yowling from almost underneath them.

'Why do they sound so scary?' Tom attempted to laugh. 'I can see why they associate them with witches.'

Their footsteps sounded loud in the silence that followed. The evening light was fading, but soon there was a glimmer from the canal ahead.

'Round here,' Nick whispered. 'It wasn't far from this end.' He found the window. They had not been able to flatten the metal grille back over the opening as completely as it had been before they broke in. Nick's fingers closed round the rusted metal and tugged.

The grille sprang open. The gap was wide enough to let them through. Nick straightened up and looked at Tom in the dusk.

'I'll go first. Stay here. I'll call if I find anything.'

'Thanks, but I'm coming in too. We've no idea how many of them there are. If necessary, one of us can take them on, while the other gets Mum out.'

'If she's here.'

'Those phone calls as good as said she was. He was goading you to come and find her.'

'That's what worries me. Why?'

'If those slogans on the walls are his – or theirs – then they're not quite sane. They *want* to see the end of the world.'

Nick kept his private fears to himself: that this was personal. That the bomb maker wanted to punish the Fewings family for discovering his factory. That he was going to make them the first victims of his device.

The crazy thing was that they had had no idea what was going on in the mill. All their attention had been on Hugh Street and the criminal activity there. If the bomb maker had not made those threatening phone calls, their break-in at the mill would have passed off without further thought.

Nick drew a deep breath to steady himself. Whoever had made those threats, he was in there now. He must be driven by a death wish to wreak havoc on an evil world, even if he killed himself with the rest of them.

He put a leg over the sill into the darkness beyond.

# TWENTY-FIVE

As his foot connected with the floor, Nick had the uncanny feeling that he was stepping into another world. The former weaving shed was in almost total darkness. The deepening grey sky of evening should have glimmered through the ranks of high windows that had once cast light on the weavers' intricate play of weft and warp. But most were obscured now by boards or grilles.

He sensed, rather than saw, the rows of looms rising on either side of him.

Then he saw it. A thin line of light at floor level, far down the end of the vast room. It was so faint he had to blink to be sure he was not imagining it.

'Do you think he's got a battery lamp in there?' Tom's voice murmured at his elbow. 'Or has he patched into the mains supply?'

'Go back!' hissed Nick, startled.

'Like I said. Two of us are better than one.'

Nick felt a cold uncertainty. It had seemed simple from outside. Break in, find Suzie, free her and flee. The gloom of the weaving shed was silent around them. He had no idea where Suzie might be held.

'I should have brought a torch,' he cursed himself.

Tom was whispering. 'That guy was taunting you to find him. Now's your chance. He's got to be the other side of that door, where the light is.'

'I was rather hoping to avoid a confrontation. Just get Suzie out and run.'

'What's that?' Tom stopped abruptly.

'What? I didn't hear anything.'

'Over there. Among the machines . . . No, it's gone now. I thought I heard a sort of thump.'

They listened intently. No further sound came from that direction. But ahead of them now rose the sound of voices from the other side of the end door.

'Sounds like they're having an argument.' Nick could almost hear the grin in Tom's voice. 'So much the better for us. The bad news is that there's more than one of them. The good news is that they're falling out with each other. Should add to the confusion when we meet them.'

'I only wish the way out wasn't such a long way back.'

'Maybe there's a door at this end of the mill. We went round the far end. But from what I saw, you could probably break out through any of these windows and the grilles would just give way.'

'I hope you're right. I wouldn't want to be trapped inside. I'm not as sure as you are that they won't be armed.'

'Have you noticed something?' Tom muttered.

'No. What?'

'It's not just quiet inside here. I can't hear a sound outside either. What's happened to the police? I thought they'd come screaming after us when Millie told them where we were going.'

Nick stopped again. Now that he tuned his ear to the wider distance, he realized that Tom was right. The derelict area around the mill was ominously silent. He thought of Millie waiting out there alone in the gathering dusk and felt guilty. It was growing harder to know what to do to keep his family safe.

His attention was suddenly wrenched back to the scene in front of him. Some twenty paces away, the door at the end of the weaving shed burst open. The artificial light in the room beyond was not brilliant, but it seemed to flood the space with unexpected dazzle. Huge shadows of the looms were thrown back on either side.

Directly in front of him, where the light was strongest, stood two men.

Within the small room was a ginger-haired young man with an angry face above a stubbled chin. He wore glasses and a stained and ragged jersey. Nick was not sure whether the first impression was of an impoverished student or a down-and-out. But something about him was naggingly familiar. The face within the shadow of the cyclist's hood? He didn't think so. That had been thinner, younger.

The student type in that fair-isle jersey, lingering in the precinct yesterday afternoon.

He had a frightening glimpse of a workbench behind the young man. An array of parts which might be the things Tom had read out from that list. A small collection of tools. A bundle from which wires protruded.

But it was the other man, now coming through the doorway, who seized his attention. Nick's jaw fell open. Striding towards him, then stopping abruptly as he saw Nick and Tom, was the plump-faced figure he had confronted before. Harry Redfern, the Baptist minister who had driven the blue Honda.

Nick was consumed, for a moment by disbelief, and then by rage. He lunged forward and fastened his hands around the thick neck.

'It was you all along! And I let myself be convinced by you – or at least by your wife. I thought it was just a coincidence that you were following us. A Baptist minister having a day off with his kids. And all the time . . . it was just a cover! *Where's Suzie?*'

His thumbs were pressing on the minister's windpipe, throttling him.

'Dad!' he faintly heard Tom cry.

But he had eyes only for the purpling face in front of his eyes, the heavy perspiration breaking out. The frightened, bulbous brown eyes. The man was struggling to tear Nick's hands away from his throat. He was quite a big man, but not athletic. He was no match for Nick's rage.

Harry Redfern was fighting to speak, but Nick's hands barely allowed him to breathe. A harsh laugh came from the lamplit room behind the pair.

'Well, now! There's a turn-up for the book. The Reverend Henry Redfern, pillar of the Baptist Church, prison visitor and general do-gooder, cast in the role of the horseman of the Apocalypse!'

From the very first words, Nick recognized that hoarse voice, the taunting tone. His pressure on the Reverend Redfern's windpipe slackened, though he did not let go.

'You! You made those phone calls. Is this some diabolical plot you two have hatched up between you? But what the hell has this got to do with Suzie? Let her go!'

His eyes flew past the younger man in the ragged jersey. He was searching the small room behind him. It might once have been the mill office, but it had clearly been turned into a laboratory. Nick tried to shut his mind to the horrible significance of the bundle of equipment on the bench. He scanned the narrow space for anywhere that might be hiding Suzie. There were floor cupboards. Could she really be crammed inside one of those, unable to move? He shuddered at the exquisite pain this would cause her after so many hours.

As Nick's hands slackened, Harry Redfern managed to gasp out his first words.

'Mr Fewings! Nick! You've got the wrong man . . . I've no idea where your good wife is . . . I only wish I could help you.'

'Then what in God's name are you doing here?'

'I know . . .' He panted for air. 'I know Dominic.' His head jerked in the direction of the young man in his makeshift laboratory. 'I was . . . his prison chaplain. I've been trying . . . to help him sort himself out, after he was released. That's why, when you came to my house . . .'

Another piece of the puzzle fell into place. A single glimpse over Harry Redfern's broad shoulder into his sitting room. The glowering young man the minister had been talking to.

That same name. Dominic.

Uneasily, afraid that he was being tricked yet again, Nick released the minister. Harry Redfern stepped back thankfully and rubbed his bruised neck around his dog collar.

Nick stared at the bespectacled Dominic. The young man was frowning now. The mocking laughter had gone from his stubbled face. He was glancing uncertainly at the large windows on either side of the darkened weaving shed. A ghost of grey twilight still crept in through the grilles. It was not enough to penetrate far into the shadowed interior among those stationary looms.

'Where are they, then?' he asked sharply.

'Who?'

'The police. You've told them, haven't you? You must have told them when you found out it was here.' He took a step towards them, anger darkening his face. 'You tricked me! I don't know what all that was, going on in Hugh Street. But it certainly wasn't me. It took you longer than I thought, didn't it, to work out that it was here?' His tone took on a bitter venom. 'I could curse you for that. I could have kept quiet. I could have carried it through. This wasn't how I meant it to end. A dirty bomb's no good unless you set it off where it will cause maximum panic. I was going to contaminate the Square Mile. Strike them right in the heart of London. Bankers. Tourists. Politicians! All the servants of Mammon. I told him!' He jerked his head contemptuously at Harry Redfern.

'And, God forgive me, I didn't believe him,' the Baptist minister cried. 'I thought he was delusional. Well, he is, in one way. As if God needed any of us to bring about Armageddon and the end of the world!' He rounded on Dominic. 'I keep trying to tell you. God *loves* this world. You, me, the smallest seahorse in the ocean, Al-Qaeda, and . . . the Lord protect her . . . poor Suzie Fewings. God wants to hold his creation in the hollow of his hand. But *you* want to annihilate us. If you imagine that you're a servant of God, you couldn't be more wrong.'

'Read your Bible, padre! *They called to the mountains and rocks, "Fall on us and hide us from the wrath of the Lord."*'

'A dream of the end time. Glorious symbolism. Not a scientific blueprint. First-century Christians didn't think in those terms. You're a million miles away from their mindset.'

'Listen to him!' Dominic's brown eyes flared behind his glasses. 'He doesn't even believe the Bible he's supposed to preach. But it's *you* I'm getting impatient with.' He glared at Nick. '*Where are the police?*'

The question had been nagging at the back of Nick's mind. The moment he realized where Suzie must be, he had leaped into his car to find her. Tom's reading of the notes jotted on that piece of paper had scared him into believing he must get to her and release her before the madman could set off his bomb. A saner part of his mind had always known that, even if the police didn't manage to stop him, they would come racing after him. He had hardly expected to get inside the mill before the sound of police sirens came blaring in his wake. He had left Millie outside, believing she would be safe with them.

But the dusk outside was silent.

Tom spoke quietly behind him. 'I gave them that piece of paper. Did you know you'd dropped it?' He directed the question at Dominic. 'When you found Dad's business card on the floor? You'd jotted down a whole list of things. Caesium-137, TNT, and a load of other stuff. You don't need to have a Nobel Prize in chemistry to work out what it was for. So the police aren't taking any chances, are they? They won't put their guys in danger until they come equipped to deal with a radioactive bomb. Which reminds me. If you're making it in that room behind you, you don't seem to be taking any precautions yourself.'

Dominic's lips stretched in a mirthless smile. 'I'm a Servant of Armageddon. Do you think I care what happens to me on this wicked earth? Or to any of you despicable little people? When the great day comes, the Lord will transport his own to heavenly glory and leave the rest of you in this stupid world to fight yourselves to death. When I press the switch, I'm going to take as many of you with me as I can. But *you'll* be going to eternal fire.'

'Just tell me first,' Tom said quietly, 'where's my mother?'

'Over here, you morons,' came a distant voice from the far end of the weaving shed. 'Did neither of you think to bring the torch from the car?'

'Millie!' cried Nick. He sprang towards the far-off circle of light throwing gigantic shadows among the looms.

# TWENTY-SIX

Nick raced across the floor towards his wife and daughter. He sensed as much as glimpsed the gaps between the machines. Two or three rows over he could see Suzie now, caught in the small circle of torchlight. His heart constricted with fear.

She was lying prostrate under one of the looms. Even before he reached her, he was almost sure she was bound and gagged.

He remembered keenly what it had felt like to crawl under a loom. The sense of claustrophobia. The weight of all that machinery so close above his head. It had been all too easy to imagine it springing into terrible life. The darting shuttles. The spinning leather belts. The pounding metalwork. Horrible to think of a piece of his clothing or a strand of his hair becoming entangled with that relentless dance, leaving him maimed or scalped.

This was the fear that generations of Fewings and Bootles had felt before him, when they entered the mill as children. A fear they masked by their quick tongues and ready humour.

He could understand why Millie had refused to crawl under the machine.

The weaving machinery was disused and silent now. It would stay like that, wouldn't it? There was no real danger to Suzie.

Then he remembered the footprints in the dust. The evidence that one, at least, of the looms had been cleaned and greased, the leather belt connected, ready to operate.

Was it that one?

He cast a desperate look over his shoulder. Tom was racing

after him. He had lost sight of the larger figure of the Reverend Redfern. Dominic was hidden from him by the rows of looms. Nick only knew where he was by the rectangle of light coming from the room he used as his workshop.

'Stay where you are!' the curiously hoarse voice thundered down the echoing room.

Nick paused. There was authority in that voice, young as it was.

'Nobody move until our friends from the constabulary arrive. The City of London this may not be, but since you've forced me to show my hand before I was ready, I'm going to take as many of you with me as I can. And that includes our much-vaunted forces of law and order. The principalities and powers of the Devil.'

'Dominic!' pleaded Harry Redfern's voice. 'You don't have to do this.'

'Oh, yes I do. *From his mouth issued a sharp two-edged sword.* Terrorist! That's what they'll call me, isn't it? Well, I'll show them terror.'

*He's going to detonate that bomb.* The full impact of that realization struck Nick. How much TNT was on that bench? How big an explosion in this confined space? How much radioactive caesium would it release? He had to get the others out.

He flung himself towards Millie's guiding light.

'I said STOP!' the voice from the other end of the weaving shed roared. 'One step further and I set these looms going. Think what will happen to your pretty wife then.'

Nick froze.

He heard Millie's desperate cry. 'Lie still, Mum! It's all right as long you don't move.'

Behind him, Nick heard a sudden commotion. He whirled round. Tom was no longer behind him. From the sounds, Nick knew that he was hurling himself back towards the bomb maker. He thought Harry Redfern might be doing the same. Dominic let out a cry of rage.

Fear raced through Nick's mind. There would be no antique steam boiler here needing to get up pressure, like the one in Thorncliffe Mill. No waterwheel to set turning, like Belldale.

This mill had long ago been converted to electricity. And
Dominic had somehow managed to reconnect the supply.
Where was the switch that would set this whole weaving shed
in motion?

He heard Tom's wail of failure.

Instantly, the world around him sprang into hideous life.
The noise was shattering. The leather belts that connected each
loom began their macabre dance above him. Heddles lifted
and crashed. Empty shuttles clattered across the space where
the warp threads should have been, too fast to follow. Metal
parts ground up and down.

*And Suzie was underneath one of them.*

Nothing could stop him now from flying forward to where
that circle of light shone. He was almost on them before he
caught a glimpse of Millie's pale face, dimly visible above
the brighter light of the torch she held.

She was directing it steadily on the bound and helpless
figure of Suzie. Dominic's prisoner was half obscured by the
flying mechanism of the loom that trapped her. Her mouth
was taped shut. Her hands were bound beneath her back. Her
hazel eyes were wide and terrified.

Nick threw himself on to his knees beside her.

'Hold still. We'll get you out.'

He did not know whether she could hear him over the
thunder of the loom above her head.

The torchlight was beginning to waver in Millie's hand.
Nick reached up and grasped her wrist. The girl was trembling
now.

'You've done a great job,' he shouted above the clacking
of the looms. 'We'll get her free.'

He fervently prayed it was true. Above the din he could
no longer hear what was happening at the other end of the room.

There was a report like a pistol shot. Something whipped
through the air, just missing Millie's head. She screamed and
ducked down to where Nick was kneeling beside the imprisoned Suzie.

'Has he got a gun?' she yelled.

The loom next to them had fallen silent. Suddenly Nick
knew what had happened. One of the leather belts that

criss-crossed the space above the looms had snapped. The leather must be old and dry. The whiplash of a belt breaking under power could kill anyone standing in its way.

There were other ominous sounds. A grinding of metal parts. A screeching, and then another loom silenced. Mad Dominic had not just been using the old mill to construct his bomb. In the intervals as he assembled its deadly ingredients, he must have been using his technological skills to get at least some of the looms working. But there must be over a hundred of them. He could not have serviced them all. Nick remembered the dust thick around most of them. And any one of them could fail suddenly, resulting in a flying belt or sheared-off metal.

'Keep down!' he shouted to Millie. 'It's not a gun, but it could be lethal.'

He tried to reassure Suzie, above the clatter of the heddle overhead. 'Lie absolutely still. I'm going to try to slide you out.'

It was far more terrifying than lying under the machine himself. Millie was trying to keep the torch steady. But Nick himself felt confused by the constant coming and going of the flying machinery. He knew it was possible to get under a working loom and out again. Children in his family had done it every day.

But Suzie was an adult. That much bigger. Bound and unable to help herself. It was his responsibility.

He took hold of her ankles. They seemed to be strapped together with insulating tape. Slowly, steadily, his heart in his mouth, he began to pull.

Suddenly, the deafening racket ceased. The wild dance of machinery just above Suzie's head clattered to a stop. Nick's head shot up.

Away from the torchlight, it was hard to see anything in the gloom. But something was different. The memory of sound echoed in his mind. A door banging.

Then he knew what it was. The rectangle of light from Dominic's laboratory had vanished. He had slammed the door.

Tom's voice rang anxiously down the weaving shed. 'Dad! Is Mum all right?'

'I think so.' It was hard to find the strength to shout, even though the looms had fallen silent.

The light of Millie's torch was fading. 'Oh, sugar! The battery's going,' she wailed.

'I need a knife to cut her free.' Nick had drawn Suzie's helpless body half out from under the loom. Her wrists were taped too.

'If you'd told me I'd need my handbag, I'd have had a pair of scissors,' Millie retorted. 'Hang on. There was some broken glass under the windows.'

He saw the ghost of her blonde hair in the twilight that still lingered in front of the tall windows on the canal side.

She was quickly back. Carefully, he took the broken shard she held out.

Running footsteps were coming towards them. Nick tensed. Tom swore as he bumped into a machine in his efforts to find them.

'Where are you?'

'Here!' called Millie.

The torch sputtered into life and died again.

Then two darker shadows were standing over them. Tom and Harry Redfern. Both were panting, from more than the exertion of running across the crowded floor.

'We tried to tackle him,' Tom gasped. 'But he broke away from us. He's locked himself into his lab.'

The Reverend Redfern's deeper voice cut in. 'I'm terribly afraid that can only mean one thing. The boy's obsessed with bringing about the final battle. He claims to belong to a group that call themselves the Servants of Armageddon. They're trying to precipitate the end of the world.'

'And he's at least halfway to making his dirty bomb . . . Is she OK? Can she run?' Tom's question this time was urgent.

There was a little scream as Nick tore off the tape that had closed Suzie's lips.

'I can now.'

She started to scramble to her feet, and cried out as limbs immobilized for hours began to take her weight. Nick leaped to support her tottering figure.

She gasped a shaky laugh. 'I'll be OK. Just let me get everything working.'

'No time to wait,' Tom ordered breathlessly. 'If this guy's right, Dominic's going to set off his bomb any second now.'

'Except,' Harry Redfern said, 'he seems remarkably keen to wait for the police.'

'He wants a captive audience,' Suzie sighed. 'That's what he's been saying. To take as many of us with him as he can. The police. Television cameras. He wants to make national headlines.'

As if on cue, there was the distant sound of sirens, approaching fast. Lights swept past the windows on the side away from the canal. Seconds later, more illuminated the other wall of windows. The Fewings and Harry Redfern were caught in the middle. A group of shadowy figures on the weaving floor where the lights could not yet reach.

A voice with a loudspeaker echoed from outside.

'Dominic! This is the police. Let Mrs Fewings go. Then come out quietly, with your hands above your head.'

Thinly, they heard a voice cry from the window of the room at the end of the mill.

'*The beast that ascends from the bottomless pit will make war upon them and conquer them and kill them, and their dead bodies shall lie in the street.*'

'We've got to get out!' Tom exclaimed. 'Now!'

# TWENTY-SEVEN

Tom ran past the others to one of the windows over-looking the canal. His tall figure was caught in the glare of the floodlights. Nick heard the crash as his son shoulder-charged the window. He could only hope that the covering grille had given way.

The light seemed to flood more brightly through the open space.

Tom yelled back. 'Quick! Jump as far out as you can. Get across the canal. As soon as you're on the other side, run like hell!'

A second crash. This time, the tinkle of glass breaking. Tom gave a yelp. Nick heard him kicking the broken glass away and trying again.

His own hand was already under Suzie's armpit. He was aware of Harry Redfern doing the same on her other side. Suzie cried out in pain as she tried to run. Together they half pulled, half carried her across the floor. To his relief, he saw the slender, fair-cropped figure of Millie running down the next aisle between the looms. She was making for the second window.

He and Harry lifted Suzie on to the sill. They had to duck to avoid the loosely hanging grille.

The scene that met Nick dazzled him after the gloom of the weaving floor. The area around the mill was flooded with artificial light. Away to his right, the side street seemed to be packed with emergency vehicles, their blue lights turning. Police, fire engines. His heart lurched as he saw the ambulances.

There were figures in white protective suits with respirators. Across the canal, more stood waiting.

There was no one on the towpath directly under him. The police were keeping a wide distance from Dominic's mill.

In a flash, Nick understood what Tom was telling them. On this side of the canal, there was no shelter. The adjacent mills had been demolished, leaving only a vast rubble-strewn waste. No cover there.

But on the opposite side more mills crowded the canal bank. If only they could get across to it, there would be some shelter behind those towering walls.

He started as he heard a loud splash. A rapid glance sideways told him that Millie had jumped from the next window. He had no time to search for her blonde head reappearing in the glistening water before Tom jumped too.

'Ready?' he panted to Suzie.

She nodded. He heard her gathering her breath.

There was another moan of pain as the two of them hurled themselves from the mill window. Nick had his arm hooked through Suzie's, willing his strength to propel them both sufficiently far out across the canal.

The shock of cold water hit him as he went under. He spluttered to the surface and realized he had let go of Suzie. For frantic moments he spun, searching among the waves of their dive for a sign of her. Then her brown head broke the water ahead of him. She turned, frightened, herself, at losing him, then flashed him a brief smile.

A heavier splash hit the canal behind him. Harry Redfern.

Nick struck out for the far bank.

Suddenly the night exploded in flame. The roar of noise bounded back from the surrounding mills. The water shook violently.

As Nick turned his head, he saw the far end of the mill blossom with fire. The building opposite stood out in brilliant light. Against the dazzle, he could not see the deadly debris that was flying out from that fire-burst. The next thing he knew, the water around him was bombarded with hurtling fragments of bricks, stone, metal, wood. He heard Harry Redfern cry out in pain.

Suzie was swimming ahead of him through the churning water. It must be less painful than running. He thought he could see splashes that might be Millie and Tom nearer the opposite bank. But there was so much commotion around him he could not be sure.

Every instinct wanted to race after Suzie. But that cry behind him had told him Harry was wounded.

He had to let Suzie go, praying fervently she would make it. He circled back.

Then something struck him agonisingly on the shoulder. He went under. He was struggling in the sudden blackness, swallowing foul water.

He surfaced again and bumped a length of splintered wood. It had come within a fraction of striking him on the head.

The cold was numbing the pain in his shoulder.

The brilliance of the explosion was dying already. More lurid red of flames made a macabre dance on the heaving water.

Harry was floating motionless, face down in the water. Nick swam up to him. He thought the dark streak down the side of the minister's head was blood. He struggled to turn the big man over. Then he caught him under the chin and began to tow him across the water. The terrible noise of destruction was clattering into quiet. Only a rain of lighter fragments showered the surface now.

Nick's shoulder ached. He had not thought the canal was so wide. He no longer knew if he was swimming directly across, taking the shortest line.

He bumped the bank before he realized he had made it. The weight of Harry Redfern's body was lifted from him. There were hands helping him, hauling him up.

White-suited figures were all around him. They were solicitous, but urgent.

A voice came distorted through the respirator.

'Are you all right, sir? Can you run? Let's get out of here.'

They rushed him through an alley between two mills. At the other end of this canyon of darkness more lights bloomed.

Suzie was standing beside an ambulance, wrapped in a red blanket. She lifted her dripping brown head and relief flooded her face. Her eyes flowered into a smile.

'Sorry to have been such a nuisance. Thanks!'

He hugged her wordlessly.

Nick saw a stretcher hurried past him, bearing the inert figure of Harry Redfern. He prayed that the minister was still alive.

His eyes were searching frantically for Millie and Tom. With a stab of both relief and alarm he saw Millie's slight figure almost lost in an enveloping red blanket. But she was holding her hand to her mouth and in the glare of floodlights he saw that there was scarlet on her skin that was not the blanket. He started to run towards her.

Someone got there before he did. He – she? – was as anonymous as all the others in a protective chemical suit, but Nick guessed from the green box in the gloved hand that it must be a paramedic. By the time he reached them, Millie's bloodied hand was being bandaged.

'That will need stitches,' came the muffled voice.

'Will it leave a scar?'

Nick was not sure whether this would wound his daughter's vanity or be a source of pride among her teenage friends. Her

face was pale. But then, it usually was. The damp blonde hair
was almost hidden under a fold of blanket.

'Are you all right?' He was reluctant to believe the evidence
of his eyes. He needed reassurance.

'Do I look all right? Trust me to choose the window with
the broken glass. And I swallowed half a gallon of that foul
canal. Besides which, I've probably got enough radioactivity
to fry an egg. Honestly, Dad!'

'Sorry!' He put an arm around her thin shoulders, over the
blanket. He was afraid to hug her as hard as he wanted to, in
case he hurt her more.

'Let's have you both in the wagon,' the paramedic ordered.
'They'll need to run some checks on you before they let you
get any further.'

Of course. It had been enough for the moment to escape
the terrifying aftermath of the explosion relatively unscathed.
Except for Harry. But Dominic's bomb had only been meant
as a means to a more frightening end. The scattering of radioactivity over as wide an area as possible. Tom, at eighteen,
had seemed to know so much more about it than Nick did.
How bad was the contamination they had been exposed to?
What would happen to them now? Suddenly, joy at seeing
Suzie apparently safe on the further bank, Millie with only a
gash in her hand and a stomach full of foul water, drained
from him. Words like 'radiation sickness' and 'cancer' tolled
in his mind. Frightening enough for him and Suzie, but Tom
and Millie were only on the threshold of their lives.

What had he done to them, with that obstinate, self-righteous
visit to the police?

On the other hand, how much worse might things have been
for his children if he had not?

Tom. He was jolted back into the immediate danger of that
frantic swim away from the mill, with masonry and metal
from the explosion crashing down into the water all around
him. He had assumed that some of the splashing he had seen
ahead was Tom powering his way across the canal.

*Where was he?*

Nick spun round. For a moment joy rose in his heart. It
took a second to recognize that the second blanketed figure

behind him was Suzie. Somewhere along the line, someone had thrown a blanket round Nick too. But there were only the three of them. The ambulance with Harry Redfern was drawing away. Millie was climbing into the next one. He and Suzie were being shepherded after her.

'*Where's Tom?*' he yelled at the paramedic.

'Ahead of you,' came a cheerful voice from inside the ambulance.

Tom was sitting on a padded bench. Someone had given him a steaming mug. His bright blue eyes grinned at Nick over the edge of it.

'Something to tell the guys about on Monday. Gerry's gone rock climbing. Dan's on an archaeological dig. They're going to be killing themselves with envy when I tell them what I've been doing.'

'Harry's injured,' Nick said sternly. He felt unaccountably angry that Tom was, after all, safe and sound. 'He was hit on the head.'

'Gosh! Sorry.' The grin was wiped from Tom's face.

Suzie was climbing into the ambulance ahead of Nick. He turned for a last look at the floodlit scene behind him.

The flames were dying down in the mill across the water. The end that had held Dominic's laboratory was shattered. Jagged stacks of brickwork stood out against the lurid red glow. The other end of the weaving shed was in darkness. But the side streets beyond, where Nick had parked the car, were brighter than they had ever been with street lamps. In the distance were many more emergency vehicles. Behind them, he could make out crowds of people lining the edge of the wasteland that must once have held a dozen mills. Probably the families who still lived in the terraces of millworkers' cottages, like the ones in Hugh Street. The police must have moved them out into a safer zone.

How safe was that?

He was sitting on a bench in the ambulance. Someone was handing him a mug of tea. He curled his cold hands around it as the ambulance began to move.

It had seemed an eternity that they had waited in the mill, alone with the malevolent presence of Dominic, and Harry

Redfern vainly trying to talk sense into him. All that time, Nick had been longing for the blast of police sirens and the sweep of headlights. For pounding feet outside. For armed response. But when he looked back at the army of officers in protective clothing, the fleet of ambulances, the evacuation of the local population, he was astonished at what they had done in so short a time.

The doors closed. He fastened his seat belt awkwardly over the blanket. The wool was already sopping wet. He felt enormously tired as he let the ambulance carry the Fewings away from the darkening mill with its messages of doom spray-painted across its walls.

'Guess the end of the world has been postponed,' Tom said cheerfully.

# TWENTY-EIGHT

The room was brightly lit. The walls were painted pale yellow. It was bare, clinical.

The paramedic had left them. Two more figures in white suits were moving Geiger counters over Suzie and Millie. Nick listened to the high-pitched clicking and heard a rise in the rate. His own heartbeat accelerated in panic. What did that change mean? How badly were they contaminated?

A larger figure came towards Nick. He – Nick assumed from the bulk it must be male – stood out from the others in a blue protective suit. Like the two in white, a respirator masked his face.

Again, the careful sweeping of the counter over every part of Nick's body. He felt cold in his wet clothes, without the comfort of the blanket. He guessed that they had not wanted to give the Fewings fresh clothes until they knew how badly they were affected by the fallout from the bomb.

Weren't you supposed to shower?

Canal water dripped on to the bare floor. His shoes were sodden.

The man was lifting the Geiger counter higher, assessing meticulously every part of Nick's wet body. Now Nick tried not to listen to the rising of the sound. Across the room, one of the white-suited figures had started on Tom.

Was the nausea Nick was starting to feel only anxiety and shock? How long did it take for the symptoms of radiation sickness to make themselves felt?

The big man in the blue suit had finished his task. He let his arm fall away from Nick's head. He looked across at one of the other figures, who nodded. The man in blue laid the counter aside and pushed away his mask. With a jolt of surprise, Nick recognized the perspiring face of Detective Superintendent Mason. His features looked drawn and weary.

Mason went over to his colleagues and had a brief muttered consultation. Then he turned back to Nick with the ghost of a grim smile.

'You're lucky. You must have panicked him into setting off his bomb before he was ready. Ordinarily, a dirty bomb works by mass hysteria, rather than by actual physical harm. Ideally, you'd want to set it off in the open air in a high-density area. Somewhere high up, so you'd get the maximum fallout. That way, you'd immobilize a key area of a city. Have thousands of people mobbing the hospitals to get themselves checked. Transport gridlocked, as people try to escape. Water declared unsafe. As it is, he let it off in a confined space, in a run-down part of town. From what these guys tell me,' he nodded to his colleagues in white, 'I'd say you were more at risk from pollution in the canal than from any radioactive fallout.'

Nick had not realized the enormity of the fear he had been bearing until he felt it slipping away from him. He could almost picture it mingling darkly with the pools of canal water on the floor.

'Well –' Mason's voice sounded lighter – 'I dare say you could do with a change of clothes. If you don't mind the regulation police issue, we can get you showered and kitted out and on your way home.'

Home? Nick stood petrified with shock.

When he could move again, he spun round to Suzie.

'Thelma! When we worked out where you were, I just

jumped into the car and we hared straight off after you. None of us thought to tell Thelma where we were going. What time is it?'

Tom consulted his watch. 'Sorry, Dad. We've been gone at least two hours.'

Nick reached for his mobile and tried to switch it on. The screen stayed ominously blank. He turned urgently to the detective superintendent. 'If I could use a phone? And if you'll get us some clothes as soon as possible, we've got an awful lot of explaining to do.'

'We'll run you back as soon as you're ready. Was that your Mazda outside the mill? If you'd give me your keys, someone will return it to the house.'

Nick felt in his trouser pocket for anxious moments. Then his fingers found the familiar bunch of metal in a corner of the wet lining. He held them out.

As they were led away to the showers, he paused on the threshold. 'Harry Redfern. The minister. Is he going to be OK?'

The Baptist chaplain's face had not been covered when they carried him past on the stretcher, but Nick was afraid of the answer he would hear.

'They've taken him to St Mary's hospital. From what I've heard, he was still unconscious. I can't tell you more than that, I'm afraid. He had a sharper eye for trouble than we did. Dominic Walters was sentenced to three months in prison for sending the Reverend Redfern letters threatening his children. He painted his doomsday graffiti on the Reverend's church and disrupted his services. I gather he was shouting how Armageddon's on its way and we're all heading for damnation. We wrote him off as religious nutter.'

'I've been an idiot!' Nick exclaimed. 'He told me he knew how I felt. That he'd been on the receiving end of menacing letters too. It never for a moment occurred to me that they might be from the same man.'

'In spite of all that, Mr Redfern visited him in prison and tried to talk sense into him. Didn't do much good, by the look of it. They let young Dominic out after six weeks. And we missed a trick. None of us picked up on the same graffiti on that mill. But Harry Redfern obviously made the connection. How else did he know where to find him?'

'*That's* why he was there before us. Both of them must have got in by a door at the end where the workshop was. We never saw it. And I thought *he* was the one on my tail. The one who was making those phone calls.'

'Yes, well. He's a good man. He'll have known how you felt. Dominic Walters was spouting hellfire over his children, and they're younger than yours. So he was willing to put himself in harm's way to stop it. Should have left it to us.'

'I suppose that's what you think I should have done.'

'Professionally speaking, yes. But it wasn't my wife tied under that loom.'

'If we hadn't burst in, he wouldn't have set off that bomb.'

'Oh, yes, he would have, sir. But not until he'd got it ready and positioned to have maximum effect. He'd have set it off somewhere a lot different from an old cotton mill.'

'The City of London.' Tom said. 'That's what he was aiming at.'

'*Dad*!' Millie's urgent voice came from the corridor behind him. 'What about Thelma?'

Nick saw anger battling with thankfulness in Thelma's face. But what broke through the surface was bewilderment.

'Whatever are you doing dressed like that?'

The four Fewings had been kitted out with identical tracksuits, blue and silver-grey.

'Probably regulation issue for prisoners,' Tom had muttered.

'Or the police athletics team,' Millie giggled.

DSI Mason had assured them that their clothes and the contents of their pockets would be cleaned and dried and returned to them before they left on Sunday.

'When forensics have finished with them,' Tom had suggested.

There was so much to explain to Thelma, Nick hardly knew where to begin.

'We fell in the canal.'

'All four of you?' She looked blankly from one to the other. Then pent-up emotion got the better of her.

'I've been off my head with worry! That detective sergeant went haring out of the house. Next thing I knew, the lot of you were tearing off down the road in your cars, like the Keystone Cops. And I'm left here with not a clue about what's going on. I knew you were in danger, or else why would you have the police guarding you? And . . .'

Suddenly the significance of seeing all four of them in front of her struck home.

'Suzie! They've got you back! I know Nick told me over the phone from the police station, but . . . well, I could hardly take it all in. But here you are safe and sound, thank the good Lord!'

She threw her arms round the younger woman and hugged her.

'And Millie! What have you done to your hand? You're hurt!'

'I had four stitches,' Millie said proudly.

'And I thought you couldn't stand hospitals . . . What am I doing, keeping you all on the doorstep? Come along inside, the lot of you.'

Tom's low voice came from behind Nick. 'Dad, you can still see it.'

Nick turned. In the valley below, one small area of the town was unnaturally brightly lit. Within it, fire still glowed like a red flower.

'I wonder what happened to Dominic,' came Millie's voice.

'Shouldn't think he stood much of a chance, with the force of that explosion,' Tom said.

'But the police will be looking,' Nick told him. 'Come on. We've kept Thelma waiting long enough.'


# TWENTY-NINE


'You'll want to go back and see Dad this afternoon,' Thelma said at breakfast. 'All of you.' She cast a penetrating look at Millie.

Millie blushed. 'Of course I will. It was just . . .'

'Well, you've come a bit nearer to death than you expected. I dare say you can spare a thought for someone who's a lot closer to it than you are.'

'He's not going to die, is he?' Millie exclaimed.

'Of course he is.' Then Thelma softened. 'We all are, pet. Sooner or later. But Dad's ninety-three and he's had a nasty stroke. He's closer than most. You want to make the most of it, while we've got him.'

Nick ran his hands through his hair. 'There's so much I still want to ask him. I'm kicking myself that I didn't come back here sooner. I know that sounds kind of selfish. As if I only to want to talk to him to get some more family history out of him. But when we saw him yesterday – gosh, was that only a day ago? – he seemed like he'd been storing up everything for all these years and he couldn't wait to tell us.'

'You're right there. He was tickled pink when he heard you were coming, and that you wanted to find out about the old days and all the people he used to know. He was tired of talking to me about it, I suppose. As far as I was concerned, it was just the same old stories I'd heard for years. I didn't pay proper attention. Not like you, with your family trees and your computer files. I think it's marvellous the way you've got it all down, like a book.'

'There's a whole lot more I need to find out,' Nick said. 'He was born just after the First World War. But he'd have heard the older ones talking about it. And what about the Depression in the twenties and thirties? Did he have a job then? Was he ever on the dole?'

'Far as I know, he went into the mill at thirteen, and stayed there. Same as everyone round here did in those days.'

'He must have been called up in World War Two.'

'In the Lancashire Fusiliers. There's an old cap badge some-where. But he never would talk much about it.'

Nick played with the crumbs on the table. 'It was the same with most of them. They saw too much. Didn't want to inflict it on their families. I feel a bit guilty now. I was so keen to find out about our family in the nineteenth century. I didn't think enough about the twentieth. I couldn't believe that he actually knew people who were on the censuses in the 1800s.'

'Like Millicent Bootle?' Millie supplied.

'Yes. So I didn't spend enough time asking him about his own life. Well, I had other things on my mind at the time. Never mind. We'll do that today.'

'What will you do with yourselves this morning?' Thelma asked.

Nick grinned across at Tom. 'I've always wanted to take the kids up Skygill Hill. It's sort of family mythology. My dad always used to talk about family expeditions up Skygill.'

'You're on,' Tom said. 'How high is it?'

'Five hundred and fifty metres. That's eighteen hundred feet in old money.'

'There's just one problem. It's all right for the rest of you. You brought spare clothes. All I had for the weekend was what I stood up in. And the police took them off us.' He looked down ruefully at the regulation issue tracksuit. 'But I guess I can make it up there in police trainers. I just hope they get our stuff back to us before I have to go back to uni.'

'You've a grand day for it,' Thelma said. 'How about you, Suzie? Are you up to it, after all you've been through?'

Suzie smiled at Thelma. 'I've just about got the use of my legs back. I'd be glad of a breath of fresh air to blow the memories away.'

The morning's brightness darkened for Nick. All her life, Suzie would carry the memory of those hours imprisoned underneath the loom. The captive of a madman obsessed with his apocalyptic vision of hastening the end of a sinful world. Armageddon.

He had his own nightmare fears to contend with, but those dark hours he could not share with her.

'Come on, then,' he said, with enforced cheerfulness. 'We have to make the top of Skygill in time to be down at the hospital for Uncle Martin.'

'What about Harry Redfern?' Suzie asked. 'He was unconscious when they took him in. Do we know if he survived the night?'

Nick was silent for the moment, aware of the others' eyes on him. 'I'll ring the hospital. If he's come round, maybe we can see him too.'

He flinched from the pain in his bruised shoulder. In his imagination he saw the gouts of flame, the debris raining down on the crimsoned water. How easily any one of them might not have been taken out of the canal alive.

The morning on Skygill Hill was everything Nick had hoped it would be. A soft blue October sky, with low sunshine that lit the flames in the autumn woods. The higher they climbed, the wider the towns and countryside of the north-west spread below them.

The path Nick had chosen was steeper than he remembered. Or else, in his forties, he was not the agile boy he had been when his father brought him up here. His damaged shoulder ached.

Millie, her bandaged hand in a sling, was lagging behind. Nick stopped and turned to enjoy the view, giving her time to catch her breath.

'Having a cut hand shouldn't make it harder to walk, but it does,' she explained.

'I guess the sling is throwing you off balance. You can't swing your arms to help, the way you usually would.'

Tom, predictably, was almost galloping up the hill ahead of them. To Nick's joy, Suzie was purposefully following behind him. There seemed to be no lasting physical effects from her ordeal of yesterday.

The wounds lay deeper. He had come so near to losing his wife and children. His own death was of little importance. The thing that mattered was that they were all here, where he had meant to bring them. He felt an enormous thankfulness as he drank in the keen air.

'It's a pity Thelma wouldn't come with us. I did try to persuade her. But she said she had the weekend shopping to do. I told her we were definitely treating her to a meal out tonight, but she's still set her heart on providing a slap-up Sunday lunch tomorrow, when Uncle Martin comes home.'

A celebration of their safe return. And Great-uncle Martin's. The Fewings family reunited.

Nick surveyed the town far below them, misted in the soft autumn light. The haze was no longer the pall of smoke that would once have lain over it, when a hundred boiler houses spewed their breath from tall chimneys.

'I've been thinking about James Bootle, brewing his herbal remedies when nobody wanted the fine cloth from his hand loom. Do you wonder if he ever wished he could concoct a bomb to blow all those mills that were stealing his living to kingdom come? But he didn't. Instead of that, he reinvented himself. Making stuff to heal people.'

'You're thinking about that Dominic nut.' Millie glanced at him sideways.

'Yes.'

'I'm with Harry Redfern. I think Dominic's read the wrong bits of the Bible. The gospels are all about loving your neighbour, not blowing them up. Do you think he's going to be OK? Mr Redfern, I mean?'

'When I rang the hospital, they wouldn't tell me much, because I'm not a relative. But they did say he's on Arkwright Ward.'

'So he's still alive? Thank goodness for that.'

'We'll look in on him this afternoon, shall we?' He cast an anxious glance at Millie, but there was none of the rebellion of yesterday. 'Look, we don't have to climb all the way to the top. It's a grand enough view from here.'

'Try and stop me.'

She set off up the path in pursuit of Tom. Nick followed. They caught up with Suzie and Tom on the summit. Nick threw Suzie an admiring grin.

'You fairly steamed up here. We couldn't keep up with you.'

She gave him a half smile, though her eyes were clouded.

'Yes, well. I needed to work it out of my system. I was angry. This is the day he didn't want us to see. Look at it! All this is what he was going to take away from us.'

'He's dead now, love,' Nick told her quietly.

'I'm angry that I let myself be frightened of him. When he came up behind me in the shopping precinct he said he'd hurt Millie if I didn't come with him quietly, and I believed him. I didn't understand how he knew so much about us. It didn't occur to me about you dropping your business cards. It made it seem there was something . . . *supernatural* . . . about him. I went as quietly as a rabbit. I should have screamed and shouted for help.'

'I felt the same. It was uncanny. When I knew he was following us, nowhere seemed safe. You thought I was behaving like a madman with the Redferns.'

'He went looking for Dominic, didn't he? Harry Redfern? He wasn't just going to be a passive victim. He really wanted to change him.'

'And nearly died for it.'

'We'll see him this afternoon. And meanwhile . . . we've got this.'

She stood in silence, turning slowly to take in the ranks of the Pennines, the distant peaks of the Lake District, the glint of the sea in Morecambe Bay.

Nick followed the circuit of her eyes. His home country, on his father's side. Where generations of them had come to breathe the clean, keen air, far above the taint and smoke of the cotton mills.

On the way down, he was trying to think of all the questions he wanted to ask Uncle Martin this afternoon. He ought to take a notepad, write the answers down. After lunch tomorrow they would have to set off for home. This would be his last chance to ask.

Nick paused at the hospital entrance and glanced at Millie anxiously.

'You're all right? About doing this?'

'Of *course*. I want to see if Mr Redfern's come round. I like him. And there was no need for Mum to stand guard outside my bedroom door. I wasn't going to run away again. Well, I didn't know, did I? Nobody *told* me there was a madman trailing us.'

'Yes, I'm sorry about that. We didn't want to scare you. It didn't occur to me that you needed to know.'

They asked at the desk and found their way to Arkwright Ward. Nick felt a cloud of apprehension at the door. He still did not know how badly Harry Redfern was injured. He had taken a massive blow to the head from the falling masonry.

He might still be unconscious. He might have taken a turn for the worse.

Nick's eyes raked down the ward. He was afraid of seeing closed curtains around the Baptist minister's bed. He was just about to ask a nurse for directions when Suzie gave a low cry at his side.

'There he is!'

Harry Redfern was propped up on pillows. His plump face was dwarfed by the huge swathe of bandages round his head. Nick's joy at seeing him awake was tempered by the fact that he was not alone. Bethan Redfern sat beside him. Of course, he should have realized Harry's wife would be at his bedside.

'We won't stay long,' he told the others. 'Just say hello. I don't know if they have a limit on the number of visitors. We don't want to look like a congregation.'

He led the way towards the bed. Harry Redfern looked up. Under the bandages, the brown eyes twinkled with warmth. But when Bethan Redfern turned her head, the expression on her hollow face was anything but pleased.

'You again! What do you want here?'

Harry laid his hand over hers. 'I'm sorry, love. I'll explain it all to you one day. When I've got less of a thumping head-ache. It's a long story. But don't be too hard on Nick. This is the man who saved my life.'

'Dad!' gasped Millie. 'You didn't tell us that!'

'It was nothing much. I just wanted to get us all across that canal as fast as I could.'

'And the police tell me that meant towing me, after I was knocked unconscious by a piece of the mill. Under the circumstances, you could have left me to drown.'

Bethan Redfern blushed. She held out her hand. 'I'm truly sorry, Mr Fewings. I had no idea. When you came storming after Harry that day . . . and after we'd been through all those threats from Dominic . . .'

'Harry told me you'd had hate messages. It just never occurred to me that ours had come from Dominic too.'

'He threatened the children. That's what really scared me.'

'Well, he's out of it now, poor boy,' Harry Redfern sighed.

'God rest his soul. He's got the short cut he wanted to Kingdom Come, but only for himself, thank God.'

'You really think that?' Tom asked incredulously. 'That he's on his way to heaven, after all he did to us? And not just us. He'd have made half London radioactive if he'd carried through his plans for the bomb.'

'*Forgive us our sins, as we forgive those who sin against us.* Who am I to act as judge?'

'That's what he did,' Millie said. 'Judged everybody else.'

There was a silence. Then Suzie said, 'Look, we don't want to take up your visiting time with your wife. We just came to see you were OK. I'm glad it wasn't worse.'

'So am I.' Harry smiled. Then, more soberly, 'You had the worst of it, I think. Tied up under that loom, with a bomb maker in the next room.'

'Never mind that. Actually, you're not the only reason we've come. We're on our way to see Nick's great-uncle. He's in the next ward.'

'Old Martin? Give him my love. I'll be round to see him when they let me up.' Harry looked up at Nick. 'I haven't thanked you properly, have I?'

'There's no need,' Nick said awkwardly. 'I'm only thankful you're alive. When they pulled you out of the canal, I couldn't tell.'

'We were all lucky – except Dominic. Though we could have an interesting theological argument about what "luck" actually means.'

'Harry!' admonished his wife.

He winced as he turned to smile at her. 'Sorry, love. Maybe not this afternoon.'

Nick felt tense with anticipation as he led the way along the corridor. It was only a short step from Arkwright Ward to Haworth.

He felt self-conscious about the clipboard and notepaper in his hand. Would it have been better to bring a small portable recorder? He was new to this business of recording family history. He was afraid to trust his memory, or even the combined memories of the four of them.

They reached the door into the ward. Nick's eyes were going ahead, seeking the bed towards the far end with the frail old man. Would he be sitting up in the chair again, in his blue dressing gown?

His view was blocked by a woman hurrying towards them. She was holding a tissue to her face. He almost collided with her as she reached the door. Shorter than he was. Grey, permed hair. A flowery scent of face powder.

Suzie recognized her a split second before Nick's preoccupied mind.

'Thelma!'

Nick's eyes flew back from the line of beds to the woman directly in front of him. With slowly registering shock, he took in his cousin's face. The eyes behind her pink-framed glasses were red.

A cold fear was knotting his stomach.

'Thelma? What's wrong?' Though he knew.

'They rang me. He's . . .' She gestured helplessly at the ward behind her. 'He had another stroke.'

The line of beds swam into focus now. The curtains around the one where Great-uncle Martin should have lain. He felt a bitter grief.

Into his mind came the elderly man with his shrunken face distorted by the stroke. But, too, the sparkle in his blue eyes. The sense of the tall, upstanding man he must have been in his army uniform. The overlooker patrolling the mill with a keen eye for quality cloth. The boy spinning down the dales on his bicycle with the youth club.

A handful of precious memories.

'Is he dead?' Millie's wondering voice came to him from a great distance.

'Are these friends of yours, love?'

For the first time Nick became aware of the nurse following Thelma.

'My cousin and his family.' Thelma's voice was surprisingly strong and steady. 'They're staying with me.'

'That's a good thing.' The nurse turned to Suzie. 'There's a waiting room over there where you can get a cup of tea. Can I leave her with you? Come back when you're ready and

Sister will tell you about the arrangements. I'm sorry, but you know . . . the paperwork.'

'We'll handle it,' Suzie said. 'Come on, Thelma. You could do with a sit down.'

'I always knew, of course.' Thelma dabbed her eyes with a tissue. 'After the first stroke. At his age. It's not as if I wasn't prepared for it.'

'We're none of us really prepared until it happens. It takes a while for the reality to sink in.'

Nick's voice detained the nurse who was hurrying away. 'I wonder . . . Would it be all right if I had last look at him?'

She looked momentarily uncertain. 'Yes, I suppose so. Do you want me to come with you?'

'No. That's all right. It's the bed with the curtains round, isn't it?'

'Yes.' Still she hesitated. 'Better not to touch anything.'

'I won't.'

Suzie was already leading Thelma away to the seating area. Tom was following them. His hands were in his pockets, shoulders hunched. For once, his merry command of any situation had deserted him.

Only Millie still stood in the doorway. Her grey-blue eyes were very bright as she raised them to Nick.

'Can I come too?'

'Are you sure? You didn't . . .'

'No. I bottled out, didn't I? And I haven't seen a dead person before. But like everybody keeps saying, it happens to all of us. Yesterday, it might have been me.' She glanced down at her bandaged hand. 'I'm sorry now that I ran away. I should have come to see him when I had the chance, shouldn't I?'

He put an arm round her shoulders. 'We all have regrets when someone dies. All the things we could have done and said, and didn't. Me, too.' He gestured with the clipboard in his other hand. 'The questions I never asked. I guess we have to accept that we're not perfect, and just try to do a bit better next time.'

They walked along the ward, past all those other beds, where visitors sat talking to the patients. Eyes followed them.

Nick moved the flowered curtains aside.

Great-uncle Martin's face looked grey and sunken as it lay
back upon the pillows. It had looked a little like a death's head
when Nick had visited before. But then it had flowered into
a welcoming smile. There had still been a merriment in his
expression then, a ghost of Tom's. The eyes had been as bright
as Millie's, sharp and full of intelligence as he warmed to his
memories of the past. It struck Nick with a pang of both regret
and gratitude that Great-uncle Martin had really enjoyed having
someone to talk to who genuinely wanted to hear him remin-
isce about the past.

Just half an hour they had stayed yesterday. There had been
so much more he could have told them.

Nick put his hand out and closed it briefly over his great-
uncle's cold and bony one.

Millie stood quietly, looking down. 'I wish I'd come. He
actually talked to Millicent Bootle, didn't he? I still can't
believe that.'

'He went to her eightieth birthday party.'

She looked up at him seriously. 'Do I have any other
great-great-uncles?'

'Not on my side of the family. You'll need to ask your
mother about hers.'

'I will.'

She gave him a grave smile and put her undamaged hand
in his. They closed the curtains behind them and walked away
to find Thelma.

# AUTHOR'S NOTE

The people, places and institutions in this book are fictitious. But I am indebted to many real-life people and
organizations who have done so much to help my own
family history research in ways which have inspired and
informed this book. They include the following:

www.ancestry.co.uk

www.rootsweb.ancestry.com

www.freecen.org.uk

Queen Street Mill Textile Museum, Burnley.

Helmshore Mills Textile Museum, Lancashire.

The Weavers' Triangle Visitor Centre, Burnley.

My son, Mark Priestley, for the history of the Priestley and
Tootle families.

National Institute of Medical Herbalists. www.nimh.org.uk

Slater's Directory for Burnley, 1865.

My mother-in-law, Annie Priestley, née Tootle, weaver.

Edith Judson, née Tootle.

My husband, Jack Priestley.

Correspondence between the Priestley brothers of Goodshaw
and Heald in Rossendale, 19th century.

www.howstuffworks.com and others, for information on
dirty bombs.

*A Village in Craven.* William Riley. It includes a picture of
a herbalist.

While I have given free rein to my imagination here, many
details owe their inspiration to people and places in my husband
Jack Priestley's family history.

James Bootle, handloom weaver turned herbalist – John
Tootle of Padiham, Burnley.

Millicent Bootle – Robert Tootle, who was a cotton factory
worker at nine.

Nick's grandmother – Annie Tootle, cotton weaver of Burnley.

Hugh Street – Moore Street and Perth Street, Burnley.

High Bank – Green Bank, Earby, Yorkshire.

The letters of the Fewings brothers – letters between the Priestley brothers of Goodshaw and Heald, including their refusal to pay church tithes.

The brothers who helped set up cotton mills in Russia – the Priestley brothers of Goodshaw.

Skygill Hill – Pendle Hill, Lancashire.

Briershaw Chapel, where the pews were carried over the fells – Goodshaw Old Chapel, Rossendale.

The musicians who carried their instruments over the fells – the Larks of Dean, who carried theirs to Goodshaw Chapel in the 18th and 19th centuries.

The sheep in the churchyard – Thornton-in-Craven, Yorkshire.

Enoch and Hannah Fewings' headstone – James and Alice Priestley's tombstone, Sunnyside Baptist Chapel, Reedsholme, Rossendale.